I0676643

The leading tank, with a second tank following close behind, entered the cut and with contemptuous ease started pushing the truck blocking the road out of the way. Grissom pushed the plunger and the explosive laden truck blew up, taking the lead tank with it. The trailing tank started to back up when Dane leaped to his feet, took a running jump and landed on the moving vehicle. With German bullets ricocheting around him he frantically shoved three hand grenades into a port and jumped off. The exploding tank gave impetus to his jump and he lit and rolled over on the north side of the cut.

# Dane Shaw Series

Dilemma in the Desert- revised 2025
Steadfast in Sicily- revised 2025
Intrigue in Italy
Normandy Knockout- coming 2025

Future books:
Freedom for France
Attack in the Ardennes
Bastion in Bavaria
Conflict in Korea
The Fox and the Vixen

# Steadfast In Sicily
## Dane Shaw War Adventure Book 2

By Dwayne Straw

Revised 2025

Dwayne Straw

Copyright © 2014
All rights reserved

No reproduction, copy or transmission of this publication may be made without written permission from the publisher except for brief quotations in reviews.

ISBN 978-0-9911167-3-7

This is a work of fiction and, except for historical personages, any resemblance to persons living or dead are purely coincidental.

Terrain may be altered to fit the story.

For Darwin, Ray, Carroll, Roy, Dean, and Bob,
my uncles.

Cast of Characters
Sergeant Dane Shaw-squad commander
Maria-Italian guide
Corporal Gates-second-in-command
Tennessee-backwoodsman
Braun-German-American
Rosario-Hispanic
Hemphill-racist
Chilvers-ladies' man
Conners-chronic complainer
Raymond-kind-hearted
O'Halloran-Irish-American
Patterson-new recruit
Zimmerman-platoon leader
Lassiter-platoon leader
Jones-platoon leader
Grissom-platoon leader
Milne-shrewd sergeant
'Doc' Pavel-American medic
Mueller-German medic
Crawford-pilot
Feodant-German prisoner
Reissenhoffenberger-engineer
Colonel Schoerner-German commander

# Table of Contents

# Historical Background

In mid-January, 1943, the British and American leaders met at Casablanca, North Africa, to come to an agreement about war strategy for the year. The Americans, led by General Marshall, wanted a cross-channel invasion into northern France and not be bogged down in a Mediterranean strategy to re-establish the British Empire. The British were just as adamant that the Allies were not ready for such an invasion and wanted to open the Mediterranean Sea to convoys between England and India. Churchill in particular wanted to invade the 'soft underbelly' of Europe and perhaps knock Italy out of the war. In the end, President Roosevelt sided with Churchill, and an invasion of Sicily was decided on.

Plans were made for the taking of the small islands south of Sicily and for the invasion of Sicily itself, but no plans were made for what would happen after the amphibious assault. British General Harold Alexander, commander of the 15th Army Group, preferred to wait upon the results of the invasion before issuing new orders for subjugating the island. As it happened, the forceful personalities of General Montgomery of the British 8th Army and General Patton of the American 7th Army made the decisions for him.

Because of their poor showing at the Battle of Kassarine Pass, the British possessed a low opinion of American fighting ability. Alexander wanted to give them a minor role while the British took the major role in trying to capture Messina, the goal of the invasion. Instead, General Patton got permission to launch a limited offensive, circled the island, and captured Messina before the British reached it.

Whether or not a 1943 invasion of France would have succeeded has been hotly debated by military experts and historians ever since. The bottom line is nobody knows. The extra year of planning, battle experience for the Americans, and the million causalities the Germans suffered on the eastern front all played a part in the success of the Normandy invasion.

Churchill was both right and wrong. A simple look at a topographical map of southern Europe shows no 'soft underbelly.' The Balkans are all mountains and forests, excellent for defense, which would have tied up the Allies for a long time. They would have then simply joined up with the Russians, leaving Germany to fight a one front war. Italy, as proven during the war, is a mountainous country with innumerable rivers forming natural defensive positions. After a long slugging match up the length of Italy, the Allies found themselves at the foot of the Alps, Europe's greatest defensive barrier. Only the south of France offered the possibility of an easy invasion, and the islands of Sardinia and Corsica guarded it.

Churchill was correct in realizing the opening of the Mediterranean Sea to Allied shipping was imperative. They needed a shortened shipping time of needed supplies and manpower between England and India. In 1944, when the Japanese invaded India, it was because of the Mediterranean convoys troops and supplies arrived in India in time to halt the Japanese drive.

# Prolog

Operation Husky, the Allied invasion of Sicily on July 10th, 1943, included the men of the American 1st Infantry Division. They landed near Gela on the southern coast and pushed their way inland. A furious German counterattack sent them reeling back almost to the beaches before naval gunfire halted the attack. Then on July 20th the Americans went back on the offensive and reached the center of the island, the city of Enna.

A separate offensive moved to capture the western half of the island. When the Americans captured the west coast of the island and turned east to move along the north coast, General Patton split his forces. The main force followed the coast road while a secondary group advanced along Route 120, which laid further inland and paralleled the coast road.

On July 24th the sun looked down on an island where hundreds of thousands of soldiers were on the move, including a lonely American company making its painstaking way across the countryside.

# Chapter One

The men of King Company, 26th Regiment, 1st Infantry Division, staggered and tripped over loose rocks as they forced their way along a dry riverbed. Sergeant Dane Shaw of the Third Squad, 2nd Platoon, the last squad in the column, wiped his sweaty face with an already wet handkerchief. He gave the sodden piece of material a disgusted look and shoved it in his pocket. The banks, fifteen to twenty feet high, reflected and magnified the temperature to over a hundred degrees. The twenty-three-year-old felt the broiling heat sapping his strength. As his agile stride carried his five and a half foot, one hundred sixty pound frame along, he lifted his helmet and brushed his hand through his wet dark brown, almost black, hair.

Worried how the ten men in his squad were affected by the heat, he replaced his helmet and stopped to give the leading man a searching look. Tennessee, the long, lanky woodsman, met his glance and grinned. *No trouble there*, Dane thought to himself. But Patterson, near the end of the line, staggered and almost fell under the weight of his eighty-pound backpack. Raymond, following behind Patterson, grabbed his arm and kept him upright. When Patterson regained his balance

13

Raymond released his hold but followed close behind, ready to lend a helping hand.

Dane knew behind Raymond's smallpox-scarred face, which made him look as mean as all get out, lay a heart of gold. He proved to Dane it didn't always pay to go by first impressions.

Dane fell in step beside the last man in line, Gates, his steady and no-nonsense corporal. Both men mopped their faces with their shirt sleeves and looked at each other.

"The squad's doing the best they can, under the circumstances," Dane said.

"Yup." Gates paused. "Do you know anything more about our mission?"

Dane snorted. "Just what you already know." His eyes examined his men as he continued speaking, more to himself than the fair man at his side, whose square, solid bulk spelled reliability. "The company is supposed to race ahead of the general advance and seize a vital bridge over the Salso River before the Germans blow it up. We're to hold it until relieved. Headquarters thought about a paratroop drop, but the last two were so scattered they dropped the idea. If we don't get a move on, the relieving force will get there ahead of us."

Gates grinned at the pun and then sobered up. "This is a race?" His face screwed up in disgust. "The heat is taking such a toll we're slowing down and falling behind schedule."

Dane glanced up at the top of the slope. "We got a break when the Italian platoon surrendered and let us use the riverbed to go through the hole in the Axis line. We should get out of here, though, before we bake. It's got to be cooler and there might be a breeze blowing higher up. Down here the air isn't moving. We need to have scouts out. We have no idea what's up there. With everyone in this river bed I feel like we're in a trap." He grimaced and shook his head. "Don't mind me, I'm just blathering away."

\*\*\*

George Gates looked at his shorter superior as he tried for the umpteenth time to figure out what made the sergeant tick. When assigned to the squad back in Tunisia, he knew Shaw to be the last survivor of the original squad. Gates, naive at the time, believed this to be the reason for Shaw's promotion to sergeant. When he first met Shaw, he thought the soft spoken man unimpressive. He and the replacements showed up at the camp one morning to find the sergeant reading his Bible.

It took less than twenty-four hours for Gates to change his mind, which also proved to him not to rely on first impressions. Shaw assigned them their quarters, visited with them, and mentioned something about each of them. Not until later did

Gates find out Shaw went to the company clerk and read the replacements' service records.

After lunch they began training exercises. Shaw didn't yell or curse, but showed great patience with the new recruits. When O'Halloran decided to test the sergeant by pretending not to hear an order, Shaw ripped into him. They watched in stunned amazement as the sergeant's brown eyes flashed with green flecks, and he gave the Irishman a tongue lashing which cowed the rebellion. Shaw delivered it without a swear word and a voice which snapped with authority. A menacing aura emanated from the man. Later, when O'Halloran tried to unjam a 50 caliber machine gun but couldn't, he cursed it. Shaw came over and in a quiet voice showed him the problem.

As days went by the men noticed Shaw didn't carry a grudge. When someone deserved a reprimand, they got it and then it was over. But they also discovered they needed to do things his way, or else. Later on, in Sicily, they learned the reason for following his instructions: the squad suffered fewer casualties than any other squad in the battalion.

When they were training for the Sicily invasion, Shaw showed patience Gates never saw in a sergeant before. When Rosario tried to drive a jeep starting from an uphill position, he killed it over and over. Shaw repeated the instructions and demonstrated several times. When another sergeant would have cursed and called Rosario stupid and an idiot, Shaw put his arm around him and said, "It's hard, but I know you can do it. All it takes is practice. That's what we're here for." Rosario learned, and became Shaw's staunchest supporter. But the men discovered any insubordination or faking would be met with the rough edge of his tongue. After a while, it became noticeable he only needed to give an order once in his quiet voice and the men jumped to obey. They learned the danger sign. When green flecks in his eyes started to burn, they needed to shape up or else.

When they practiced hand to hand combat, the men were shocked at the sergeant's quickness and agility. They never saw anyone strike so fast their hands became a blur. During one-on-one drills, he taught them combat tricks he'd learned from experience.

Once O'Halloran with an innocent expression asked, "What if we're attacked by two men at the same time?"

Shaw looked at him and said, "Okay, choose someone and the two of you take me on."

O'Halloran chose Tennessee and the fun started. Fun for Shaw, that is. Gates and the rest of the squad watched in growing awe as Shaw blocked or ducked every blow O'Halloran or Tennessee launched. They couldn't touch Shaw. Gates saw several times when Shaw pulled his punches so not to hurt either of the men. It took a full minute, but Shaw put both of them on the ground.

Gates and the rest of the squad learned of Sergeant Shaw's tactical prowess in the desperate battle at Gela. During the retreat from the German assault, he kept his squad together as a cohesive fighting unit. He never let it break apart and proved adept at setting up supporting firing bases to cover the retreat, leapfrogging the men back in pairs. Twice he set up a killing field, stopping attacking Germans in their tracks and sent them reeling back. But more enemies showed up and the Americans were forced back.

When they reached the heights near the beaches and received the 'no further retreat' order, he placed the squad in the most advantageous defensive position possible. He even advised their platoon leader, Lieutenant Enderhall, on defending their front. In the hand-to-hand fighting which followed, he showed again and again his deadly fighting skills. Twice Gates watched Shaw beat back assaults, fighting two or three enemy soldiers at a time as they surged into the American line, holding the squad's position almost by himself.

Gates realized Shaw to be self-effacing about his advice, and not just about advice. On occasion,

Gates observed the sergeant merge and disappear into a group of men, unnoticed by those around them. He seldom pushed himself into the limelight, but when necessary would snap with authority, drawing all attention to himself. Most of the rest of the platoon didn't realize who planned the defense at the Gela heights, but Lieutenant Enderhall promoted Shaw to staff sergeant on the spot. Before Enderhall's wounding and evacuation, Gates overheard his recommendation to Captain Carter for Shaw's promotion to technical sergeant when an opening occurred.

Gates shook his head, puzzlement on his broad face. In the five months since he met him, Shaw never swore, smoked, drank, or chased women. His single recreation seemed to be reading a couple of books on tactics he'd picked up somewhere and his Bible. He spent time with a sergeant buddy from the 1st Armored Division. Once Gates walked into Shaw's billet and saw them on their knees, praying together. Shaw later tried to talk to him about the Bible and God, but Gates preferred his own religion, and Shaw didn't press it.

Another time they were in town together and he heard Shaw catch his breath. He followed Shaw's gaze to see the back of a slender, black-haired woman walking down the street, and saw pain in his eyes. "Do you know her?" he asked.

Shaw shook his head. "No, she just reminded me of someone."

*He must have been hurt by a woman in his past,* Gates thought.

Gates came back to the present as the column came to a stop. The squads in front of them dropped down to rest. He watched Dane order, "Everybody down, get the weight off your back." He went to help Raymond remove Patterson's pack, while Patterson leaned against a rock with a pained look on his face. Gates turned his attention to the rest of the squad.

\*\*\*

Dane gave a worried look at the short, scrawny 19-year-old who needed his combat boots on to tip the scales at 110 pounds. Fear shone out of the kid's eyes. Fear of battle. Fear of failure. Fear of dying. Dane had seen the look too many times.

"What's wrong?" Dane asked.

"I think I twisted my ankle, Sarge."

Dane knelt down to feel Patterson's foot and noticed the men taking out their canteens. "All of you, just take one mouthful of water and hold it in your mouth. Let it soak in. We don't know how long it will be before we find more water."

"But Sarge," Conners complained, "I'm so dry I can hardly talk."

"Good," Dane heard Gates mutter. Dane hid a

smile. In the short time since Conners joined the squad here in Sicily, more complaining came from him than everyone else put together. Dane felt a constant irritation from Conners' laziness and the habitual sly look on his narrow face.

"Put a pebble in your mouth, it will keep the saliva flowing," Dane ordered. "It's a trick I learned in Tunisia." Conners looked at him in disbelief while Dane felt Patterson's boot. Sure enough, he felt the tightness around the ankle as it swelled. "Yep, you've twisted it alright." Dane stood up and looked around, wondering what to do about the injured man. He breathed a silent prayer for wisdom. "Sit here and rest until we start moving again."

"Sergeant Shaw, Sergeant Shaw, where are you?" Dane heard the querulous voice asking from up ahead.

"I'm back here, sir." Dane answered. Second Lieutenant Galow, Lieutenant Enderhall's replacement, came tripping up. Dane and Gates saluted their ninety day wonder, as second lieutenants fresh from their three months training course were termed by their men. Dane knew Galow to be a typical product of the rushed program which the army used to supply needed officers. Inexperienced, with poor command skills and yet brimming over with his own importance, Galow

21

needed to be curbed by Makins, the platoon sergeant, or else he would become as much a hazard to their platoon as the Germans were. Not all second lieutenants were this bad, but unfortunately too many were.

"What are you doing at the back of the line?" the lieutenant asked with a scowl.

"I'm checking the men, sir," Dane replied in a noncommittal tone of voice.

"Captain Carter has called for a conference with the lieutenants and their platoon sergeants. You're in charge of the platoon until Sergeant Makins and I return."

Surprised, Dane stared at him until the lieutenant's scowl deepened, and then saluted. As Galow walked away, Dane and Gates exchanged puzzled glances and moved away from the men so they couldn't be overheard.

"Why in the world would the captain be calling for a conference now?" Gates wondered out loud.

"Beats me. We need to be moving faster, not stopping to have meetings. What's so important to necessitate all the company leaders huddling together?" Dane never learned why.

They returned to their men, and Dane checked the rest of them. All were hot and thirsty. Most tried the pebbles and found they helped. Only Patterson suffered from an injury. Dane issued orders, "When we move out, Rosario and Hemphill carry Patterson's pack between you. Meanwhile, sit and relax." He lowered himself and leaned back against the same rock on which Patterson sat. The 'crump' sound of an exploding mortar shell filled the air.

# Chapter Two

The Americans were stunned with surprise, then guns started firing and men screamed.

Dane yelled, "Take cover!" He rolled behind his rock and looked for targets. Patterson still sat on the rock, gaping at the sudden noise when a bullet took him in the chest and he tumbled off. Dane saw German helmets sticking up over the top of the slope and shooting down at the Americans. He scanned the slopes opposite his squad, surprised to see no enemy soldiers. They were all ahead of him.

"Gates, lead the squad to the top of the right hand slope and sweep forward. Everybody, drop your back packs! Go!" Dane bellowed. He waited until his men were scrambling up and then dashed ahead to the next squad in line just as another mortar round exploded amid more screams.

"Where's Sergeant Ardivan?" Dane yelled to the squad ahead of him.

One of the men turned frightened eyes to him. "He's down," he screamed over the noise of the firing.

"Second Squad, drop your backpacks and follow me! First Squad, covering fire, odd men to the right, even men to the left," Dane roared in a voice both squads heard. As the Second Squad got to its feet, German bullets peppered them and a man stumbled and fell. Then the American fire took effect and drove the Germans to cover. Dane led the squad up the slope as another mortar round burst in the riverbed.

Once up on the high ground he shook the men into a skirmish line and moved forward. At once they ran into a couple of Germans who traded shots with them before retreating ahead of the Americans. Dane waved the squad on while he grabbed the two nearest soldiers. "Follow me," he told them. The three of them slid down into a gully about thirty yards away and roughly parallel to the riverbed just as another mortar round exploded. In the back of his mind, Dane wondered at the slow rate of fire of the enemy mortar. Under normal circumstances they were fired off as fast as someone dropped the shells into the tube, about every five or ten seconds. These were being fired about once a minute.

They ran, bent over, down the gully as a crescendo of firing erupted behind them between the Second Squad and the Germans at the top of the slope. *Lord, please protect us, don't let us be spotted,* Dane prayed as they ran.

Nobody shot at them or sounded an alarm.

When Dane thought they'd traveled far enough, he stopped and motioned the other two men to follow him. They crept up the side of the gully and heard the 'whoop' of another mortar shell firing. Dane peeked over the edge and saw the mortar crew about twenty yards away, and the reason for the slow rate of fire. The crew needed to reposition the mortar after every shot because it didn't have a base plate and a damaged support arm caused it to lean over each time it fired.

Dane whispered, "Grenades," pulled one out, and squirmed on his belly towards the Germans, followed by the other two GIs. When they got within range, he pulled the pin and held up three fingers. He hefted it once, twice, and threw it at the same time as the other two. The three explosions rang out as one. Dane sprang to his feet and charged, firing his Thompson submachine gun at the survivors. The mortar crew went down, but then four Germans on the far side of the mortar position jumped to their feet from their firing positions overlooking the riverbed. Dane leaped among them.

With breathtaking quickness he rammed the barrel of his gun into the midsection of one who collapsed like a broken folding chair. Then Dane ducked under the rifle butt of another who slipped, lost his balance, and fell on his face. Dane clobbered the third with the butt of his gun who then flopped into the fourth. Both of them went down in a welter of arms and legs, leaving Dane standing there with the same surprised look on his face as the other Americans. All four Germans were down on the ground tangled up together and he'd only hit two. They made such a ludicrous sight the three Americans broke out in laughter. The Germans decided to stay down.

Disarming the prisoners and leaving one of his men to guard them, Dane and the other GI made their way back to the firefight going on between Second Squad and a German group. The two men snaked their way behind the Germans, hugging the ground. There were about ten enemy soldiers. Some of them were firing down into the riverbed while the rest shot at the American squad. What looked like an NCO began to pull his squad back when the two Americans opened up. Three of the Germans fell. When the NCO turned around, he looked down the barrel of Dane's gun. Discretion proved the better part of valor and he raised his hands, followed by the rest of his squad.

\*\*\*

Gates and his squad reached the top of the ridge without suffering any more casualties. He waved his arm and screamed above the racket, "Form skirmish line! Advance!"

Two Germans spun around to face this new threat. They fired off a round apiece before retreating. As they fell back more men joined them from where they'd been shooting down at the trapped Americans.

"Go, go, move forward," Gates kept yelling. "Drive them back." A corner of his mind registered the fact the mortar stopped firing. The shooting from below became heavier, and he noticed some Americans scaling the bank.

A green flare trailed smoke into the sky ahead of him from his side of the river bank and made a lazy curve back to the ground. Realizing it must be a prearranged signal for retreat, Gates hollered, "Attack! Charge!" He raced forward but a burst of firing drove him to the ground.

O'Halloran, who carried the squad's Browning Automatic Rifle, or BAR for short, dropped beside Gates and blazed away. Three Germans fell and the rest fled.

Gates jumped to his feet, then dropped back down as bullets zinged past his head. The bullets came from the Americans trapped in the river bed. Realizing they didn't know the attack was over and continued to shoot at the top of the banks, Gates waved for the squad to stay down. Afraid of endangering his men to friendly fire, he stopped the pursuit.

He glanced over to the other side and saw Shaw squirming to the edge, being careful not to expose himself, and hollering, "Stop shooting! Stop shooting!" Gradually the firing died down. Dane stood up and saw Gates. "What happened over there?"

"There were a couple of squads on this side, most of them escaped. How about you?" Gates hollered back.

"We got the mortar and one squad. Stay up there with your squad and guard the slope, I'll leave this squad here." Dane said something to the corporal of Second Squad and then slid down the slope. *I wonder how much damage the company suffered*, Gates thought.

# Chapter Three

Almost an hour later Dane kneeled beside Lieutenant Jennings, the last conscious surviving officer. The lieutenant suffered multiple wounds but refused to be medicated, preferring to endure the pain and help organize the company. Dane gritted his teeth at the torn and suffering man and gave him a respectful salute. *You're one of the good ninety day wonders. We can't afford to lose men like you.*

"What's the story?" Jennings wheezed.

"I've got one of my men who understands German interrogating the prisoners, but we're not going to learn much more. We were been spotted by the Germans and a platoon ambushed us. It looks like they suffered about twenty casualties before breaking off."

The lieutenant gasped in pain. After catching his breath, he added, "I heard you caused seventeen of them."

At the obvious signs of acute pain, the medic standing by inserted a hyperemic needle into the patient's arm. As the morphine took effect, Dane watched the tortured lines in Jennings' face smooth out.

Dane shrugged at the complement and went on, "There're guards on each side of us and scouts are out looking for a place to take our wounded." He mopped his face with his shirt sleeve. "If we stay down here they'll cook. There has to be farmhouses or other buildings nearby. As for casualties, the company's been beheaded. Captain Carter, Lieutenants Galow and Wilson are dead and the medic says Lieutenant Oosterkamp probably won't survive his wounds. The First Sergeant and all four platoon sergeants are down, as well as seven other sergeants and five corporals. We have a total of 14 dead and 36 wounded, almost one third of the company."

\*\*\*

Jennings looked at Sergeant Shaw through half closed eyes. The morphine shot the corpsman gave him started taking effect and his mind tried to drift away. He'd noticed when all the officers were down, Shaw issued orders which were effectual, economic, and brought organization out of the chaos.

Jennings' mind went back to the first exploding mortar shell. Either through incredible bad luck or very good aiming, it exploded right in the middle of the meeting called by Captain Carter. The second landed close by. They devastated the command structure of the company. He could still hear the screams of the wounded and dying men and the pain as the shrapnel ripped into his own body.

He forced his mind back to the matter at hand. He'd been funneling orders through Shaw until now, but he wouldn't be able to hold up much longer. "Sergeant," he licked his dry lips, "you're gonna have to take command of the company, you're the senior surviving sergeant. I suggest we turn back." He sighed in resignation. He didn't like it, but he didn't know what else to do.

Dane pursed his lips. "Since we haven't seen any other American units, I expect the Germans have plugged the hole in their defenses and are between us and our lines. Has there been any radio contact with battalion?"

Jennings sighed. "We haven't been able to raise them, radio problems again." He paused. "They might have broken through and be following us."

Dane shook his head. "We can't rely on that. We have to assume we're on our own with a mission to accomplish. By the way, do you know where we are and where the bridge is?"

Jennings blinked in surprise. "Captain Carter carried the map. Didn't you get it?"

Dane looked grim. "We didn't find it with his body, and I never saw it. So am I right to assume we don't know where we're going?"

Jennings grimaced again. "It looks like we can't go back, can't go forward, and can't stay here." He shot a look at the sergeant. "Maybe you should have a council of war with all the sergeants and see what they think."

"Sir," Dane hesitated and then with a dogged expression plowed on, "if I'm in command then I will command. I'm not going to stop and have a vote every time there needs to be a decision made. I'm open to ideas and suggestions, but I'll make the decisions."

Jennings looked at the determined face, satisfaction at Shaw passing his first test easing his mind. Jennings sagged. "Do you know what you're going to do?"

"Not yet, but God will show me," Dane replied, confidence in his voice.

Jennings drifted out again. What did Sergeant Shaw say, something about God? His mind retreated into a drug induced haze, blocking out the pain.

\*\*\*

Corporal Winans came up, followed by Private Braun, the German speaking man from Dane's squad. Like many people of German descent, Braun possessed brown hair and brown eyes. Winans saluted, "Lieutenant, burial detail is finished digging the graves." He stared at the lieutenant's white face and closed eyes.

Dane turned to him. "Lieutenant Jennings has turned the company over to me." He sighed. "I'll be there in a couple of minutes for the burials."

"Yes, Sarge," Winans hurried away.

Dane turned to Braun. "Did you get anything more out of the prisoners?"

Braun shook his head. "Just names, ranks, and serial numbers mostly."

"How about any other German units around, like their company?"

Braun hesitated. "I'm not sure; the company might be close by. Somebody said something before another prisoner hushed him up which might have meant they're an advance platoon for their company."

"Oh no," Dane moaned. "So we might be attacked by a company at any time." He looked around. "We have got to get out of here quick. Go join your squad for now; I'll need to detach you for guarding the prisoners later. Let Corporal Gates know."

After Braun left, Dane considered his next action. With the loss of all the officers he needed to appoint four new platoon leaders. He closed his eyes. *Dear God, please give me wisdom. Direct me as to which four men I need to promote. In Jesus' name I pray. Amen.*

He went over his mental notes of which sergeants kept their heads and which ones were overwhelmed by the disaster. Of course he knew all of them, kind of. His mind shied away like a nervous colt from the reason why he didn't know them better. *Zimmerman was a lumberjack foreman from Minnesota. He keeps his men in line. Grissom is a heavy weapons sergeant. He needs to stay there. Lassiter's a tough Texan. He's a good fit. Jones is the senior surviving sergeant of his platoon and a good one.* His choices made, he looked around and spotted one of them.

"Sergeant Zimmerman," he called out. He saw Zimmerman look up when he heard his name. Dane waited while Zimmerman finished giving instructions to Corporal Winans and then wasted no time in getting to the point. "Lieutenant Jennings has turned the company over to me. I'm putting you in charge of First Platoon, Sergeant Grissom over the Heavy Weapons Platoon, Sergeant Lassiter over the Second Platoon, and Sergeant Jones over the Third. There might be a Kraut company nearby. If there is, the Germans who ambushed us have warned them. I need you to send a detail ahead and find a place where we can take the wounded out of this riverbed and defend ourselves from an attack."

Zimmerman nodded. "I'll send out a squad right away. Anything else?"

Dane added, "I want to hold a conference with the four of you. I'll need to round the others up. Do you know where they are?"

Zimmerman looked at him. "Um, you could send runners to find them."

Dane looked at him with a blank stare and then shook his head in self-disgust. "You're right, I didn't think about them." He looked around. "Do you know where they are?"

Zimmerman chuckled. "I'll send them out. Where and when do you want to meet?"

Dane glanced up and pointed to a big rock at the top of the slope. "Meet there in ten minutes," he looked at his watch, "at 1045 hours. I need some fresh air. Now I have to hold the funeral."

Dane moved off and pulled his well-read Bible out of his pocket. When he got to the grave site, some of the men were standing around. He started reading from Psalms 104, starting at verse 13: "Like as a father pitieth his children, so the Lord pitieth them that fear him. For He knoweth our frame; he remembereth that we are dust."

***

When Braun climbed the slope to return to his squad, he met Conners standing watch.

"Did you learn anything from your cousins?" Conners asked, his ever-present cigarette drooping from the corner of his mouth.

Always sensitive about his German heritage, Braun swore and turned on him. "Don't call me a Kraut!" he yelled and swung a punch, catching the surprised Conners in the face, giving him a bloody lip and smashing his cigarette. The two men started punching each other. Braun dropped his rifle and swung a right at Conners' head. Conners ducked, the blow missed, and then hit Braun in the face, snapping his head back.

In a rage, Braun rushed Conners, smothering him with a succession of rights and lefts. Conners put up a desperate defense, trying to block the blows with his forearms as he gave up ground. Then his heel caught on a rock and he tripped and fell down with Braun on top of him. Braun felt hands grabbing and pulling him off before he could land another blow. Rosario held him while O'Halloran yanked Conners to his feet.

Gates came storming up, yelling "What's going on here?", or words to that effect.

"He called me a Kraut," Braun accused.

"I just asked if he learned anything from the prisoners," Conners whined. "I didn't call him a Kraut."

Gates looked at both of them in disgust. "If you want to fight somebody, there's a whole German-Italian army out there. Go fight them. Braun, stop being so thin-skinned. Conners, get back to your post." Rosario and O'Halloran released their grips and Conners wiped his mouth. When he saw the blood on it, he glared at Braun and slouched away, pulling out another cigarette.

Braun mopped his sweaty face and looked at Gates while the other two went back to their posts. "Sergeant Shaw wanted me to tell you he's going to dispatch me to guard duty over the prisoners."

"Did he say when?"

"No." Braun shook his head, and then added, "What a mess. We got whipped, a sergeant's in command of the company, and I don't think he knows what to do."

Gates gave him a cold stare. "You've only been with the squad a couple of weeks. You'll soon find out Sergeant Shaw always has a plan. As for being whipped, you're only beaten if you think so. Now get back to your post."

\*\*\*

Although Dane didn't hear what Braun said, he saw the words echoed in his men as he moved among them. The body language and the side-long looks let him know the men were dispirited by the defeat and disquieted at being led by a sergeant. A sergeant many of them knew little about. Since becoming promoted to sergeant, he'd held himself apart from most of the men for personal reasons. As a result they didn't know him. Expressions told him some of the men were whipped, but a disgusted comment he overheard summed up the attitude of many others: "Ambushed by a platoon. A platoon, for crying out loud!"

When he gave orders to prepare the wounded to be carried up the slope, he noticed just the hope of them getting out of the oven of the riverbed made the men perk up. Many of them weren't beaten yet, but if he didn't come up with something soon, they well might be. *If only I knew what to do?*

He noticed the group of sergeants standing at the meeting place. He climbed up to give them their new assignments.

While Dane talked to the new platoon leaders, Tennessee and Hemphill were out scouting for someplace to take the wounded: a farmhouse, an empty barn, something. They were about half a mile away from the company and hadn't seen anything yet. They were climbing a rocky ridge when they heard movement on the other side. They froze, listening. Tennessee motioned for Hemphill to cover him. He crawled up and peered around a rock, to see a face staring back at him from a few inches away.

# Chapter Four

After breakfast Maria Calvoratti skipped out to water the sheep and found one of them gone. "That Pepecita," she said aloud, "she snuck out again." Dancing back to the house, she found her father preparing to check the orange trees and her mother carrying a hoe out to the garden. "Naughty Pepecita ran off again," she announced. Unless other people were around, they spoke in English to each other.

For an instant strain showed on her parents' faces. "You best find her, Maria," her father answered, trying to hide the gruffness in his voice.

"Yes Papa." Maria gave them her infectious smile and sped off. Before searching for the elusive sheep, she stopped at her grandparents' graves and dropped to her knees. Most mornings she would spend some time tending the daisies, roses and lavender which decorated the gravesite. It made her feel close to them, especially her grandmother. Today, as she absentmindedly pulled some weeds, her mind wandered to the past.

Her father, Antonio, immigrated to America some twenty years ago to seek his fortune and wound up in Omaha, Nebraska. He held a good job when he met and married her mother, Lucia, the epitome of a good Italian girl. Maria's mouth formed a tender smile as she recalled her parents telling her how happy they were at her birth. They were sure they would have a number of children and a secure life ahead of them.

Then came the 1929 stock market crash and subsequent depression, and Papa lost his job. Her smile disappeared as she recalled the hard times as they survived on the few temporary jobs Papa could find, as well as some handouts from Mama's family. They lived hand to mouth. At last Papa secured a job working at a cattle yard. Things were looking up. But then came the terrible accident when a steer ran over him and shattered his leg and their lives.

Once his leg healed to the point where he could leave his bed and hobble around with a crutch, Papa discovered a cripple could not find any kind of employment. He needed operations to be able to walk properly again, and they didn't have the money. They were in a dilemma: he couldn't walk without the operations and he needed to walk to be able to pay for them.

Soon after Papa semi-recovered, a letter came from his parents saying his father was dying. Papa and Mama talked it over. Despite the dark clouds of impending war in Europe, they decided to move back to Sicily and take over the farm. At least it would provide a livelihood. Since the prospects of warfare in the sparsely settled middle of the island seemed unlikely to them, they thought it would be safe. Between selling everything they owned and his parents sending them money, they were able to pay for the tickets. They moved back to Sicily and Papa became a farmer again. But farm life is hard work, and Papa with his crippled leg had his limitations. The farm deteriorated to where they possessed half a dozen sheep, a few orange and olive trees, a garden, a donkey and a wagon. She needed to find the wandering sheep.

Maria blinked from her reverie, shivered, and jumped to her feet. She had work to do. Before leaving, however, she looked at the grave of her small, brave grandmother and whispered, "I promise, *Nonna,* this farm will be prosperous again."

After checking all the sheep's normal hiding places and coming up empty, Maria stood looking around with her hands on her ample hips. "Now where did you go this time, Pepecita?" she said.

As she gazed over the Sicilian countryside, she saw the brome grass, downy oaks, and hackberries. She threw her arms out. Although duly instructed in the household chores by her longsuffering mother, she loved being outdoors, working with the trees and sheep, running up and down the hills. She gave a skip of pure joy and laughed out loud, not caring she spent a lot of time alone. After all, she had herself and the sheep to talk to, although the sheep were poor conversationalists. She giggled at the thought.

She heard a low 'boom' in the distance and looked up, searching for the source of the thunder. There wasn't a cloud in the sky. Puzzled, she listened some more and heard another boom, and then some kind of noise, almost like a rattle. It came from the west and she hesitated, curiosity over the strange noises fighting against the need to find Pepecita. Curiosity won out. Telling herself Pepecita might have gone that way, she started off. After a few minutes the noises stopped, but she continued on, being sure to check any place where the sheep might be hiding. It took over an hour before she came close to where she thought the noises came from.

As she climbed up a slope, she heard what sounded like somebody on the other side. She stopped, and they stopped. Perplexed by the sounds, she resumed climbing, reached the top and peered around a rock to see a man's face in front of her. She squeaked in surprise and the man jumped. His jaw dropped open and he stammered, "What…who are you?"

"Maria, who are you?" she returned in English, which made the man even more astonished. He stood up to his full, lanky height, and darted a look around to see if there were any more surprises like her popping up. She looked up at his six foot frame, rather long face, well-muscled shoulders, and felt her heart doing strange flip-flops.

"Tennessee," he answered without thinking.

She frowned, "That's not a name, that's a state." She thought for a second. "Or a river."

"It's mah nickname," he said in his southern drawl, and then he realized what she said. "How do you know that? How come you speak English?" he asked in amazement.

"I was born in the United States."

He looked her up and down. For the first time in her life she became conscious of her black hair tumbling down her back almost to her waist. Of how her well-developed figure filled out her loose necked scarlet blouse and brightly patterned skirt. She noticed her head came between his heart and shoulder and she felt her heart skip a beat.

They became aware of Hemphill, who stood up and joined them with the same look of amazement on his face.

"Who're you?" she demanded.

"Hemphill, Jonas Hemphill, ma'am."

Tennessee looked around but could see no sign of habitation. "Whatcha you doing out here?" he asked.

"Looking for a sheep."

"A sheep?" he asked with dumbfounded expression on his face.

"Yes," she nodded, "a sheep. You know, stands about this tall," she held her hand waist high, "has wool, goes 'baa'."

Tennessee flushed. "Ah knows what a sheep is." A wicked smile spread across his face. "If you done lost yore sheep, then you must be Little Bo Peep."

She looked at him, threw back her head and laughed. Then she became serious. "What are you doing here? Are you American soldiers?"

"Yes ma'am, we are. Do you live around here? We have a passel of wounded needing shelter."

At once she felt concern. "We live about three kilometers that way," she said, pointing east. At their blank looks she translated, "About two miles. You can bring them there."

"Let's go tell Sarge. Will you come with us?" Tennessee asked.

"Of course," she nodded, and thought to herself, *you couldn't drag me away.*

As they approached the dry riverbed, Tennessee said, "The sergeant is over thar."

Maria looked in the direction he indicated. She saw five men standing together looking at her, stunned surprise on their faces. She wondered which one Tennessee would lead her to. She saw a big blond man, at least six feet tall, with powerful arms and shoulders. The second man, almost as tall, had a slender build and bowed legs. *A cowboy*, she thought to herself. The third man had brown hair, average height, and wore glasses which made Maria think of a storekeeper. The short fourth man looked almost as broad as tall. The fifth man standing behind the others appeared so unobtrusive she ignored him. She decided the first man must be the sergeant and stared at him, while Zimmerman returned the interest. She felt flummoxed when Tennessee led her to the fifth man.

"Sergeant Shaw, this is Maria. She's an American and lives nearby. She says we can take the wounded to her home."

All the sergeants were as flummoxed as her. "You are? We can? Where do you live?" Shaw stammered.

She pointed. "We live about two miles over there." She looked down into the riverbed and saw the wounded lying there. "Oh," she said and paled.

"It would be a big help, miss," Shaw replied, pulling her attention away from the bloody sight. "Would you also happen to know where the bridge over the Salso River is?" he asked, hope in his eyes.

She frowned in thought. "Do you mean the big one on Road 120?"

"Yes," he nodded with an eager look while the others paid even closer attention to her.

"*Si,* but it's far away. You'll need to go east about four kilometers to catch the road clear to Leonforte and then back north. You'd never make it," she shook her head. "There are many soldiers there."

"What if we go cross country?"

"Well, yes, you could go that way," she said, doubt in her voice, "but it's confusing with all the hills and ridges and gullies. I think I could do it, but to try to tell you?" she shook her head again.

\*\*\*

As she spoke, a runner from the squad Zimmerman sent out scrambled his way up the bank and stopped, flummoxed to see a pretty girl talking to the sergeants. He stammered out his report while not taking his eyes off of her. "There's an easier way out of the riverbed about a hundred yards on up."

"East side or west side?" Dane asked. *There seems to be a lot of flummoxing going on*, he noticed.

"Huh?" The runner tore his attention from Maria, "On the right, uh, east side."

"Good, we can start moving out." Dane turned to the girl, "Maria, is it? Would you lead us to your home?" Maria nodded, but then they were interrupted when two scouts hurried up the bank, puffing as they came.

Dane saw Lassiter's lip curl at the sight of the leader and knew the reason why. When informed about a full-blooded Apache, nicknamed 'Pache of course, in Lassiter's squad, Captain Carter selected 'Pache to be the chief scout. He didn't bother to find out 'Pache, raised in Phoenix, Arizona, needed a compass to tell east from west. A fact most of the company knew. As chief scout 'Pache always assigned someone to go with him so he could find his way back to the company. *Just another sign of Carter's ineptitude*, Dane thought to himself.

'Pache reported to Dane, "There's a German company headed in our direction." He pointed north.

Dane froze. "How far away?"

"A mile, maybe a mile and a half."

The other scout added, "Be here in twenty or thirty minutes, they're moving pretty slow."

All eyes were on Dane as he looked around. He made a silent prayer. *Lord, I need your help. I need you to tell me what to do, Lord. I need your wisdom and guidance to protect these people you put into my care.* He pointed to the low ridge to the east, about a quarter mile away, "What's on the other side of that ridge?"

Tennessee answered, "Nother ridge about a

quarter mile further on, that's where we run into Miss Maria. Nothin' between them ridges, just open ground."

A plan formed in Dane's mind. He spent about twenty seconds looking at the lay of the land, the curve in the riverbed, and the ridge to the east, checking it out against his thoughts. He faced the others. "Gentlemen, God gave me an idea," and told it to them. They were stunned at the audacious and risky plan. But since none of them had a better option, or any other suggestions at all, and the only alternative must be a futile defense where they stood, they went for it. Dane snapped express orders to the four platoon leaders. As he talked, his face hardened into one of ferocious and ruthless determination.

\*\*\*

Maria stared at him with a shiver of fear going down her spine. When she approached the five men, this one appeared almost invisible. The other four, including the storekeeper, overshadowed him. Then the others made their reports to him, and he seemed in some obscure way to grow. Now she watched the transformation continuing and he became the one in command, the cynosure of all eyes, impossible to overlook. Even she got an order, "Miss Maria, please go with Sergeant Grissom." Though phrased as a request, she knew it for an order. She noticed as he spoke, he didn't really look at her, but stared over her shoulder. She wondered why, because he looked everyone else in the eye when he talked to them.

He glanced around and beckoned to a nearby man. "Chilvers, have Braun meet me at the prisoners, on the double." She glanced over to the newcomer and her eyes widened. *What a handsome man,* she thought to herself as Chilvers gave her a wide smile. She took in his baby blue eyes, Adonis-like features and wavy blond hair which made other females itch to run their fingers through it. He gave her another smile from his perfect, white teeth before he left.

As everybody scattered to obey their orders, Dane turned and ran down the bank. Maria's jaw dropped. She liked running up and down slopes, but to run down that steep bank? *Why, I would never have tried it!* But he did it with such unconcern, as if it were nothing. She looked down and saw him giving orders to someone by the wounded, having reached the bottom without mishap. *Why, the man must have the agility of a mountain goat,* she thought in awe.

# Chapter Five

In five minutes Dane had the company on the move. The extra backpacks from the dead and wounded and from Grissom's platoon were stacked in piles in the riverbed. They were hidden from the approaching Germans by the curve in the riverbed, unless they came down the riverbed past the place where the Americans were debouching. His plan accounted for that eventuality, unless the Germans refused to take the bait. Sergeant Grissom's platoon led the way, with eleven stretchers carrying wounded. The lead bearers for each stretcher were the German prisoners. Maria went with them. They hurried as fast as they could down the riverbed, up through the cut in the bank, trotted over to the low ridge, and disappeared over the top. More of the company followed them with the rest of the wounded, of necessity moving somewhat slower than the lead group.

When Dane exited the cut, he looked first in the direction the Germans were coming, then at the ridge they were heading towards. He called 'Pache to his side. "Do you see the dead tree on top of the ridge and the bush next to it?" pointing towards a silverbush shrub. 'Pache looked and nodded. "Run over to the bush and hide behind it. Don't let the

51

Germans see you. When the Germans are in a position to see us, give the bush a shake. Just one and not a big one, I'll see it." 'Pache took off running.

As the men exited the cut, Dane reminded them over and over, "Keep going and don't look around. Keep looking forward or down to the ground." He kept them moving as fast as they could while he counted down the minutes. Fifteen minutes had passed since 'Pache told him about the German company, but they were only a third of the way to the ridge. With a grim look on his face Dane kept the men moving as fast as they could go. Five more minutes, six minutes, seven minutes. The leading men reached the base of the slope but still 'Pache didn't signal.

"Okay," Dane barked, "drop down to a walk." Obeying his command, the men slowed down. They reached the slope and started climbing it. Men disappeared over the top of the ridge. Dane walked with the last group, nearing the base of the slope, when the bush shook. Keeping his head down, forcing himself not to turn and look back, he prayed again. *Lord, have the Germans follow us, don't let them look around.* The end of the line had, by design, three stretchers to draw the German's attention. As Dane climbed the slope he felt tightness in the middle of his back, waiting for a bullet to hit. But he made it over the top of the ridge without any shots being fired and let out his breath in a long 'whew'.

"Go! Go!" he barked out and the column double-timed to the next ridge. Dane joined 'Pache behind the bush and peered back the way they'd came. He saw some Germans standing on the far bank of the riverbed. They were looking his way, so Dane knew they'd seen the Americans. Would they follow them? Dane felt his throat tighten as what looked like an officer joined the group. Dane went over the plan in his head again while he watched the Germans converse. There were so many variables in the equation. What were the original orders of the commander and the company's mission? Is the commander cautious or bold and daring? Is he green or experienced? Has he seen every trick in the book, plus other devices Dane couldn't imagine?

In his place, Dane knew he would send scouts to check out the riverbed to make sure there were no surprises hiding there. But if the platoon that ambushed them told the German commander how the American company had been surprised, and seeing the same company making its escape, and maybe with orders to run this unit to the ground, maybe the commander would take the bait and chase them. There were a lot of maybes in that sentence. It was up to the Lord now. He put the plan in Dane's head, and He would have to make it work.

After what felt like an eternity, but actually took only a couple of minutes, the officer pointed in Dane's direction and nodded. Soldiers poured down the bank and came up the cut. He couldn't see anybody following the river downstream. Relief flooded him as he murmured, "Praise the Lord."

Out of the corner of his eye Dane saw 'Pache give him a surprised glance at his words. ." Dane interpreted the look. *He's thinking I talk to and about God a lot.* Dane gave himself a mental shake and concentrated on the mission at hand.

He turned and slid down the slope, followed by 'Pache. Dane looked at the next ridge, towards which his company streamed. He pointed to a shrub at the top of the ridge. "See the bush with the yellow flowers? Hide behind it and give it a shake when you see Germans come over this ridge."

'Pache nodded and took off. Dane ran up to the front of the line, checking his men as he passed them. They rushed along, panting, hampered by their heavy backpacks. But he couldn't allow them to be seen without their packs. Any commander worth his salt would be suspicious at seeing an enemy force, miles from their camp, not carrying spare supplies.

Nevertheless, men were helping the walking

wounded by giving them an arm. In a few cases a man on each side grabbed the wounded man's belt, lifted him and almost ran. They knew they had to reach the next ridge and safety.

There were at least four men trotting along carrying each stretcher. The unfortunate wounded were jostled about. As Dane ran, he winced at their moans and screams of pain. He felt their suffering, but he needed to save their lives.

Dane counted off the minutes again, and after fifteen minutes yelled out, "Walk, heads down or look ahead." He slowed to a walk, letting the others pass by and keeping an eye on the yellow-flowered bush. The last of the line almost reached him when the bush shook. The men at the front of the line were climbing up this taller ridge and almost reached the top. Again he felt the tightness in the middle of his back. Would the Germans open fire this time? He thought not. The range was still too great, although the Germans were closer this time. He prayed they would be content to play catch up for the time being. Without a doubt they were closing the gap while his men climbed the ridge, but as long as nobody appeared to notice the approaching Germans...

At last he topped the ridge and went down the other side. He saw his men strung out below the top of the ridge, hidden from the approaching Germans.

The prisoners were tied and gagged at the bottom of the slope. Maria's colorful clothes showed where she sat separated from them. Dane spotted Sergeant Grissom peering out from behind a bush, looking towards the approaching enemy. He noticed the mortar tubes were sticking almost straight up. *Good, it means the enemy would be close when we open fire.* He saw where the 30 caliber machine guns were placed. It would only take a minute for them to be sited and firing.

He scrambled over to Grissom and peered through the bush. The German commander showed his experience by having a skirmish line of about a dozen men a couple of hundred feet out in front of his main force. The rest of his men were not spread out in a line or in a column, but were scattered in depth. But because the men hurried across the open ground, the distance between the skirmish line and the main group shrank, and clumps of men formed.

Grissom turned his head towards the mortar crews, and using hand signals made them adjust their targets. Everybody waited with bated breath for Dane to give the signal.

# Chapter Six

Tennessee lay with his cheek pressed against the hot ground, his rifle in his hand. He watched Sergeants Shaw and Grissom from his position. They were the only two soldiers able to see the enemy coming. Everyone else, like Tennessee, lay on their stomachs below the ridge line, out of sight.

Tennessee, like Corporal Gates, served with Shaw back in Tunisia, and also like Gates, had every confidence in Shaw's plans and ideas. Shaw had been tough but patient in training the squad, and it paid off here in Sicily. During the invasion and the weeks of battles since then, the squad suffered just four casualties. They'd received three replacements a couple of weeks ago, Braun, Conners and Patterson. *Poor kid, he didn't last a month,* Tennessee thought of the slain soldier.

He saw the all-around glance Shaw gave when the sergeant came over the top and took cover. Tennessee knew from experience Shaw saw more in a glance than most men would see if they stopped and stared. Now Tennessee waited for the signal to poke his head over the top of the ridge and start shooting. He wiped his sweating hands on his pants and gripped his rifle again. Everyone who could handle a rifle lay hidden behind the top of the ridge, waiting, waiting…

Then Shaw shouted, "Fire!" and the mortars shot their missiles. Tennessee squirmed up to the ridge top, and to his surprise saw a German a few feet from him, climbing the ridge. Tennessee shot him through the chest. Rifles, BAR's and Thompson submachine guns blazed away and the German skirmish line went down. One of the mortar rounds hit one group of Krauts while the other round caused little damage. Grissom yelled out corrections. The 30's opened up and Germans dropped in swathes. Tennessee fired as fast as he could at the exposed enemy, and more mortar rounds found targets. The enemy line sagged back under the relentless hammering. An officer tried to restore order, but he fell. The Germans saw the best defensive position lay behind them. They started retreating back to it, amid the hail of bullets and exploding mortar rounds.

"Charge!" yelled Sergeant Shaw, and Tennessee jumped to his feet, running down the slope, shouting and shooting as the Germans broke and ran. As the first Germans reached the base of the slope of the first ridge, rifle barrels appeared at the top. Zimmerman's platoon opened up, with the other 30 caliber machine gun. Another swathe of Germans fell.

"Hit the dirt!" someone screamed and

Tennessee flopped down. He aimed and hit another German. He saw Shaw and a handful of men run to outflank the enemy, then drop to the ground and start shooting. Tennessee saw Grissom grab a 30, run to the other flank and plant it. He shot anyone trying to escape in his direction.

The Germans were trapped by Zimmerman's men on the ridge, the rest of the company on the opposite side, while Shaw and Grissom blocked the ends. Hands were raised and the bloodbath stopped. The rest of the German company surrendered.

Tennessee stood up, surprised at the accomplishment. In less than ten minutes they trapped and wiped out an entire enemy company.

Shaw got to his feet and barked out orders, "Round up the prisoners, get the wounded attended to. Gates, sweep the area between the ridges."

Gates spread out his men in a skirmish line. They paced across the open ground, checking bodies. Most of the wounded were easy to spot, groaning or holding various parts of their anatomy. Several times Tennessee heard a yell, "Here's a wounded man," at an unconscious body. Tennessee spotted two Germans lying face down. Neither showed any blood stains and their rifles were under their hands. Suspicious, he circled around them without seeing any wounds. Without warning, he jabbed hard at one of the bodies with his rifle and jumped back. The victim yelped in pain. The other man rolled over to point his rifle in Tennessee's direction. He stopped moving when he saw Tennessee's rifle aimed at him. "Playing possum, were ya?" He motioned with his rifle. "Git up." Crestfallen, they joined the rest of the prisoners and were all led back to the second, higher ridge.

When they reached it, Tennessee saw Maria sitting on a rock, watching them. "You weren't sitting there durin' the shootin', were ya?" Tennessee croaked.

Maria shook her head. "I waited 'til it ended."

He didn't realize how dry and scorched his throat felt until he talked. He'd done a lot of yelling during the charge. He took out his canteen and took a long drink. Then he noticed Maria's eyes on the water.

"Please, may I have some?" she asked.

"Oh! Oh, of course." He started to hand her the canteen, then stopped and carefully wiped the neck clean before handing it to her.

She lifted it to her mouth took a swig, and then made a face at the warm liquid. "It's wet," she announced. They both laughed at the release of tension.

***

Braun walked among the prisoners and listened to their talk. Doc, the American medic, called to him, "Braun, come here." Braun moved to where Doc bent over a wounded German soldier.

The soldier jabbered away at Doc, desperate to communicate something, and pointed to his blood-covered right arm.

"What's he saying?" Doc asked.

Braun talked to the distraught man and calmed him down so he could understand what the German said. Braun looked at Doc. "He asks please don't amputate his arm. He's a musician and can't make a living without it."

"Humph," Doc snorted. "He should have thought about that before he joined the army." Unlike his harsh words, his fingers were gentle as he examined the wounded man. At last he said, "You can tell him not to worry, I can save his arm." Braun passed on the message and the soldier sighed in relief.

The German medic happened by during the exchange and he looked at Braun. "You speak German gute," he said in guttural English.

Braun flushed. "My parents came from Germany," he answered with reluctance.

"What part of Germany?" Doctor Mueller asked as he examined another patient.

Braun hesitated and then answered, "Magdeburg."

Mueller looked up in surprise, "That is vhere I

am from." Braun muttered something under his breath and hurried off, leaving Mueller staring after him in surprise. The German turned to more pressing matters.

\*\*\*

Dane met Zimmerman on the first ridge. Zimmerman told Dane, "We almost didn't make it in time."

"What happened?"

"We had to capture them first," he said, and pointed to the other side of the riverbed. Dane looked and saw three wagons with horse teams. He cocked an eyebrow in query. "A kitchen and two loads of supplies," Zimmerman smacked his lips. They laughed.

The other platoon leaders joined them. Jones grinned in ecstasy. "What a victory! What a fight! I've never seen the like before!"

Lassiter joined in, "Your man Braun says the platoon which ambushed us is part of the company. The two groups of prisoners recognized each other. He said you should hear them chatter about what happened."

Dane gave them a sober look. "What were our casualties?"

The others looked at each other and came up with, "Three dead and six wounded, an incredible price to pay for knocking out a whole Kraut company."

Dane's lips tightened. "Ten percent casualties and we aren't any closer to our objective than we were an hour ago. It'll be another hour or two before we can be on the move again." He looked at the four men, whose faces changed from jubilant to crestfallen. "I'm sorry," he apologized as he rubbed his forehead, which pushed his helmet back. "Please forgive me for grousing. God gave us a great victory and with minimal losses. We needed to take on the company or it would have prevented us from reaching the bridge. Grissom, you did a magnificent job with your mortars. There at the end, when and where you placed your 30 at just the right spot to block their escape was wonderful. Zimmerman, you appeared on this ridge with impeccable timing. I realize how hard it must have been for you and your men to sit there in the riverbed, not knowing if you were going to be discovered and shot down like pigs in a poke. Jones and Lassiter, both of you did a great job moving the troops over the ridges, not too fast and not too slow. This operation would not have succeeded without your efforts. Thank you.

"But," he went on, "we can't rest on our laurels, we have to keep moving. We can celebrate later when we have the time." He snapped out orders, "Zimmerman, get those wagons on this side of the riverbed." Dane looked at his watch, "We'll need to make a lunch halt, the men need it after all what's happened this morning." He looked around. "We'll make camp on the other side of the second ridge. After you get the wagons over, have your men get their backpacks. You're in charge of lunch. Lassiter, you're over the prisoners and perimeter security. Grissom, pick up all the German weapons and ammo lying around. Have your men grab their backpacks first. Jones, help with the wounded. I'll have a talk with the medic." He stopped and looked at each one in turn. "I want to thank each and every one of you gentlemen again for your help and support." He turned and left them.

Lassiter summed up the feelings of all of them in his Texan drawl, "Wal, if thet don't beat all." He straightened his shoulders, "Gentlemen, ah think we got our orders."

Jones added his admiring observation, "He sure outfoxed the Krauts." They moved in their various directions.

# Chapter Seven

Maria couldn't remember the last time she felt so happy. All of these nice Americans to talk to, and they were all so friendly. They crowded around her, talking and laughing. Besides giving her compliments and their names, they chattered about this battle they just fought. She noticed the difference in these young men from when she first met them. Earlier they were quiet and slumped shouldered. Now they were jubilant and happy. Young men? A lot of them were boys not much older than her.

She looked around for Tennessee. *I have to find out his name. There he is, helping to guard the prisoners.* She bounced over to him and gave him a big smile. His answering grin lightened up his whole face and sent a tingle up and down her spine. She didn't notice when her court started to follow her, a look from Sergeant Lassiter sent them back to their duties.

She looked over the crowd of prisoners. "How many are there?" she asked.

"Sixty-five, give or take a couple," Tennessee answered, keeping an eagle eye on them.

She became serious. "There's a lot of wounded too, isn't there?" She saw the American doctor working beside a German doctor as they treated the injured.

"Yes, Miss Maria, there's a total of about forty of our boys and seventy of them. We found about forty bodies, too."

Behind them they heard someone call, "Chow! Come and get it."

She looked at him. "Are you going to eat now?"

He hid a smile. "Ah has to wait until ah'm relieved."

"I'll wait with you, then." Before he could protest, she asked him a question. "What's your name?"

"Ah told you mah name, it's Tennessee."

She shook her head and said with a stubborn look, "No, it's not. It's just a nickname. What's your name?"

"It's Norton, miss."

She looked at him with her head cocked to one side, "First or last?"

He looked ill at ease. "Last."

She put her hands on her hips, "What's your first name?"

With visible discomfort, he shifted his weight from one foot to the other. He looked up at the sky, down at the ground, at a German who thought Tennessee wasn't paying attention and started to sidle away. When Tennessee pointed his rifle at him, the German realized his mistake and stopped sidling. Maria tapped her foot. Tennessee looked miserable. "Please, miss, just call me Tennessee."

She looked up into his face and demanded, "Tell me your name," and then cajoled, "it can't be that bad."

He had such a hangdog expression she almost giggled, and then at last he said, "It's Octavian."

She did giggle then, but clapped her hand over her mouth. "I'm sorry, nobody should laugh at someone's name. Why were you named Octavian?"

He looked into her face and saw only curiosity "Ma read somewhere about a Roman emperor and she liked his name. Ah wish she'd picked somebody else to name me after," he added with some heat.

She almost giggled again. "How about if I call you Van?" she asked.

"Van?" He hesitated. "Well, if you want to."

Tennessee looked over her shoulder and she turned to see Sergeant Shaw walking towards them. Puzzled, she watched him come closer. *What's different about him? Oh, he walks like a cat, on the balls of his feet.* A shiver went down her back as she thought of a tiger, or maybe a wolf.

He came up to them. "Tennessee, how are the prisoners?"

"Wal Sarge, they're not very perky right now.

Every so often one of them tries to wander off, but ah kinda discourages it."

Dane grinned and Maria looked in surprise at him. *Why, he's good looking when he smiles, much more human like.*

"You keep on discouraging them. We went to a lot of trouble to get them and we don't want to lose any of them now." Tennessee grinned back. "When this bunch finishes eating, then you'll be relieved to go eat, and then we'll feed the prisoners."

While they talked, Maria looked at the two men who were soon going to be very important in her young life. And whose lives she would impact. Tennessee stood much the taller, six feet in height, with brown hair and coal black eyes which hinted at a different heritage. She noticed his loping, ground covering stride, his broad shoulders and ropey muscles. Though six inches shorter, the sergeant's shoulders were as wide as Tennessee's. Of the two men, she much preferred the company of the taller man. Somehow she felt the other man could be dangerous.

The sergeant finished talking to Tennessee and turned to her. He glanced at her face, then away, then back again and then away again. He wore a puzzled look on his face, and seemed to have difficulty in starting a conversation with her. With a shock she realized he felt as uneasy in her company as he made her feel. The realization took away her reserve and she gave him a wide and natural smile, "Hello Sergeant."

"Uh, Miss Maria, where is it you live?" He glanced back at her face.

"Almost two miles that way," she pointed northeast. He glanced in that direction and back to her.

"How long have you been away from home?" he asked, concern on his face.

"Oh, I left early this morning. I went looking for a lost sheep. Pepecita is naughty and runs off every so often."

"Your parents must be worried about you. I need to see about getting you back home," his voice changed to paternal concern.

"They won't worry, sometimes I'm gone all day," she tried to put him at ease. "I'll lead you to our house after we eat."

He frowned, "You wander all alone out here all day long? Young lady, don't you realize how dangerous it is? With fighting going on all over the place it would be better to stick closer to home and make sure your parents know where you are."

"You sound like *Zio* Rudolfo," she pouted. "He says the same things to me. 'Maria, you shouldn't be running the hills by yourself. That is not the way young ladies behave. You need to stay in the house and learn to be a proper Italian young woman.'"

Tennessee burst out laughing at her tone and expression while Dane asked, "*Zio* Rudolfo?" with a puzzled look.

"Uncle Rudolfo. He's Papa's uncle, and very strict."

"Well, he's right," Dane agreed, although the corners of his mouth twitched. Maria took a close look at his face and saw the laughter in his eyes.

She grinned at him and said, "You should be called *Zio* Sergeant." She laughed at his expression.

He became serious again. "I mean it, Maria. It's not safe to be alone. There are small groups and individuals running around who are desperate and likely to do anything. Some of them are deserters and some have been separated from their units, but any of them could be dangerous."

"Since I'm with you, then I must be safe, *Zio* Sergeant," she teased.

"Imp," he retaliated, laughter in his eyes again.

She grinned back at him, feeling herself relax in his presence and amazed at the turn of events. She couldn't believe her change of opinion of '*Zio* Sergeant' in the last few minutes.

# **Chapter Eight**

Dane made his rounds and looked over the men. Their spirits were rebounding, not just due to their recent victory but also attributable to the presence of the young lady. He smiled at her evident pleasure in their banter and hurried on.

He checked with the medic, 'Doc' Pavel, on the condition of the patients. Doc, a big man in his thirties with unruly black hair and a perpetual fierce expression on his face, tended to growl when he spoke. But Dane knew his rough exterior concealed a caring heart for the broken bodies he tended.

Doc glared at Dane from under bushy eyebrows. "Sergeant, all this moving 'round is bad for them. If we don't stop and rest we're gonna to lose some of the men."

"I think there's a place for them to stay a couple of miles away. How is Lieutenant Jennings?"

"He's holding his own, but Lieutenant Oosterkamp is dying. He won't last the day."

Dane tightened his lips. "I'm sorry to hear it. How is the German medic doing?"

"Good doctor, he understands English and studied in England for a while. What do you mean, 'there is a place for them to stay'? Are you leaving

71

the wounded behind?" Doc demanded.

Dane gave a weary smile. "What else can I do? It's a farm, there should be shelter and water there, and it's the safest place to hide that I can come up with."

"And if not?" Doc asked.

"Then I'll decide what to do."

Dane went to see the half-conscious Jennings and then visited with Grissom. "What did you find?" Dane asked.

Grissom smacked his lips like Zimmerman did about the food. "We got six light machine guns, four mortars and one *panzerfaust*, plus all the normal rifles, side arms, and ammo."

"Good." Dane thought a moment and added, "Keep them in your platoon for now. I'll decide later how to divvy them up."

When Dane walked over to get his lunch, the last of the Americans were being served and he joined the end of the chow line. A burst of laughter caught his attention and he looked over to see Maria in the midst of GIs, who were all talking and laughing. He frowned when he saw Don Chilvers, the lady killer, sitting next to her. His string of conquests went clear back to the States. Something stirred deep inside of Dane. Something he hadn't felt for many months. *I'll have to make sure it goes no further,* he thought as he regarded the two of them. Surprised, he saw Tennessee, normally shy around women, on her other side. Dane felt better with Tennessee close by her.

He noted with relief the complete lack of profanity in the men's conversation. He always tried to block it out, but at times it became difficult.

He got his food and a cup of coffee, saw Zimmerman by a wagon and walked over to him. "Are you ready to feed the prisoners?" Dane asked.

Zimmerman nodded. "I sent someone to tell the guards to bring them over. The wounded are being fed now."

Dane sipped his coffee. "I noticed. As soon as the prisoners have finished eating we'll get started." He glanced around. "Speaking of which, I'd better eat my own lunch before I get left behind." The two men chuckled and Dane walked away.

Dane found a seat away from the others. He bowed his head. *Lord, you are so good to me and You have blessed me so much. Thank you for the victory and the few casualties. Please give me wisdom for the decisions I still need to make before the day is through. Please guide and direct me. May you be glorified in everything which happens. In Jesus' name I pray. Amen.*

Dane finished his prayer and began to eat. He looked over at Maria with the same puzzlement he felt earlier. Always before, whenever he saw a pretty, black-haired girl, he felt heart-wrenching pain, but not when he looked at Maria. Could he at last be getting over her? After all, it'd been five and a half months since he'd last seen her. Or maybe because Angelique's elegant grace contrasted so much with Maria's exuberance.

Angelique's image exploded into his mind. Unbearable heartache tore at his soul and he hunched over in pain. He saw again the horror on her white face as she stared at him, standing among the bodies of the men he'd killed to save them, and saw her turn from him to another man. He forced the emotions back into their hiding place and hardened his face. He stared down at the meal which now nauseated him. But he needed the strength the food would give him, and he forced himself to eat.

***

As Zimmerman supervised the feeding of the prisoners, he thought about Shaw. He knew him to be a good sergeant. But since taking over the company he'd been surprised at how fast Shaw grew into a company commander. In Zimmerman's opinion, if Shaw could find them a resting place to go along with the recent victory, it would put him head and shoulders above Captain Carter.

***

Maria saw Dane sit down and bow his head,

74

and wondered why he did so. She saw someone, she thought Corporal Gates, start to get up like he would join the sergeant. But when he kept his head bowed, Gates sat back down. She wondered why the sergeant ate by himself, and why Gates hesitated about joining him. Then she watched agony flow across *Zio's* face. Her chin hardened in resolute determination. A look her parents knew all too well. *I will find out why he sits alone and what caused his anguish.*

Chilvers pulled her attention away. "What were you doing when we found you?"

She launched into a vibrant discussion about the wandering Pepecita, much to the amusement of her listeners. She turned to Chilvers and asked with a smile, "What do you think about sheep?"

"Sheep are alright in their place, I suppose," he answered in his smooth voice.

Maria's practical side rejected his answer and she turned to Van. "What do you think about sheep?"

Tennessee answered, "Wal, they can be almighty stubborn animals, and purty dumb, but mighty useful. We raised a small flock of sheep. Ma made clothes out of their wool."

Maria's practical side approved of the answer and her romantic side approved of the man. She loved listening to his accent. *Is he the answer to the plans I made years ago?*

# Chapter Nine

After everybody ate, Dane issued the marching orders. "Lassiter, start off first with two scouts out in front. Jones, you help the wounded and put two scouts to the right. Zimmerman, take the wagons, guard the prisoners and send two scouts to the left. Grissom, you're last in line and have two scouts trail the column. Tell the scouts to keep their eyes peeled, I don't want to run into another ambush." A chorus of "Yes Sarge's" answered him and the sergeants scattered to obey their orders.

It took an hour to march the mile to Maria's home. The men were overburdened, and the relentless afternoon sun poured down its heat. The men soon stopped their lighthearted chatter and settled down to the grim business of putting one foot in front of another, climbing up and down ridges. Dane watched them and knew they would never make it to the bridge on time at this rate. Something had to be done. He continued to pray.

At the top of the last ridge, Maria, at the front of the line, pointed and said, "There's my home."

The slight breeze molded her clothes against her more than ample curves. Dane saw her silhouetted against the skyline. He turned to Lassiter and said in a voice loud enough for the nearby men, but not Maria, to hear, "If anybody touches her, I'll skin them alive. Pass it along." Lassiter nodded and repeated the order to his corporals.

Maria skipped down the hillside and waited at the bottom for the others to catch up. When Dane reached the crest, he saw the house and a couple of outbuildings. From here he saw they were in need of paint and repair. With a sense of foreboding he went down the slope.

When they were close to the house, Dane heard someone shriek, "Maria! Maria!" A woman ran out of the house, grabbed Maria and with a sob say, "Did they hurt you?" She patted Maria all over and turned to glare at the column of men. Dane saw a man coming from the nearby orchard, hobbling as fast as he could on a crutch.

"Mama, Mama, of course I am all right. These are Americans, they are our friends," Maria soothed her mother.

Dane stepped up and touched the brim of his helmet, "Uh, Mrs..." and stopped, embarrassed that he didn't know Maria's last name. "I'm Sergeant Dane Shaw, in command of this unit."

Lucia hugged Maria close, and looked as fierce as a lioness protecting her young as she glared at Dane. By then Antonio hobbled up with a surprised look on his face at the Americans and the tableau in the yard.

"This is my Mama and Papa, Lucia and Antonio Calvoratti," Maria introduced her parents. "This is Sergeant Shaw, and this is Sergeant Lassiter and this is *Signore* Norton and *Signore* Chilvers and..."

"Enough, enough," her father protested. "What is the meaning of this?"

Dane answered him, "We met your daughter in the hills, and she indicated we might find some shelter for our wounded here."

While Dane and the Calvoratti's conversed, the two doctors huddled by Lieutenant Oosterkamp, who drew his last labored breath and exhaled. The two doctors frowned at each other and rose to their feet. "I have to talk to the sergeant," Doc growled and stalked over to the conference, followed by the German medic. Doc interrupted Antonio's vehement objections to the Americans' presence. "Sergeant Shaw, Lieutenant Oosterkamp just died. I demand we stop travelling and rest up before any more men die. Some of them cannot continue on." He glared at Dane from beneath his bushy eyebrows.

Lucia looked over at the huddled group of wounded, and her eyes fell on a young GI with an anguished look on his white face. He couldn't have been more than nineteen. Her mother's heart tore at her and her eyes moistened with tears. "Oh, those poor *bambinos*. Antonio, we must help them," she beseeched her husband, who shut up and looked at them too. He looked miserable.

"How many wounded do you have?" he asked.

"About a hundred and ten," Dane answered.

"But we have no room for so many in the house," Antonio protested.

Dane indicated the barn. "Can we use that? We don't want to be a bother to you. We wouldn't think of intruding in your house."

Antonio looked more miserable. "The barn, she is not in good repair and not very big. I don't think you could get twenty or maybe thirty at the most in there."

"We'll take anything you can offer," Dane soothed, and turned to Doc. "Put the most seriously wounded in the barn, as many as you can. The rest will have to stay outside, but at least they can rest."

Doc looked at him." Do you mean put the American wounded in the barn?"

Dane gave him a puzzled look. "No, I said the most seriously wounded, German or American." Doc gave an approving nod and headed back to the injured. Mueller gave Dane a long, thoughtful look before following the American doctor.

"German? You have Germans with you?" Lucia shrieked.

"Yes ma'am, we have German prisoners with

us," Dane answered, his mind already on the next problem. He looked around and spotted the fenced lot he'd noticed from the top of the ridge. The fence, made of sections of woven wire, stood five feet high. "May we use the pen?" he pointed as he asked Antonio. With a dumfounded look, Antonio nodded. Dane turned to Zimmerman and Grissom, who came up. "Zimmerman, put the prisoners in the enclosure. Grissom, put a machine gun on the rise overlooking the enclosure. It should keep them quiet. Ma'am, may we use your water?" he asked Lucia while he indicated the well.

"*Si, naturemente*, of course," Lucia answered with as much bewilderment as her husband at the way this strange man took over their lives.

"Thank you," Dane replied and turned to Lassiter. "Have the men start filling their canteens." He turned back to Antonio, "There is one more thing. I need to get to the bridge on Highway 120, over the Salso River. Can you tell me how to get there?"

Antonio looked surprised but answered, "You take this road," pointing to the rutted path leading out of the farm, "to the main road which goes through Leonforte and on to Route 120."

"No, not that way," Dane shook his head, "overland, not by the road."

"Overland?" Antonio's mouth dropped open.

"Through those ridges and gullies? *Signore*, there is a reason the road curves around the area. It is so cut up it is hard to get through."

Dane frowned. "We have a compass. If you gave us the direction, couldn't we just go that way?"

Antonio shook his head. "There are many dead end gullies. To go down the wrong one could mean kilometers of backtracking."

"I could guide you," Maria said. Everybody ignored her.

Dane gnawed his lip. "Is there anybody who could guide us?"

"I can guide you," Maria repeated in a somewhat louder tone, with the exact same result.

Antonio and Lucia looked at each other, "Old Guiseppe could do it."

"I could do it," louder but with no better result.

"Where is Guiseppe?" Dane asked with an eager expression.

Antonio answered, "He is following his sheep somewhere. Somebody maybe could find him in two or three days and bring him to you."

Dane frowned, "I don't have two or three days, I have to leave today. Is there anybody else who can guide us?"

Maria shouted, "I can guide you!"

The other three looked at her in surprise.

"There is no need to shout, Maria. We can hear you just fine," her mother scolded. "What did you say?"

Maria glared at them and spaced out her words. "I--can--guide--them."

"Out of the question!" Horrified, her mother refused.

"No!" her father shouted.

Maria stood firm. She held her body straight and her chin up. "There is nobody else who can help, only me." Then she switched to Italian, "We have to help them, they are Americans. Don't you want to rid this country of tyranny? Besides," a blush came over her cheeks but her eyes were steady on her mother, "I may have met my future husband. I need time to find out for sure."

"What?" screamed her mother.

"No! You are too young. You are only sixteen." It became her father's turn to be horrified. With a fierce expression he stammered, "Who is trying to, to, turn your head?"

"He hasn't tried to turn my head. He hasn't done or said anything which you would find amiss. Besides, I am not too young. When Mama met you, she was fifteen and said she was going to marry you."

"That was different," her father sputtered. "We met under the full view and approval of her family."

"I heard Grandpapa wasn't happy at all when

you first met her," she retorted, her Italian temper rising.

"That was different," her father repeated in a stiff tone. "I forbid you to make eyes at any of these young men," his temper also spiraling.

Dane saw when they switched languages, faces turned red and voices raised, but of course he had no idea how far the conversation had strayed from his need of a guide. He interrupted, "Maria, will you please leave us so I can speak to your parents alone?"

Angry, Maria spun towards him, "I won't!" Then she saw his face change. She saw the steel in his hardened face, green flecks start to show in his eyes, and she caught a glimpse of the dangerous man which she'd seen before. She stared at him for a second before she turned and flounced away.

When Dane turned back to her parents, he saw Maria's mother give him a strange look before her father launched his attack. "What are your intentions towards my daughter?" he roared.

This flummoxed Dane. (Obviously, the plague of flummoxing had not yet run its course). His mouth dropped open accompanied by such a look of bewilderment Antonio realized this man must be innocent. "What intentions, what are you talking about? I have no feelings for your daughter, I'll swear by anything you want," Dane protested.

Antonio subsided. "Well, if you don't, do you know who does?"

Dane shook his head in emphatic denial. "Nobody I know of. She hasn't been alone with anyone."

Lucia broke into the conversation with an oblique statement, "You aren't old enough to have teenaged daughters."

By now Dane wondered if he'd wandered into a madhouse. "I raised my sister," he answered in confusion.

"That accounts for it," she nodded.

Dane took a deep breath and tried to bring the conversation back to the problem at hand. "You say I need a guide to get to the bridge, but there are no guides available. Am I correct?"

Antonio nodded but Lucia added, "Except for Maria."

Dane hesitated, and then said, "But I need a guide right now, and she's the only one."

"No!" Antonio glared, but Lucia kept her eyes glued to Dane's.

"How important is getting to the bridge?" she asked.

"Very," he replied, a grim look on his face. "It could save many lives and shorten the time Germans are on this island by a lot."

She nodded, "If she were to go with you, would

you guarantee her safety?"

"No, I forbid it!" Antonio announced again. It was his turn to be ignored.

"Ma'am, I can't guarantee anyone's safety. If she stayed here, I couldn't promise any of you would be safe, with or without us to protect you. The enemy isn't far away and a battle might be fought here. But I will promise to do everything I can to protect her, and I promise to send her back as soon as," Dane paused, "as soon as it is safe to do so." He'd been about to say 'as soon as we come in sight of the bridge', but thought better of it. "And I promise to send guards back with her."

Lucia nodded while Antonio sputtered. "Papa," she addressed her husband in Italian, "we must let her go. We must help both of our countries in this way. I trust this man to protect our Maria to the best of his ability, and I think he can do it much better than either of us can," she added. Antonio growled but gave in. He knew that look of his wife's, and he shared her opinion of the forceful sergeant.

"Maria, come here," commanded Lucia. Maria joined them and looked at their faces to gauge the mood. "Maria, you may go with them if," Maria squealed with joy while her mother frowned her down, "you promise to obey orders."

Maria peeked at the sergeant and, to her relief, saw no sign of the scary man. She gave him a big smile and said, "Of course I will obey *Zio* Sergeant." Antonio looked puzzled, Lucia looked wise, and Dane's eyes laughed.

# Chapter Ten

Dane hurried to see Doc. After discussing the condition of the wounded, Dane asked, "Do you trust the German?"

Doc considered, then said, "He's a good doctor, and takes care of his patients, whichever side they're on. I think he's a good man. Why do you ask?"

"I'm thinking about leaving him here in charge of the wounded and taking you with us. Would you trust him with them?"

Doc pursed his lips, eyes narrowed in thought, then nodded. "If he gave his word of honor, I would accept it."

Dane turned, spotted the German and called, "Doctor Mueller, come here, please."

Dane felt Doc's look of surprise at knowing the German's name.

Mueller walked over and Dane said, "Doctor, I want to leave you here in charge of the wounded. I want you to give me your word of honor you will treat all the wounded to the best of your ability and you won't use your position to help any escape attempts."

Mueller looked at him and with a thick accent said, "You vould trust me?"

Dane replied, "Doc here says he would trust your word of honor, and therefore I will too."

The two men stared at each other and then Mueller said, "You gafe orders for the vounded to be treated alike." He nodded, "*Ja*, I vill give my word."

Dane held out his hand, and after a slight hesitation, Mueller shook it. Dane added, "These people living here are good people; I would take it very amiss if anything bad happened to them."

Mueller stared into his eyes and said, "I understand."

After the doctors returned to the wounded, Dane thrust his hands into his pockets and stared off into space, deep in thought. *I need to leave a guard. Who should I choose, Lord?* He went over the remaining sergeants in his mind. *Milne, he's shrewd, I'll bet he can keep the prisoners under control.*

Dane watched a wagon being pulled out of the barn, Antonio keeping a watchful eye on the operation. Dane walked over to the wagon and inspected it. "Mr. Calvoratti, can we use your wagon? I'll leave the kitchen wagon here for your use."

"What about my poor donkey? Such a trek would be hard on him."

"You keep the donkey, we'll use the horses we

captured."

"All right," Antonio shrugged his shoulders.

Dane glanced around. "Rosario, call the platoon leaders together for a conference in the orange grove."

"Yes, sergeant." Rosario scurried away to find his quarry.

At the meeting, Dane laid out his plans. "I'm splitting the company into two parts, a flying column and a support column. I'll lead Sergeant Lassiter's platoon of two infantry squads and one squad of heavy weapons with three machine guns and one mortar. We'll take two days rations and ammo. We need light backpacks to make it to the bridge on time. The support column will be under Sergeant Zimmerman and follow with the wagons. We'll leave the kitchen wagon for the wounded and prisoners. Sergeant Milne and a squad will stay here to guard the prisoners. The Calvoratti's offered us their wagon. Zimmerman will use it and the other two wagons. Load them with five days rations for the support column and three days rations for the flying column. They'll also carry the rest of the weapons and ammo. Since we only have one radio left, Zimmerman will have it. I'll leave a clear trail for you to follow. Any questions?"

"What happens when you get to the bridge?" Jones asked.

"We'll capture it and hold it until you arrive. If the enemy garrison is too strong, we'll wait for you and then take it. Any other questions?" Dane looked around the circle. The men shook their heads and Dane dismissed them.

When Maria said her goodbyes, her father hid his emotions behind a gruff voice and held her tight like he might never see her again. Her mother hugged her and whispered, "Make a wise choice."

"I will," Maria whispered back.

Dane led the thirty men of the flying column, followed by Zimmerman and his eighty men. They included eight wounded whom Doc patched up enough to go back into combat. They left in the hottest part of the day, with the temperature flirting with the hundred degree mark. As they set off, Dane asked Maria, "Which direction is the bridge from here?"

"North and a little west," she replied as she bounced along.

Unlike her, the men didn't bounce as they walked. They were wearing backpacks, and although they were carrying a lot less than the eighty pounds they started with, the heat slowed them down. Even so, they outpaced the support column. Soon sweat ran down their faces and dampened their shirts. After a while, Dane stopped and watched each man walk by, checking to see if any were not sweating, which would indicate sunstroke. *Praise God, no one is suffering, although there are some red faces.* Then he hurried back up to the front of the column.

After an hour on the march, Dane called a halt for a ten minute break. While the others rested, he again looked over the men, and then sat down by himself.

# Chapter Eleven

Maria, sitting with Corporal Gates' squad, looked at *Zio* and frowned. "Why does he go off by himself like that?" she wondered out loud.

"He has a lot on his mind; maybe he needs the solitude to think," Rosario defended him.

Conners snorted as he lit up a cigarette. "Nah, he thinks he's better'n us."

Gates shot him a stern look. "You don't know him, he doesn't think like that. He's more of a loner, is all."

By the looks Conners received from most of the rest of the squad, Maria knew he held a minority opinion. She asked Gates a blunt question, "Are you his friend?"

He looked startled and then said, "Well, no, I wouldn't call us buddies." He gave Shaw a long look and added in a pensive voice, "I think he would make a good friend, though."

At that point, Shaw stood up and announced, "Time to go." He headed north again as Maria scrambled to her feet.

"Not that way, we go this way a little bit," she pointed east.

"East?" he queried, turning to look back at her as she hurried to his side. "I thought you said the bridge lay a little to the west?"

"It is," she gave a firm nod. "But we go east first."

He shrugged and then stopped her. "We need to leave a sign for the others." They made an arrow out of stones and left a stick with a bit of white cloth attached to draw attention to it. After making sure the flankers were aware of the change of direction, they moved off.

Until now they'd traveled up the same valley which held the Calvoratti farm, but now it narrowed and the side ridges were higher. They came to a saddle on the east side which offered an easier way to cross the ridge. They walked up and over it, crossed a wide gulch, and then climbed a steeper ridge. They came to a wider valley which reached to the northwest. "Do we take this valley?" he asked Maria.

She shook her head. "A little ways ahead the sides become steep, and in five or six kilometers it ends in a V-neck which can't be climbed by wagons, maybe even men with packs. We go on."

After another fifteen or twenty minutes of traversing more ridges, they came to a narrow valley heading north. Brush cloaked the entrance, but a path led through the undergrowth. "We go this way," Maria announced, pointing to the path.

Shaw shook his head. "I do did need a guide,

more than I thought." He eyed the path. "It's not wide enough for the wagons." He turned to Lassiter. "We'll cut back some of this brush so the wagons can get through.

While men cut down brush to ground level, Maria watched Shaw and wondered about him. From the conversation during the break she thought most of the men respected him, but he didn't appear to be friends with any of them. *I'm sure Corporal Gates would like to be his friend, but why does he push people away?* She remembered how he acted when he was *Zio* Sergeant. *Why isn't he like that more of the time?* She determined to get to the bottom of this riddle.

After fifteen minutes of working, Dane looked at his watch and announced, "That's enough. The others can finish the job when they get here." They'd cleared much of the smaller brush. Maria heard him say to Lassiter, "Those small trees need to be removed. There are axes in the wagons. They can finish the job. I'll leave another arrow with a stick and a piece of white cloth to mark the turn-off."

"Do you think it's necessary with all the cut brush lying around?" Lassiter asked.

"Maybe not, but I don't want any mistakes."

They proceeded up the gradual slope of the valley floor, rising towards the hills in the distance.

After about fifteen minutes of walking, Shaw called another rest halt and everyone collapsed to the ground. Maria watched him as he checked all the men. One man's beet-red face and labored breathing spelled a warning. Shaw knelt beside the sufferer, took the man's handkerchief, soaked it with water out of Shaw's own canteen, and laid the handkerchief on the back of the sufferer's neck. "Lie down and rest," Shaw ordered. After he finished, he again sat down by himself.

*It's obvious he cares for his men, so why does he act like this?* Maria wondered.

She plopped down next to Raymond. Once, after scrambling down a steep ridge, she turned back to see O'Halloran slip and Raymond catch him. Then Raymond helped O'Halloran carry the big gun. Intrigued, she wanted to learn more about this rough looking man with the scarred face.

He smiled at her, which didn't make him look any better. "Hello, Miss Maria."

"What's your name," she asked.

"Chug Raymond, miss."

"Where are you from," she asked with her head tilted to one side.

"South Dakota."

She screwed up her face. "Isn't it, um, in the south?"

He chuckled. "No, miss. It's up north."

"Why is it called South Dakota?"

"Because it's south of North Dakota."

She threw back her head and laughed. "Oh, I'm thinking of South Carolina."

They shared the merriment and Maria recognized the friendly warmth in his eyes. *He's much nicer than he looks.*

Under her probing questions, she learned Raymond came from one of the poorest families in one of the poorest counties in the state. Too many times bad weather wiped out much of the crop. But still, if anyone needed help, you could always count on the Raymond clan to be there. Grandpa Raymond raised his family to be a help meet to their fellow man. When he died people came from miles around to honor him. His funeral procession stretched for a mile.

An outbreak of smallpox left eight-year old Chug marked for life. Most women steered clear of him because of his looks, but Maria found him delightful.

She looked over her shoulder at *Zio* Sergeant sitting by himself. Her curiosity boiled up inside of her. *I'm going to find out right now why he's showing such antisocial behavior.* Taking her courage in both hands, she sprang to her feet, flounced over to him, and plopped down.

He looked at her, surprise written all over his

face.

"Why do you do it?" she asked.

"Do what?" his expression changed to puzzlement.

"Sit alone like this?"

He looked away. "Oh, I don't know."

She gave him a stern look. "Yes, you do know. Why do you shun people and push people away? I think Corporal Gates would like to be your friend, but you won't let him. Why?"

Fury changed his features as he glared at her. "I don't push people away," he barked. "I need some time to myself. Now go back to the others and bother them with your chatter."

She stood her ground, figuratively speaking since she was sitting down, and lifted her chin. "Yes, you do. See, you're doing it to me. I want to know why you refuse to be involved with people."

He glared at her and retorted, "You don't know what you're talking about." He sprang to his feet and hollered, "Let's move it!" and stalked off.

# Chapter Twelve

Dane stormed away, white hot fury erupting up from within him like a volcano. *How dare that little so-and-so criticize me? What does this upstart girl know about anything? What gave her the right to pry into my affairs? Isn't it bad enough I've been hurt by Angelique? I haven't been pushing people away; I needed some time to heal. I involve myself with people, and I witness to them.* For several minutes he raged before calming down.

He panted and sweat poured off of him. He wiped his face with his shirtsleeve and then looked back over his shoulder. The column marched far behind him. *I must have been hurrying along*, he thought to himself. He slowed his pace to allow them to catch up.

A small voice in his head spoke up, *You were running away from the truth.*

'She doesn't know the truth,' he argued to himself.

*When was the last time you just sat and visited with anyone?*

'Jeff Slater, my buddy,' he answered with a proud lift of his chin. 'We visited and prayed for our men and opportunities to witness to them.'

*That was back in Tunisia and months ago. Who*

99

*have you witnessed to lately?*

'I witnessed to Gates.'

*Again, that was back in Tunisia and months ago. What about your other men? What about your new replacements?*

Dane mentally squirmed; he did not like the bent of this conversation. 'I haven't had time; we've been rather busy fighting Germans the last two weeks.'

*And now Patterson is dead and he may never have heard the gospel. Why haven't you witnessed to Gates again? Why haven't you witnessed to the others?*

Dane squirmed some more. He hated to think Patterson might be in hell because he'd never heard of Jesus' saving grace. A tiny portion of his brain registered the column catching up with him, but after sidelong glances the men were avoiding him.

'I haven't had an opportunity.'

*It's because you don't visit with them. You're always by yourself. Why?*

'She hurt me, bad. It takes time to recover from these things.'

*Too hurt to be friends with people?*

He trudged along for a few moments, wrestling with that question. 'I call Jeff my friend.'

*It's good to have Christian friends. Do you have any others?*

'Well, there's Drew and Angelique, they're Christians,' he added, for some reason reluctant to mention the couple.

*And how do you feel about them?*

'How should I feel about them?' Dane felt another spurt of anger. 'I led them to the Lord. I rejoiced when they got saved.' He stopped as he realized something deep down inside him. He added with genuine thankfulness, 'I still rejoice.'

*Good. But how do you feel about them?*

'I--I--I don't know.' Dane hung his head.

*You're jealous of them.*

'No! No I'm not!' Dane screamed to himself.

*Yes you are, and you are hiding behind your hurt.*

Dane stomped along, now angry, now shaken, as memories flooded his mind. The argument ran around and around in his mind. Did he feel jealous of Drew and Angelique? Did he use her rejection of him to, in turn, reject all others?

The small valley they traversed sloped uphill. They reached the head of it and Dane's mind switched into command gear. He didn't have time to think about himself. He had a job to do.

Before them the land dropped away and he looked into mixed maze of ridges, hills and narrow valleys. Where he stood wasn't any higher than some of the other hills he saw, but he looked into a region of ridges, hills and narrow valleys, all mixed up together. The broken terrain before him contained jumbled hills and draws leading to dead ends. Some of the slopes were quite steep. He saw ahead and to his right a draw which ended in a dead end with banks too steep for his overburdened men to climb. He couldn't see a clear way through.

"Which way do we go now?" he demanded of Maria. They could follow the ridge to the east, to the west, or go down the hill.

Maria bit her fingernail and looked to the left and then to the right. "One direction leads to the way through and the other winds up in a series of dead end gullies and steep ridges."

"Well, which way is the right way?" Dane snapped at her, and then felt guilty at the wounded look she gave him.

"The last time I came here, I went to the gullies to dig up some wild flowers to take back home for Mama," Maria answered. Dane stirred but held his peace. He couldn't care less about the flowers, but he didn't want to rattle the girl. "When I went to get them, the sun shone in my eyes. Now did I go in the morning or afternoon?" She snapped her fingers. "Morning, my shoes were wet from the dew. Therefore we go west." She turned and skipped in that direction.

Dane said, "Wait a minute, we need to set up a

sign post." While a couple of men formed an arrow of rocks and Lassiter stuck a stick in the ground with another piece of his handkerchief attached, Dane glanced at his watch. *Wow, that late already?* He checked the sun. *Still plenty of time before dark to travel further.*

They traveled on the ridge for about ten minutes before Dane called the hourly halt. He checked on the earlier sufferer. *I'm not sure of his name. Is it Wilbers?* Dane's heart bumped in alarm at the man's even redder face and his evident distress. Dane ran a quick eye over the rest of his men and saw two more showing signs of overheating.

"Corporal, see to these men. Get them into shade, have them drink plenty of water and put damp cloths around their necks," he ordered a nearby non-com. He realized he hadn't prayed for healing for the first man earlier and felt shame for his lack. *Dear God, please heal these three men and make them well. In Jesus' name I pray, amen.*

He finished his silent prayer and started to sit down by himself again. He caught himself with a guilty start and went and sat by Gates, who looked at him with surprise on his face, but with pleasure also. Dane felt guiltier.

From his position he could see and hear Maria as she sat with his squad. He saw the smile on her face as she observed him beside Gates. He glanced down at the ground, feeling ashamed of his previous aloofness, and then looked back at her. He saw her attention pulled away by her neighbors.

"Did y'all find yore sheep before we left?" Tennessee asked her.

Maria turned to him with a sparkle in her eyes, "Papa said he found Pepecita in the orange grove. She's a bad sheep and escapes out of the pen sometimes. Papa and I have looked but we can't find where she gets out."

Then Tennessee regaled the group with a tale about him and a sheep. "We had a sheep that took me fer a ride once. Mah older brothers told me the funnest thing in the world is ridin' a sheep. We corralled one and ah got on it. Ah must have been three or four. They let go and we went off lickety-split right through the garden. When the sheep reached the crick she turned one direction and ah flew off the other." All the listeners burst out laughing.

Dane, listening to the conversation, looked at Gates in surprise, "They're talking about sheep?"

"Yep," Gates nodded. "Tennessee and Hemphill ran into Maria as she searched for a lost sheep."

"Huh," Dane grunted. Then he grumbled with a dark look in her direction, "Doesn't she ever just walk? All I've seen her do is skip and dance and bounce. She doesn't walk like normal people do."

Gates burst out laughing, which caused heads to turn in their direction, including Maria's. Dane saw the happy expression on her face, then she turned to Tennessee. Dane caught the funny side of what he said and his own lips quirked.

Dane continued to look at her with a puzzled look. Why did she catch his attention? He didn't have anything like the same emotion for her which he'd felt for Angelique, but he did feel something. Did she make him think of, maybe, a younger sister, or perhaps a niece? He felt protective, but not as if she belonged to him or anything. Not like Amy, his sister, before she married. What did Maria call him, *Zio* or Uncle Sergeant? Somehow, it fit.

# Chapter Thirteen

Tennessee noticed Shaw looking at her. *Is the sergeant attracted to her?* Tennessee asked himself. Somehow the thought bothered him, almost as bad as the sight of Chilvers whispering in her ear. *That rascal could charm a coon out of his tree.*

***

Dane glanced at his watch and stood up. "Time to get moving again," he said to Gates. Dane checked on the three men. They were doing better, and one of them stopped him with a question, "Sergeant Shaw, did I see you praying for me?"

"Yes, you did."

He looked up at Dane with a haunted expression on his face, "Am I going to die?"

Dane looked at him in surprise. "Of course not, I just asked God to make you feel better."

"Oh," the man plucked at his shirt in embarrassment. "Ma's the only other person who ever prayed for me."

"If you like, I can keep praying for you," Dane pitched his voice low so the others couldn't hear. The man looked down and didn't answer. Satisfied the man didn't say no, Dane asked, "What's your name."

"Tony Wilbers."

"Okay," Dane squeezed his arm and moved off. Dane felt ecstatic. For the first time since, well, since Drew and Angelique, someone wanted him to pray for them. Could it have something to do with what Maria took him to task over? He had a sneaking suspicion it did.

For the next two hours, they forged their way through gullies and over ridges. The further they went the more uncertain Maria became of the way, but she still did not make a mistake. By the time they stopped to make camp she thought they'd covered half the distance to the bridge.

Suppertime lacked the banter of lunch. The men were worn out after marching all day and fighting two skirmishes in the heat. They ate at dusk, and after posting guards the camp became quiet.

Almost.

Loud snores from Gates rent the night. Raymond covered his ears. O'Halloran, lying next to Gates, kicked him which caused Gates to roll over on his side and stopped the snoring. The nightly ritual over, peace descended on the camp.

Maria slept in a tent which somehow appeared out of nowhere. She had a shrewd idea it came from *Zio* Sergeant. She felt perfectly happy and perfectly safe. Van, as she called Tennessee in her thoughts, lay nearby and *Zio* Sergeant and *Signore* Raymond and *Signore* Gates and…she fell asleep. Most of the men fell asleep just as fast, but not all.

George Gates opened his eyes. He hadn't been quite asleep when O'Halloran kicked him. He never reprimanded O'Halloran for the kicks. They reminded him of his wife. On their wedding night he fell asleep first and started snoring. The loud noise kept Eliza from sleep. After an hour of tossing and turning she had enough. Being a lass with spunk, she gave him a kick. He rolled on his side, stopped snoring and they both slept. After that, most nights she gave him a kick.

Jorge Rosario thought of his home back in California. Although a simple field hand, the blood of conquistadors flowed in his veins, and he felt a kind of thrill as he remembered today's battles. He almost never talked about it, but four hundred years ago some of his ancestors came to California from Spain and wrested it from the native people. The rest of his ancestors had lived there for a thousand years or more and were the ones whose land and freedom were taken. Then about a hundred years ago came the gringos, who took the land from the sleepy caballeros. Rosario's people traded masters, though a much more lenient people who did not make his people slaves. He felt mixed emotions about his forbears. He felt pride about a relative handful of fighters conquering whole continents, but also shame in how they drove the natives into the dust. He sighed, turned over, went to sleep and dreamed of his Maria back home.

Sully Conners crumpled an empty pack of cigarettes and threw it away. *Down to my last pack.* He glanced around the camp trying to decide where he could filch some more. The tent caught his eye and he scowled at it. *Thought she was too good for him, did she? She spent all of her time with the hillbilly, that know-it-all Sarge, and the two -timing Lothario. She even talked to ugly old Raymond, but not to him, not Sully Conners. One day, one day he would show them all, her and her kind, when he became rich. Just give him a lucky break and then let the women who ignored him all of his life come begging for some attention. Then let them see!* He dozed off and dreamed of becoming wealthy (by unspecified means) and dozens of beautiful women throwing themselves at him.

Sabine Lassiter, named after the Sabine River which formed one of the boundaries of the family ranch, used his backpack for a pillow. He let his mind drift back home. Dad's arthritis in his broken bones made it hard for him to get around some days. He wanted to hand over the ranch to his oldest son last year, but Sabine had been drafted instead. Now Dad, Sabine's wife, teen-aged brother, and a crippled old Mexican were trying to hold the ranch together. All the ranch hands quit after Pearl Harbor and joined the military. Restless, Sabine rolled onto his side. He recalled his last letter from his wife, how she claimed to enjoy riding around the ranch, making light of the little jobs she found to do. But he read between the lines and knew the long hard hours she must be working along with trying to care for their baby. His son, whom he'd never seen! She tried to hide the problems they were facing so he wouldn't worry, but he knew. The tough Texan blinked back moisture in his eyes. He ached to go back home, hold the two of them in his arms, and settle down to ranch life again. It took a while for him to drop off to sleep.

*** 

Several hours later Maria woke up. She heard movement and low voices, and knew the guards were being changed. Wide awake now, she realized she needed to take a walk. She eased out of her tent and moved as quiet as she could towards the outskirts of the camp. Judging from the night sky, it must be somewhere between midnight and four in the morning. She rounded a tree which had deep shadows under it. Her eyes couldn't penetrate the darkness and she tripped over someone's feet.

"What?" two strangled voices whispered together, hers and a man's.

"What are you doing out here?" She recognized

*Zio* Sergeant's whispered voice as the form scrambled to his feet.

"Some voices woke me up, and I needed some fresh air," she whispered back. "What are you doing here?"

"I'm checking the guard." She waited; he couldn't check the guard while sitting under the tree. "I'm thinking," he added after a pause.

"About what I said to you?"

"Yes." As if by mutual consent they both sat down with their backs against the tree. "You're right, I do push people away."

"Why?"

"Someone hurt me."

Maria dared to press her questions. "Tell me her name?"

"Angelique."

"Did she die or jilt you?"

"Neither, she chose someone else."

"Tell me about it," Maria suggested with a soft tone.

Maria felt him stiffen in rejection, but then the story tumbled out. How Captain Drew Matthews and Dane were on a mission behind enemy lines. How Dane rescued Angelique from the Germans and Arabs. How they fought off attacks and completed the mission. He told about the treachery of a fellow American, and rescuing Drew and

111

Angelique. How they accepted Jesus as their savior. The wild night ride to freedom only to be caught within sight of their goal and the final climatic battle in which he killed their adversaries. How he fell in love with her but she recoiled in horror from him and turned to Drew.

When he finished talking, his cheeks were wet with tears. His hurt, until now buried deep within him where it festered and began to poison his system, now lay exposed to the fresh air where it could heal. With wisdom beyond her years, Maria left him without a word and went back to her tent. As she left him she heard him pray, "Dear God, please forgive me for my selfish actions."

In her bed, she thought over what he said and wondered what 'accepting Jesus as their savior' meant.

# Chapter Fourteen

Unbeknownst to Dane and company, a fierce battle had raged behind them during most of the day. After the Italians stumbled forward with raised hands that morning, two phone conversations occurred, one American and one German.

Major Hammond, the American battalion commander, ordered attacks on the open enemy flanks to widen the breach. Then he contacted the regimental commander.

"Colonel, there's a small breach in the enemy line." He listened to his orders with a scowl. "Yes, sir, but I'm going to need reinforcements." His frown lifted at what he heard. "Okay." He slammed the receiver down and hollered for a runner. "Tell Captain Carter to come on the double."

When Carter arrived, puffing, Hammond told him, "Division wants the bridge over the Salso River seized before the Germans can blow it. You're to take your company through the gap and take the bridge. I'll be on your heels. It shouldn't take more than an hour to smash a hole in the enemy line."

"Yes, sir. Uh, do you have a map to the bridge?"

"Yes, here it is." Hammond handed it over.

"Now, hurry."

The second conversation began when a German officer snatched up a ringing receiver. "Colonel Vessler speaking." As he listened, a scowl appeared on his face. "An Italian unit surrendered, opening a hole in our lines and some Americans slipped through?" he repeated. "Send an infantry company to seal the breach and another to hunt down the Americans," he ordered, then slammed the receiver down.

Hammond's estimate of time proved to be too optimistic. Just as the tail end of Carter's company disappeared up the draw, the German defenders on the left side saw the situation. They occupied the heights overlooking the draw, sealing off the breach. Since the departure of Carter's company reduced his strength, Hammond could only muster a platoon for the attack. The Italians on the right side were made of sterner material than the ones who surrendered and they, along with the Germans, withstood the attack.

Hammond waited for almost an hour before the promised reinforcements, an infantry company, arrived. He threw them into the firefight, but as the enemy began to waver, the German company summoned by Vessler appeared on the scene. Again, Hammond was stymied, and he called for more reinforcements.

All morning long, the battle swayed back and forth. Charge and counter-charge followed each other. The only result being rising casualty counts as neither side achieved dominance.

The battle took on a life of its own. The fighting spread to each flank, sucking in the reinforcements on both sides as they trickled in.

Hammond, unable to mass enough troops for a knock-out blow, radioed regiment for help, who in turn reached out to division. All morning long and into early afternoon the fighting raged. The experienced Germans stood their ground, inspiring the Italians to do the same.

About 2:30 in the afternoon, the assistant division commander, Brigadier General Theodore Roosevelt, arrived on the scene with a battalion in support. Skinny and cantankerous, son of one president and nephew to the current one, he cursed out the mishandled offensive and all those involved. He organized and launched a massive attack backed by powerful artillery support. Step by step, he forced the enemy back. But by nightfall when the fighting ended, the Americans were only able to advance half a mile.

\*\*\*

Before dawn broke the next morning, July 25th, the camp roused up. Fires were lit, coffee boiled, and the aroma of cooking food spread throughout the camp. Dane rattled the tent, "Rise and shine, imp."

A sleepy, smothered voice answered, "Go 'way, I'm asleep."

He grinned, "You'd better not be when the tent comes down in five minutes."

She shrieked, "You wouldn't!"

"Wanna bet?" He grinned again and walked away. Tennessee, Hemphill, and Rosario overheard the exchange and stared after him, surprised at his lighthearted mood.

Maria crawled out of the tent, glared at Dane's unresponsive back, gave a sunny smile to Tennessee, flounced over to them, and plopped down. "What's for breakfast?" she asked, her face bright with anticipation. The three men laughed.

As Tennessee and Rosario went to get their mess kits, Dane scanned the camp, listening to the conversation between Maria and Hemphill.

Maris sat with her elbows on her knees and hands cupping her chin. "Jonas, you like cooking over an open fire, don't you. I can tell from the expression on your face."

Red colored his cheeks, and not just from the heat from the fire. "I guess you found out my secret, Miss Maria. I do enjoy it. My family used to camp out on weekends sometimes." He stopped and stared off into space. "Those were fun times." He resumed his cooking and added with a smile, "Besides, I'm the best cook in the squad."

"Where did you come from?"

"A small town in Mississippi you never heard of."

"In Nebraska we heard stories of how black people were treated by white people in the Deep South. Are they true?"

Hemphill snorted. "Blacks, they're a third rate class of people. Miss Maria, there are three types of people: respectable white folks, poor white trash, and colored people."

Maria frowned. "What if the colored family was cleaner or more honest? Doesn't that make a difference?"

Hemphill scowled. "No, doesn't matter if white trash would steal the buttons off your shirt. They're better than colored. We'd be better off if they were still slaves, and they should be treated as so. Them wearing the uniform of our country is a disgrace." He stirred the pan so hard food almost spilled out.

Dane scowled as he listened to Hemphill's words. He'd caused trouble in the past about his bigotry. Dane hoped there wouldn't be any in the near future, he faced enough problems already.

Rosario walked up and dropped branches he'd picked up for the fire. He looked around as if searching for a job which needed doing. "*Senorita,* if you are finished with the tent?" He motioned to it.

"*Si*," she nodded. She got up and followed him to it. As he began to take it down, she asked him, "What is your first name."

"Jorge, miss."

"Where are you from?"

"California."

She asked, "You're a Mexican, aren't you?"

He replied without expression. "You could say so."

She cocked her head to one side. "What do you say?"

"I'm an American."

She giggled. "Of course you are. But all Americans have a heritage, where they came from. Mine is Italian." She screwed up her face in thought. "Jorge, isn't it a Mexican name?"

"Or Spanish," Rosario replied, a twinkle forming in his eye.

"I see," she giggled again. "Half of your ancestors emigrated and the other half met them?"

Rosario chuckled. "Yes, miss."

"But the Spanish wasn't at all nice to the natives, were they?" She asked, concern in her voice.

Rosario sobered up. "No, they made slaves out of them. Slavery is a stain on our country." He stopped folding the tent and glanced at the campfire. "It still is."

Dane pondered Rosario's words. *Why can't everyone understand we are one race, the human race? It doesn't matter the color of your skin. God made us all in His image.*

Dane walked up to beside Gates. Dane's eyes narrowed as he ticked off the names of the squad in his mind: Hemphill, Gates, O'Halloran, Rosario, Tennessee and Chilvers. *Braun and Raymond are on guard duty. No Conners.*

Dane turned to Gates. "Where's Conners?"

Gates looked around. "I don't know. He offered to go get firewood, but I haven't seen him since."

"I see," Dane said in a dry tone. Both men looked at each other, realizing what happened.

Hemphill announced, "Grubs on." Maria scooted to the fire and the rest of the squad followed. Like magic, Conners appeared too.

# Chapter Fifteen

Conners gave a sigh of relief at his successful escape from a work detail. He lived by the motto 'out of sight, out of mind' and it worked for most of his life. If those in charge didn't see you, they wouldn't give you jobs to do. Then he scowled. *But it doesn't work on the sergeant with the too-seeing eyes. He always notices when I disappear and he searches me out.*

He jumped when Shaw spoke behind him, "No wood for the fire?"

"Couldn't find any dry enough, Sarge," Conners excused himself.

"Uh, huh," Shaw gave a pointed glance at a group of dead trees not far away. "You'll supply the wood for the noon fire."

Conners scowled at the rebuke. Maria gave him a cheerful greeting, but he mumbled a reply and looked away. He never did know how to respond when a girl said something to him.

Conflicting emotions tore at him as he stood in line waiting for his food. Fury at Shaw for the way he treated him, embarrassment about Maria talking to him, and a sullen anger at his fellow soldiers for the way they ignored him. After two weeks in this stiff-necked squad nobody wanted to be his buddy.

He remembered his need for more cigarettes and glanced around to see if there were any packs lying around which he could steal.

\*\*\*

Each of the three squads possessed their own fire and cook, but as soon as the other men got their food they all gravitated to Maria's fire. Dane looked them over. Without exception, they were all on their best behavior. Some of the men Dane would not have trusted alone with her, but his warning the previous day showed its affect. The Third Squad, who took her under their collective wing, also passed on some words of their own.

As Dane moved among his men he gauged their mood. After all the mishaps of yesterday, along with the battles and casualties and the long march in the heat, after a decent night's sleep, hot food, and hot coffee, the men were raring to go. His heart swelled as he regarded them; there couldn't be better soldiers anywhere. *Thank you, Lord, for these men and their attitude this morning. Please watch over them and keep everyone safe Please bless them and strengthen them for the ordeals they will face today.* Dane knew they would need every bit of their ability and strength in the coming days.

He checked on the soldiers who'd suffered from the heat yesterday and found them much improved. "You men watch yourselves. If you start

121

feeling the way you did yesterday, or if you feel disoriented tell your corporal. Keep drinking plenty of water. When we stop be sure to rest in shade. After all, the government paid out plenty to train you and they want to get their money's worth," he smiled at them and they grinned back.

He hunkered down next to Tony Wilbers. "I prayed for you, Tony."

He looked nervous. "Are you sure I'm going to be all right?"

"I know you will, if you follow my directions." The confidence in Dane's voice allowed for no doubt. Wilbers sagged in relief and gave a more natural smile. "Is there anything else you would like me to pray for?" Dane asked.

Wilbers looked down in embarrassment. "Ma is having a tough time. Could you pray for her?"

"I will," Dane promised.

"Sarge, do you think prayer helps?"

"Yes, I've seen it happen. Not every time, but, yes, it can."

Wilbers had a thoughtful look on his face, but didn't say anything more.

Dane patted Wilbers on the shoulder and went to get his breakfast.

He picked up his food and sat down by Lassiter. While they ate breakfast they discussed flanker duties, order of the march and possible encounters along the way. "Put Gates' squad in the lead with two scouts in front," Dane ordered. "We could run into retreating enemy groups. Tell everyone to keep their eyes peeled."

When they were done eating, Dane looked for Maria. He saw her sitting next to Tennessee with their heads together. Dane called to her, "Miss Maria, come over here, please."

She looked at him, said something to Tennessee and skipped over.

"Where do we go from here?" he asked.

"We head north now. I need to watch for some landmarks."

Dane asked, "Have you ever been this far before?"

She sneaked a peek at him. What she saw in his eyes made her tell the truth. "No, I've never been this far into these hills."

Lassiter gaped at her while Dane didn't bat an eye. "But Old Giuseppe told us how he brought his sheep this way and I remember what he said," she added in triumph. Dane nodded, accepting what she said. She stole another look at him and asked, "How did you know I've never been here before?"

"You said on previous occasions you'd been away from home all day, but you never hinted at being gone overnight, so there is no way you could have come this far."

123

Lassiter gaped at Dane this time, flummoxed at his reasoning. Maria started to grasp what her mother had seen, that Dane knew how to handle teenage girls.

The meal over, men scattered to pick up their belongings, put out the fires and make a last stop at the latrines. Dane caught a stealthy motion out of the corner of his eye. Conners slipped over next to O'Halloran's backpack and palmed a pack of cigarettes sticking out.

Mickey O'Halloran came from a long line of fighters. His great-grandfather joined the Union Army almost as soon as he set foot off of the ship which brought him from Ireland. He distinguished himself in the Irish Brigade at Gettysburg. His grandfather charged up San Juan Hill with Teddy Roosevelt. His father went Over There in the Great War and forced the Germans to surrender, according to his version of the war. When O'Halloran spun around and smashed a fist into Conners' face, knocking him down, Dane could almost see three generations of O'Halloran's standing at their descendant's back.

"You miserable spalpeen," O'Halloran bellowed, "you leave my smokes alone!" He yanked Conners to his feet and knocked him right back down again.

Conners lay on the ground, not moving. "I

thought it was my pack," he whined.

O'Halloran let Conners know in no uncertain terms what he thought of that excuse.

Dane spotted Lassiter at the other end of the camp and couldn't see Gates anywhere. Dane did his disappearing trick, moving behind some bushes. Sometimes a squad handled its own internal discipline better than if the sergeant intervened. Conners crawled away and O'Halloran helped him along with a kick.

In a few more minutes, the camp broke up and the men started off. Tennessee and Hemphill scouted in front while Dane and Maria led the troops. The cool early morning air felt refreshing, but the rising sun promised another scorching day. Dane marched them until mid-morning without a break, taking advantage of the cool part of the day.

Maria pointed to a hill with a distinctive white scar in the distance. "We need to go around the east side of the hill and then we angle to the northwest. There's a spring on the north side where Old Giuseppe watered the sheep."

Dane scanned the horizon. "Okay, we'll stop for a ten minute break."

He noticed during the stop Chilvers took the opportunity to set down beside the attractive young woman and ply her with some of his well-practiced lines. She listened with wide eyes and rapt attention until Dane called for them to start again. She abandoned Chilvers without a second glance and with a happy smile skipped beside Dane. He shot her a sidelong glance, "I see you have been getting to know some of the men."

She raised innocent eyes to his. "They are all so interesting to talk to, *Zio* Sergeant."

"I saw you talking to Raymond yesterday. Sometimes people aren't too comfortable around him, I've noticed."

She nodded with a firm set to her jaw. "He has a kind heart, I'm glad to get to know him. The others don't realize what they're missing by ignoring him."

"What's your opinion about Chilvers?" Dane asked.

She screwed up her face. "He says the most marvelous things about me and I love to hear them, but I don't believe him. He's not a farmer."

Her last statement surprised a chuckle out of him. "That's something important?"

She nodded, a serious look on her face. "It's the most important thing to me."

"Why?" Dane asked, puzzled.

She hesitated, glanced at him out of the corner of her eye, shrugged and said, "It just is." Changing the subject she asked, "Last night you said something that I don't understand. What does 'accepting Jesus as their savior' mean?"

They walked for a few steps while Dane marshaled his thoughts and breathed a quick prayer. "God hates sin. God hates all sin, no matter how little it seems in our eyes. The Bible teaches us the punishment for sin is death. That's why people grow old and die, because of sin. But the punishment isn't just physical death; it's also spiritual death, which is eternal separation from God. God created Hell for Satan and his angels while God lives in Heaven. God is pure, and no sin or sinner can live with Him, so all sinners are cast into Hell to be separated from Him forever. God is righteous, so all sinners have to be punished and die.

"But God loves us, and He made a way so people can be sinless and live with Him. Jesus Christ, the Son of God, God Himself, became a man and lived on earth. He came to be the sacrifice for sin. Since He is a sinless God, His death on the cross couldn't be for His sins, because He never sinned. He died for everyone's sin, everybody who ever lived or will ever live. His blood washes away all sin. He offers it as a free gift to anyone who will accept it. Nobody can earn their way to Heaven; only by accepting Jesus' sacrifice can they become free of the bonds of sin. Accepting Jesus as your savior means admitting you are a sinner, knowing only the blood of Jesus can cleanse you of your sins, and asking Jesus to forgive you and live in you."

Dane reached into his pocket and pulled out his Bible. "Here are some verses, Romans 3:23 'For all have sinned and come short of the glory of God.' Romans 3:10 through 12, 'There is none righteous, no, not one: there is none that understandeth, there is none that seeketh after God. They are all gone out of the way, they are together become unprofitable; there is none that doeth good, no, not one.' Isaiah 64:6, 'But we are all as an unclean thing, and all of our righteousnesses are as filthy rags.' Jesus says in John 10:10, 'I am come that they might have life, and that they might have it more abundantly,' and in Luke 19:10, 'For the Son of Man is come to seek and to save that which was lost.'"

Dane looked at Maria. "The human race became lost when Adam sinned. Jesus came to save us, but we have to personally accept Him as our savior. Here," he handed her his Bible, "you can keep this and read it if you want to."

"Thank you," Maria hesitated, then took it and looked at it. "Papa said he doesn't think there is a god. He said a loving god would not have crippled him like he is."

"What happened to him?" Dane asked.

"Papa at last got a job at the stockyards when a

steer ran him over and shattered his leg. The doctor set it as well as he could, but we couldn't afford the surgery needed to make it well. Then Papa couldn't find a job again."

"Where did this happen?"

"In America. Papa emigrated there and met and married Mama and they had me. Then the depression hit and Papa lost his job. After his accident *Nonna* wrote to us *Nonno* was dying, and so we moved back for Papa to run the farm. *Nonno* died soon after we came, *Nonna* died last year."

"*Nonna* and *Nonno*?" Dane quirked an eyebrow.

"Grandmother and Grandfather," Maria explained.

Dane walked on a bit, his brow furrowed in thought, before he asked, "What would have happened to you and your mother if your father had been killed?"

"What?" Shocked, Maria stared at him.

"What would have happened to you and your mother if the steer had killed your father?"

"We... I suppose we would have had to...I guess we would have had to live with Grandpapa and Grandmamma in America," Maria replied, hesitation evident in her voice.

"And what about *Nonno* and *Nonna*?" Dane pursued his questioning.

Maria thought. "After *Nonno* died, *Nonna* would have…would have, maybe tried to live at the farm living off of the garden, or maybe live with, I don't know, somebody." Her voice trailed off.

"Now, what if your father had not been injured, what would've happened to your family?" Dane asked Maria.

"Papa would have his job and we would be living in Omaha," she answered with a happy skip. Then her expression changed, "Oh, we wouldn't be here though."

"What would have happened to *Nonna*?" Dane queried.

Maria pondered the question. "Papa would have brought *Nonna* to America, but she wouldn't have been able to sell the farm, there were no buyers then. She would have had to abandon it." She looked around at the countryside. "*Nonna* would have hated living in the city. She loved living here in Sicily, in the country."

"So for *Nonna* to stay on the farm in comfort and for you to live here, your father had to have the accident," Dane said. Maria looked at him with large round eyes but said nothing.

*\*\*\**

Maria dropped back to beside Gates, a little behind *Zio* Sergeant, her mind full of what he said. She glanced up and saw a thoughtful look on Gates' face.

"You heard what *Zio* Sergeant said, didn't you," she whispered.

"Yes," Gates whispered back.

"What do you think about it?"

"He could be right. It kinda seems logical."

"And about God?"

They paced some more steps. "Well, like a wise man once said, there ain't any atheists in a foxhole."

Maria pondered *Zio's* words. Then she thought about her conversation with Van about farm life. Happiness bubbled up in her at discovering he had as deep of love of the land as she did. Her heart skipped a beat. *Could Van being the answer to my plans?*

As they marched on in the rising heat, Maria kept thinking. At the next break, she watched *Zio* move among the men, checking for heat exhaustion. She heard him tell a few of the men to drink more water.

She overheard O'Halloran say to Braun, "Shaw's friendlier now, not so aloof."

"Yeah, didja see the long conversation he had with Maria? I'll bet she's the reason."

"He's been talking to her a lot."

Break time ended and the march resumed. Maria remained quiet, her thoughts focused on *Zio*

Sergeant's words. *Could what he said be true? Is the only reason I'm here is because of Papa's broken leg? If I wasn't here, would I have ever met Van?* The last thought felt too terrible to bear. The rest of the morning Maria spoke little, thinking about his explanation while they marched on in the rising heat.

# Chapter Sixteen

At the next break, Dane moved among the men, checking for heat exhaustion. A few of the men were showing signs of stress, and Dane made a speech. "Listen up, men. Don't waste your water, but you need to keep hydrated. Take a good swallow and then use the pebbles like I said yesterday. If anyone feels woozy tell myself, Sergeant Lassiter or your corporal. We'll make camp where there's water."

By the time they reached the hill with the spring the sun stood almost straight overhead. Tennessee and Hemphill were waiting for them. Dane walked over to get their report first.

"We looked around and found nothin' to worry about," Tennessee said.

Then Dane talked with the other scouts who reported seeing little. A few tracks were discovered of two or three small groups of men and a house had been looted not long before, but there was nobody there. They'd sighted planes during the march, but too high up to distinguish friend from foe.

"Okay men, go take a rest. You've earned it," Dane smiled at the scouts and dismissed them. He glanced around. "Sergeant Lassiter, set out guards.

Conners, go gather firewood."

Conners, stymied from skipping out of his chore, grunted something unintelligible and slouched off.

Lassiter strode up to Dane. "The guards are posted."

Dane nodded. "Good." He raised his voice, "Corporal Gates, Corporal Goldner, over here." He looked around again and saw Maria standing next to Tennessee. "Miss Maria, please come too."

When they were all gathered together, Dane first addressed Goldner. "How is your heavy weapons squad making out? Are you having any problems carrying the weapons and ammo?"

Goldner blinked at him. "We're short-handed. Another man would be helpful."

Dane glanced at Lassiter. "Sergeant, see to it." Dane looked back to Goldner. "Next time, don't wait to be asked if you need help." Abashed, Goldner nodded.

Dane turned to Maria. "How much further is it to the bridge?"

She thought and looked around. "I'm not sure, about ten kilometers, I think."

Dane looked at Lassiter. "How far do you think we've traveled since yesterday?"

He pondered the question. "Wal, we've been kinda snaking around, but I would say aboot fifteen miles," he replied in his Texan drawl.

Dane agreed, "That's about what I thought too, which would leave about five miles. And ten kilometers is about six miles, isn't it?" he asked Maria.

"*Si,*" she agreed.

"So, about another two or three hours," Gates added to the conversation.

Dane looked at Maria. "Do you know what kind of terrain is around the bridge?"

She frowned in concentration. "I remember going through a cut in a ridge and seeing the bridge. I think the other side rolled uphill, not steep."

"Which side has the ridge?" Dane asked.

"West side, this side," Maria replied.

Gates and Goldner left the group to see to their squads. Dane asked Maria, "Where do we go after we leave here?"

"Now we head straight for the bridge, northwest from here," she replied with a smile. Dane stared off in that direction while Maria and Lassiter left. He felt an overpowering urge they needed to hurry. *Lord, please show me what to do. I feel a need to hurry, is this from You? Please show me your will.* He prayed to God for help. He didn't want the men to be worn out when they reached the bridge. His original intention to have an hour's break for lunch because of the heat now felt wrong.

He changed his mind and decided to leave once the men finished eating. Peace fell on him when he made the decision.

He broke open a ration and bowed his head. *Thank you, Lord, for this food. I ask you to strengthen me and help me this afternoon. Help us reach and take the bridge without any casualties and hold it. Please guide and protect Zimmerman and Milne. Please have Zimmerman make radio contact with headquarters so they know our situation. Bring him to us as soon as possible. Help Milne to thwart any escape attempts. Keep any enemies away from the Calvoratti farm. In Jesus' name I pray, amen.*

\*\*\*

Tennessee felt puzzled. When he'd seen Maria, she gave him a brilliant smile, but when he tried to talk to her, she seemed abstracted. Now he got an earful from some of the men.

Braun began the conversation, "Sergeant Shaw sure changed, hasn't he?"

Hemphill agreed. "Yeah, I heard him crack a joke. You'd think he's getting human or something."

Braun chuckled. "I bet I know who's humanizing him."

Conners came up in time to hear Braun, dropped an armful of wood and said, "Yeah, Shaw sure talks up Maria, doesn't he?"

O'Halloran put in, "They do visit at lot." He gave a meaningful wink.

Tennessee's heart plummeted. "What do y'all mean?"

"This morning, Shaw and her talked most of the time together. He warns everyone off and then he spends all his time with her. He must be clearing the field so just he has a chance at her," Conners added in a cynical tone. "Matter of fact, I got ten bucks says he tries to seduce her first chance he gets."

Rosario and Raymond jumped to the sergeant's defense. While the argument swirled, Tennessee sat silent. At first furious at Conners for the way he talked about Maria, and then at Shaw for what his plans were. He wanted to pound them both into the ground. But then his shoulders slumped. *Ah'm nothin' but a hillbilly from Tennessee*, he thought, dejection weighing heavy on him. How could he compete with the likes of Shaw or Chilvers for Maria's affections? But then he straightened up and a glint came into his eyes. Nobody had better bother Maria with him around, whether she liked it or not.

Chilvers, silent up until now, broke into the conversation. "I for one have never heard anyone sweet talk a girl by calling her an imp before."

Raymond sided with Chilvers. "She calls him

Uncle Sergeant, there's no romance there."

Gates walked up in time to hear the last two comments. "What's going on?" he demanded.

Rosario answered, "Conners thinks Shaw is trying to sweet talk Maria."

"Knock off that kind of talk," Gates ordered. "I heard the whole conversation; they were talking about the Bible."

"The Bible?" Rosario laughed out loud at Conners chagrined tone and expression. Tennessee felt a huge burden lift off of his heart, and then a thoughtful look came over his long face. *The Bible?*

# Chapter Seventeen

Tennessee felt a thrill go through him when Maria came and sat down next to him. The men, as if to atone for their thoughts of a few minutes ago, were extra nice to her, and Tennessee didn't get a chance to have a private conversation with her.

While they were eating, Shaw strolled over to them. "Gates, under normal circumstances I'd take one of the new men with me and scout ahead of the column. But since I'm in charge of the operation, it's not my place. Take Conners and scout ahead this afternoon. Maria says we need to head northwest from here. We want to come up to the bridge from the south, so we'll head a little more north than west so we won't miss it. If we run into the river first, we'll follow it to the bridge."

As soon as they were done eating, Shaw ordered them on their way. He led the column with Tennessee and Maria behind him.

Tennessee asked Maria, "How come y'all over here in the middle of Sicily and speakin' American and everythin'?"

Maria told him of her family's story and then asked, "Van, were you ever in Omaha, Nebraska?"

"Me?" Tennessee's eyebrows shot up. "Ah never been out of Tennessee, not 'til ah joined the

139

Army." He discovered he enjoyed being called Van by her. "Why do you ask?"

Maria explained Dane's reasoning about her father's accident and added, "So if Papa didn't have his accident, we would never have met."

Tennessee dared to respond, "Wal, except for your father's leg, ah shore am glad to know you, Miss Maria."

Maria gave him a brilliant smile, "I'm glad to know you too, Van. I've told you all about me, now tell me about yourself."

"Wal, ah grew up on a farm back in the hills of Tennessee. Pa and Ma had six of us young'uns. It takes a lot a hard work to wring a livin' out of that land. All of us kids had to work hard. Ah'm the youngest and got the most education, all the way up to the eighth grade. When Pa died, the farm went to my oldest brother, Arthur. But the farm cain't support more than one family, so when Arthur and his wife started havin' young'uns and the rest of us got old enough, we packed our bags and left. Alexander married the storekeeper's daughter and they are runnin' it now. Cyrus drifted off to Californy, Esther and Rachel got married, and ah joined the Army."

He looked down at Maria and saw her puzzled look. He chuckled. "Yeah, Ma liked those old warrior names. They were named fer King Arthur,

Alexander the Great, and Cyrus the Great who whupped up on old Babylon. Ah just wished she liked something other than Octavian."

She chuckled and gave him a saucy look. "Don't you have someone back home waiting for your return?"

It took him a moment to realize the point of her question. "Nope, ah never rightly had me a girl." He turned his head and looked down into her eyes, and his heart did strange flip-flops.

Maria changed the subject by reaching into the pocket of her skirt and pulling out the Bible. *"Zio* Sergeant gave this to me to read. Do you know anything about it?"

"Yes'm, Ma used to read it to us kids every night, and all of us went to church on Sundays. Ma made sure we never missed when we were youngsters." Tennessee hesitated and then went on. "Ah kinda drifted away when ah got older, began running around, drinking a little 'shine. Ah never did read it much before ah left home and haven't read it since, but ah know Ma prayed fer me.

"What's 'shine?" Maria inquired.

"Moonshine, corn likker." Tennessee got a half embarrassed, half thoughtful look on his face. "Kinda funny, ah never did like the taste of it. Some of the guys ah ran around with drank it all the time. Sometimes they would get ornery and talk about

141

pulling some sort of shenanigans, but somehow ah was never around when they did stuff like that. Ah'd remember that Jesus died fer mah sins and as a youngster ah asked Him fer forgiveness. Then ah could almost hear Ma praying fer me, and somehow ah never got involved."

"*Zio* Sergeant told me about Jesus dying for people's sins. It seems too good to be true, that it's free, that we don't have to work for it."

"It's true," Tennessee averred. "Ah knows the Bible says that. Ah knows Sergeant Shaw reads his Bible every day and ah feel maybe like ah should too, but, wal, you know…" his voice trailed off.

Maria looked up at him, "Van, would you read it with me later?" she asked.

"Yes, ah will," he promised.

Chilvers watched them talking together, and irritated at the sight of the hillbilly making time with her, hurried up to them. He stopped when he heard them talking about the Bible. *The Bible, of all things,* he thought to himself. For once, not knowing what to say, he dropped back.

Dane, ahead of them, heard snatches of their conversation, but his mind remained fixed on the bridge and what they might find there.

# **Chapter Eighteen**

Three hours later, Dane peered over the top of a ridge at a bridge about a hundred feet away, and did not like the sight. Here the Salso River flowed south between narrow but steep banks. A mile or so to the south, it turned and flowed east. Because it being summer the river ran low. But it rushed in a torrent over rocks which caused a constant low pitched roar, and at a speed and volume which no boat or swimmer could live in for more than a couple of minutes.

The ridge ran from the northwest to the southeast. South of Dane's position it merged with the west bank of the river, creating a steep and high cliff, almost impassible to anyone trying to work their way along the river. To the north, in the broken ground between the ridge and the river, Dane's battle-hardened eyes spotted a knoll which provided a defensive position.

A hard surfaced road appeared from the northwest, west of the ridge, made a bend just north of where Dane lay, swept east through a cut in the ridge, onto the bridge and then on east past a hummock. A two story stone building, small enough to be called a hut, guarded the west end of the bridge, with a door in the west wall. On the east

143

side of the river, the ground rolled up towards some hills in the distance. Dane picked out a defensive line east of the river.

A steep slope on the west side of the river ran down six feet to a bench. From the bench it dropped straight down to the river. To the south, the bench stopped where the ridge and bank met, and some fifty or sixty feet north, it ended in a rocky tangle of rocks. It ranged from two to ten feet wide, and the bridge crossed at the widest portion, with a bridge support on the bench. The bridge looked about forty feet long and sixteen feet wide.

Dane saw three German soldiers on this end of the bridge and a couple of Germans inside the small building standing by the windows. A German truck at the far end spelled trouble to him. He squinted his eyes at four Germans busy doing something by the end of the bridge. With a shock he realized they were preparing it for demolition! *No wonder you wanted me to hurry, Lord.*

Dane slid down the ridge and related what he'd seen to the others. "We've got to take the building before the Germans can hole up in it, and also the far side of the bridge before they finish laying the charges," Dane explained.

"What we need is some kind of diversion," Gates said slowly. "Something which will attract the Krauts' attention so we can get into the building, but won't alert them. Then from the building we can provide covering fire for a charge across the bridge."

"Good idea," approved Dane. "But can anyone think of something?"

"I can do it," spoke up Maria, with more bravery than she felt.

"No!" exclaimed Dane and Tennessee in the same breath.

"It's too dangerous!" Tennessee went on.

Maria looked Dane right in the eye. "I can walk right up to them, and they wouldn't suspect anything. You know it."

Dane bit his lip. He didn't like it one little bit. He glanced around. Tennessee scowled, but dawning acceptance appeared on the faces of the others. No other plan came to mind which wouldn't alarm the Germans. "All right. Maria, work your way over to the road and then walk up to the bridge. Make sure you are standing where the Germans can't see the door. Talk to them until you don't see any Germans watching you from the building. Don't stare at it, but keep your eye on it. Then walk back down the road. Corporal Goldner, your squad will provide covering fire from the ridge. Your first targets are the Germans on this side of the bridge. Gates, your job is to help secure the building and then lay a covering fire on the other bank. Sergeant

Lassiter will take the last squad across the bridge and secure it. Cut any wires you see. I'll take Tennessee and Hemphill and sneak into the building while the Germans are distracted. Everyone keep your heads down, nobody looks over the ridge until the firing starts except for Lassiter. Any questions?"

There weren't any. When Maria disappeared along the ridge, Dane didn't notice she stopped by a man from Goldner's squad and took something he handed her. While the men waited in the hot sunshine and perspiration dripped down their faces, the Germans continued their work. Two of them on the far side disappeared under the bridge. Each passing second felt like an eternity. At last, Dane saw Maria walking down the road. Anger surged through him at her appearance. She'd pulled one arm out of her blouse, baring her shoulder, and a long slit in her skirt exposed her leg well up her thigh with every second or third step she took.

He shuttled his glance to the Germans, and saw they were all staring at her. It seemed to take forever for her to walk from the cut up to the bridge, and Dane saw all four of the Germans on the other side stop working and watch her. He checked the stone hut and saw two Germans leaning out the windows on the first floor, but then he noticed one on the second floor. He would be a problem. Maria walked up to the bridge, stopped and said something to them. He saw some confusion until one of the Germans started talking. *He must be able to speak Italian,* Dane thought.

Dane motioned for Tennessee, Hemphill, and Lassiter to join him. "Follow me," he whispered to Tennessee and Hemphill and slithered down the ridge. For several feet he could have been spotted, but Maria stood where the Germans on this side of the river had their backs to him, and the Germans on the other side kept their eyes glued on her display.

Tennessee and Hemphill joined him, and they crept to the door. Dane heard Maria mention Pepecita, and his lips twitched. He slipped through the door into a room about fifteen feet by fifteen feet with a staircase along one wall leading up to the second floor. The furniture consisted of a table, several chairs, a stove, and some cupboards. There were two windows facing the bridge, and a German looking out of each of them. Dane motioned for Hemphill to watch the stairway while he and Tennessee crept up behind the two unsuspecting guards. At the last second, one of them must have sensed something, for he started to turn his head. Dane slapped his hand over the man's mouth and plunged his knife into his back. The German stiffened and tried to pull Dane's hand away and he stabbed him again. The German slumped, and Dane eased the dead body onto the floor.

Dane glanced over at Tennessee and saw him wiping his knife clean on the shirt of his victim. Dane motioned to Hemphill to climb the stairs.

Hemphill crept up the steps until his eyes peeked into the upstairs room. There were bedrolls lying around on the floor, and a German leaning out the window for a better view. On silent feet he glided towards the window, but just before he reached it, the German turned around. The German's eyes bulged and he opened his mouth to yell. Hemphill in desperation grabbed him by the throat. The two men swayed together, Hemphill hanging on to the German's throat with one hand and trying to stab him with the other. His opponent hung on for dear life to Hemphill's knife hand and tried to pull the other hand from his throat.

Dane flashed across the room and plunged his knife again and again into the German's body until he sank down, dead. Only then did Hemphill release his hold on the man's throat. They gave each other a shaky grin.

*Step one is over, now to capture the bridge*, Dane thought to himself.

***

Maria gave a voluble description of Pepecita's traits to the leering Germans. She glanced at the building and saw the empty windows. Now came

148

the hard part, to end the conversation and walk all the way back down the road without breaking into a run or otherwise tipping off the Germans. She swallowed hard, and with a lump in her throat spoke in Italian to the Germans, "If you haven't seen her, then I'll go check over there," giving a vague wave to the north. She turned and walked away. Behind her she heard the Germans talking and then a burst of laughter. No doubt somebody made a lurid comment which she was glad she couldn't understand.

***

Dane peered out the window with one eye. He saw a burly German sergeant watch Maria walk away with a grin on his face and then glance around. A puzzled look came over the German's face as he took a second look at the lower windows. He spoke out, asking a question. No answer. He called out again and then yelled at Maria, "*Stoppen!*" The Italian speaking German then yelled "*Alt!*"

Dane pointed his Thompson at the group of enemy soldiers below him and yelled, "Maria, drop!" He sprayed the Germans below him with the gun and saw them fall. He spared Maria a glance and saw her run and drop into cover. He spotted a German raise his gun up towards him, and Dane shot him. Another one struggled to his feet and then

149

went down in a hail of bullets as the Americans on the ridge opened fire. Dane heard Tennessee and Hemphill firing at the enemy on the far bank from the east windows. Dane ran over to the window by Hemphill and opened up with his tommy gun, catching a German in full stride as he tried to run behind the shelter of the truck. Then Lassiter charged past the building and led his men across the bridge. The fight ended when the last German threw his hands up in the air and surrendered.

Dane rushed out of the hut to go to Maria and saw Tennessee ahead of him. "Are you all right?" Tennessee gasped out as Maria stood up and dusted herself off.

"Yes, of course I am," she answered.

"What do you think you were doing, dressed like that?" Dane snapped at her, the relief he felt at her safety being swallowed up by his anger.

Maria looked at him with age-old eyes. "If I'd walked up to them they would have looked, yes, but like this," and she thrust out her leg and moved her bare shoulder, "they would not look away."

Tennessee glared at her. "Don't you ever do anythin' like that again, ya hear me?"

"Yes Van," she agreed in a meek tone.

"What if those men had attacked you?" Dane thundered at her.

"Then my *Zio* Sergeant would have rescued

me," she said with outward calm, although she remembered her fear at the time with an inward shudder.

"You didn't tear your skirt, you cut it," Dane observed, still with a bite to his voice but weakening.

"*Si*, I borrowed a knife from one of the men."

"Well, you can sew it back up again," Dane ordered.

"Ah've got mah sewing kit, ah'll get it for you," Tennessee volunteered.

"Then if you *signores* will go away, I'll make the repairs," she said with a pert lift of her chin

"Oh," belated, the men realized she needed privacy. "Maria, use the upstairs room, Tennessee, guard the stairway until you're done."

Dane swung away, his eyes sweeping the terrain, his brain busy making decisions, his voice barking out orders. "Gates, get a detail to get rid of these bodies here, I want you and Braun to interrogate the prisoner. Lassiter, you dispose of those bodies over there and search the truck. Goldner, we'll need defensive positions on the east side of the river on the hummock there and along the ridge behind us here," Dane pointed to the two positions.

Lassiter interrupted, "We captured it, but the question is can we hold it?"

Dane looked at him, "We can only hold it against a small force. Anything big comes along, we'll pretend we're not here and let them through. That's why we've got to get this cleaned up now."

The men gaped at him in surprise. Goldner gulped and asked, "How soon do you think the rest of the company will be here?"

Dane looked at his watch. "It's almost 1600 hours. My guess is late tomorrow morning."

Lassiter whistled. "Thet's a long time to be alone."

"Yes it is, but we are going to hold it," Dane's face became a mask of ruthless determination. "After we get done cleaning up, start digging foxholes." The others scattered to their duties.

# Chapter Nineteen

"Hey, Sergeant Shaw," a soldier called as he hurried up to Dane. "The truck is full of mines and explosives."

"Mines?" Dane's mind grappled with the possibilities. He hurried over the bridge to the truck.

Lassiter and Braun were prowling through the loaded vehicle. "Looks like a dozen antitank mines and about a hundred antipersonnel mines," Braun reported. "There's explosives and fuse wire over there," he pointed to a corner in the truck.

Dane thought out loud, "The last intelligence report I heard said the Germans were making a fighting withdrawal to cover their retreat across the Messina Strait. They're trying to get as many men and materials out of Sicily as they can. If that's the case, then most of the traffic from the east will be ammunition and messengers. Our danger will be from the north and west. There will be skulkers and men lost from their units, wounded and prisoners, rear area troops and artillery moving through here at any time."

"Unless they find out we're here and there is a unit to the east they can send against us," Lassiter added in a matter-of-fact voice.

"True." Dane looked at Braun. "Did you find

153

out anything from the prisoner?"

"They were to rig the bridge for demolition and then wait for orders to blow it."

"Good, then they won't be missed today." Dane mused, "It would be best to plant the mines all in one field, it'll be more effective." *Lord, grant me wisdom,* he breathed a silent prayer and then spit out orders. "Lassiter, assign five men to drive the truck and lay the mines by the knoll to the north, chose men with mine laying experience, if we have any. I know Rosario does, take him. Have a half squad dig foxholes to cover the minefield.

"Split Gates' squad, put two or three men around the bridge to clean up and Gates with the rest on the ridge digging in. Take the last squad and set up a defensive position on the hummock on the east side of the river. I'm putting you in charge over there. Gates will command the ridge.

"Goldner, split your squad into three sections. Put one section on the ridge, one at the hummock and the other at the knoll. You're in command at the knoll.

"If something comes along too strong for us to handle, wave your hands. That means everyone hides. Remember they will look to the front, sides and rear so hide well and let them go through. If we can take them then wave your gun. Then we'll ambush them.

"Lassiter, tell Gates. All three of you have a man keep his eyes on the other two positions so nobody misses the signal. Okay, let's get moving."

Dane roved the area, trying to be everywhere at once. He told Maria, "After you sew your skirt, you're in charge of the food. It'll be brought in here."

At the knoll he talked to Goldner. "See how those hills tend to funnel vehicles there, there and over there?" He pointed to the three places. "Lay a diamond pattern of four antitank mines at each place. Then lay the rest of the mines from one end to the other. Place a machine gun emplacement where it will cover the minefield."

He checked the eastern defenses on the hummock but Lassiter needed no suggestions. Dane gave him a thumb up and went to see Gates.

When Dane reached Gates, the corporal struck the ground with the blade of his shovel. "The ground's too rocky to dig foxholes. The best we can do is scoop out some hollow spots."

"Okay." Dane stood at the top of the ridge and gave a long look to the left and right. "George, I see some places where attackers can take cover and shoot up at us. Why don't we lay some of those explosives we found in those places and give them a nasty surprise?"

Gates gave a start. He couldn't remember Shaw

ever calling him by his first name. "Yeah, sounds good. Right over there is the perfect place to run the fuses to. From there we can control the whole side from the cut to the river."

Dane nodded. "Good, see to it." He turned and saw Braun. "Braun, scrounge up a German uniform and put it on. You can trick any passers-by."

Braun blinked in surprise. "Where do you want me to get a uniform?"

"There are plenty of bodies to choose from."

Braun grimaced in distaste. "You know wearing an enemy uniform is against the Geneva Convention, don't you?"

Dane gave a derisive smile. "The only way we can stay here is by trickery. You don't think the Geneva Convention has stopped the Germans before, do you?"

"You know, I have an American accent. It's hard to fool a real German." Braun tried a different protest.

Dane shrugged. "Fake it."

Braun sighed and trudged down the slope. Rosario passed him running up the ridge.

"Sergeant Shaw, we found three field telephones and a roll of telephone wire in the truck," Rosario puffed.

Dane stared at Rosario while his mind raced. "We'll set up a phone here and at the hummock on the other side and tie them together at the building. I'll have Conners string the wire. He should be done digging the mass grave for the dead. Go on back to the knoll."

"Yes, Sarge." Rosario half slid, half trotted down the slope, followed by Dane.

When Dane reached the building he poked his head in the doorway. He saw Maria scrubbing away at the table and saying something in Italian which sounded uncomplimentary about German cleanliness. O'Halloran kept out of her way while he stacked rations in cupboards and made sure Conners worked, watching him out of the south window. Dane grinned and gave her a wave while she sniffed at him.

Dane walked behind the building in time to see Conners stop digging and lean on his shovel. Dane looked at the hole in the ground. It looked barely big enough to hold all nine bodies, but it would have to do. There wasn't time to dig bigger graves. "Conners, you and Braun bring the bodies back here and then you go over to the truck. Get the roll of telephone wire and run it along the ground from the ridge, to the building and then to the hummock."

"Sarge, I've been working hard in this heat. I need a break," Conners whined.

"You'll rest when all the work is done. Now jump to it." Dane snapped.

Grumbling under his breath and moving as slow as he dared, Conners joined Braun. Dane helped the two of them drag the bodies beside the grave and then led Conners to the truck.

Dane stood by the knoll and watched the men plant mines. All the men caught Dane's urgency and worked as fast as they could. *All except Conners,* Dane corrected himself. He watched Conners stagger away lugging the heavy roll of wire, making a bigger job of it than necessary.

Dane scowled at the sight of backpacks lying on the ground. "Corporal," he addressed Goldner, "get all the backpacks into the truck. Remember, it has to look like we're not here."

Goldner nodded and in turn passed on the order. "Rosario, pick up those backpacks and anything else lying around and put them in the truck."

Dane took a last look around and loped back to the ridge. Backpacks and other paraphernalia sat in plain sight. "Gates, hide that stuff. Put it the building if you have to, but get rid of it."

When Conners appeared and began to string the wire, Dane took one end and wrapped it around a big rock so it wouldn't drag away. He saw Hemphill gathering up backpacks and helped him.

\*\*\*

Conners muttered as he trudged along. "Stupid

sergeant, making me work this way. I'm doing twice as much as anyone else, but do I get thanked? No! All he does is tell me to do something else. I need a break. Working me in the heat like this is dangerous. I could get sunstroke. But does he care? No, he just tells me to carry this heavy roll."

He reached the building and saw Braun, sitting on the ground, wearing a German uniform and trying on German combat boots. The sight of someone relaxing exasperated Conners soul and he snapped, "Hey Kraut, why don't you get off your duff and do something."

Braun exploded off the ground and looped an overhand blow which mashed Conners' cigarette and split his lip again. "Do you think I had fun undressing dead bodies?" Braun roared. "I'll show you, you little..." and he let loose a torrent of expletives which made Maria, inside the building, cover her ears.

Conners howled in pain, dropped the reel and punched a left to the body followed by a wicked right to Braun's head. But Braun shook it off and kept coming. He smashed a blow to Conners' midsection which he partially blocked and then Braun landed a right to the chin. Conners staggered and tried to clinch Braun, but they tripped and both went down with Braun on top.

Dane appeared like a rocket. He wrenched

Braun off and landed a punch in his solar plexus which doubled him over. When Conners tried to scramble up, Dane backhanded him and knocked him sprawling. "Enough!" Dane roared. "There will be no more of this!"

Conners looked up into Dane's face and fear clutched at his heart. In Dane's green tinted eyes he saw something savage and untamed. It made his blood run cold. Dane glared at Braun who turned pale at his look. "If there is any more fighting between you, I'll chain the two of you together. You'll eat, sleep, and fight together, and if one of you is killed, then the other one will be too," he said in a fierce voice. "Now, get back to work."

# Chapter Twenty

All of a sudden a bystander yelled, "Look up there!" Everyone stared up into the sky to see several planes swooping and circling, one of them with smoke coming out of its engine. A piece of a wing flew off and the plane started spiraling down. The pilot ejected from the plane and his parachute opened. But then the plane made another spiral and ran into the parachute. Horrified, the watchers saw the chute collapsing and the pilot drop too fast. They saw the American star on the wing as the plane careened away to crash somewhere to the west.

While dropping beyond the knoll to the north of them, the wind pushed the pilot towards the river. Dane hollered at Hemphill, still carrying an armload of backpacks. "Hemp, come with me!" and took off running. Hemphill dropped his load and ran close behind. They ran around the minefield and panted up a slope in time to see the pilot slam to the ground, right at the edge of the steep bank. The blowing parachute began dragging him towards the river. They ran down the slope to his side, where Dane grabbed his knife and cut the parachute lines. The pilot rolled over onto his back with a muffled groan and a grimace of pain. White teeth shone in

161

an ebony face as the pilot gritted out, "I got a busted flipper," and grabbed his arm.

Dane quipped right back, "Good thing you're not swimming, then."

The pilot looked at the edge only a foot or two away, "Yeah, that's close."

Dane looked at the arm and grimaced. It needed attention, and this wasn't the place to work on it. "Hemp, help him to his feet while I stabilize his arm," Dane commanded.

Hemphill drew back. "But…but he's colored!"

Dane felt the pilot stiffen. Dane looked at Hemphill and said with quiet steel in his voice, "He's wearing an American uniform so that makes him one of us. Now pick him up."

With evident reluctance Hemphill approached and the two of them helped him to his feet. While the pilot cradled his arm and Hemphill steadied him, they walked back.

The pilot broke the silence, "I sure am glad I came down behind our lines. I don't want to sit out the war in some prisoner of war camp."

"You didn't," Dane replied, keeping a watch out for any curious enemies.

"I didn't what?" the pilot asked with a puzzled look.

"You didn't come down into friendly territory. We're behind the enemy lines, trying to hold onto a bridge."

"Oh boy, can I pick them," the pilot groaned.

"I'm Sergeant Dane Shaw, Company K, 26th Regiment," Dane introduced himself. "This is Private Jonas Hemphill." Hemp grunted an acknowledgement of the introduction with a pained look on his face.

"I'm Second Lieutenant Booker Crawford of the 99th Pursuit Squadron."

The corners of Dane's lips curled in a smile. "I guess I should have saluted before I rescued you."

Crawford chuckled. "Under the circumstances I'm glad you didn't."

Dane began to like Crawford and felt the emotion being reciprocated.

Hemphill gave a start and said in a shocked voice, "Salute him?"

Dane glared and snapped, "He's an officer, and he will be saluted."

By now, they were walking around the knoll and Dane became distracted. He kept looking at the north side of the knoll and scanning the terrain. Five men were unloading mines from the truck and planting them in the ground. Dane stopped and said, "Hemp, take the lieutenant to the hut and take care of his arm." He spun around and trotted to the truck where Rosario labored. "Rosario, has the truck been stripped and emptied?" Dane asked.

Rosario stood up. "Yes sergeant."

"Good, I want you to drive the truck over there and park it," Dane pointed out the place he meant. "Plant some mines around it here and over there and wire up some explosives so we can blow it up from the knoll. The truck can't be seen from the road and it won't interfere with our firing until the Germans come up and hide behind it."

"I see," Rosario grinned. Parked on a slope so it would be easier to push the mines out the back of the truck, Rosario climbed in the cab, started it, and drove up and over the slope without killing it. His grin got bigger; the practice in Tunisia had paid off.

As Dane checked the cleanup around the hut, he saw Braun massaging his stomach. O'Halloran walked past Braun and said. "Hits hard, doesn't he?"

"Yeah," Braun grimaced. "I don't remember being hit harder." Then he did a double take. "How do you know?"

O'Halloran chuckled. "Once, while training in Tunisia, I thought it would be fun for me and Tennessee to try him out. He didn't try to hurt us, but I wanted to hurt him. Turned out he had the fun and I didn't."

\*\*\*

Hemphill brought the pilot to the hut and faced a dilemma. He didn't want to splint up the broken arm, and of course Maria, full of sympathy, demanded to do it. But in his world, if a black man touched a white woman, it became a lynching offense.

Maria glared at him with her hands on her hips, "Well, didn't you hear me? Go get two boards or sticks so I can put a splint on him. I've done sheep before so I know how. So go!" She shooed him out and he left muttering under his breath.

Crawford collapsed into a chair, his face turning pale from shock. "Oh, you poor man," Maria rushed over and fussed over him until Hemphill came back with two boards. With Maria holding the arm steady, Hemphill fastened the boards, stabilizing the arm. "That should help until the doctor comes tomorrow," Maria announced.

"Does he make house calls," Crawford joked as sweat drops formed on his face.

"No, he's coming with the rest of the men tomorrow," Maria explained while Hemphill made his escape.

Raymond came in and began to hook up the telephone, whistling a merry tune as he worked. Maria gave him a thoughtful look. "*Signore* Raymond?"

He looked up. "Yes, Miss Maria?"

"We're in a dangerous position, aren't we?"

Raymond nodded and his mien turned sober.

"Yes, we are. It's likely a lot of us are going to be dead soon."

Crawford became a very interested listener.

"Why is everyone so cheerful then? For instance, you were whistling just now," Maria inquired.

Raymond thought for a second. "It's because of our commander. Since Sergeant Shaw took over command of the company, we've gotten hot meals and sufficient sleep. He knows how to take care of his men. He knows what he's doing, and he has a plan. Do you know how many causalities we took when we captured the bridge?"

"There weren't any, right?" Maria answered.

"That's right, nobody even got a scratch. When we wiped out the German company yesterday we suffered nine casualties. Nine! It's unheard of, Miss Maria."

Lieutenant Crawford's mouth dropped open. Since flummoxing is contagious, he, of course, was flummoxed by the information.

"I've been with him from Tunisia, and we've discovered when we do exactly what he says, our casualties are few. Since landing in Sicily our squad lost four men, five with Patterson. We heard we suffered the least in the whole battalion." Raymond shook his head in wonderment. "I don't know how he does it. You'd better believe the whole unit is aware he's not intending to fight against impossible odds to keep the Germans off the bridge. He's planning to use subterfuge and that has morale sky high."

He finished wiring the phone and reached to pick up the receiver to test it when it rang. He raised an eyebrow, "I guess it works." He lifted the receiver as Dane walked into the building. "Hut," Raymond said, and listened to the other end. Still holding the receiver he turned to Dane, "The east hill reports three trucks coming. He thinks they're carrying ammunition."

Dane thought for a second. "Tell them we'll take them here at the bridge, everyone is to hide." He hurried to the door, gave a shrill whistle to get everyone's attention and waved his gun. "Everybody, take cover," he yelled.

"Braun," he ordered, "grab a bottle and act like you're drunk. Stop them so the last truck is just past the bridge. Ask them for a pass or something." He spun towards a group of nearby men, "Hide behind the hut. When they stop, jump out and cover the drivers." He took a long look around the area and tightened his lips. All his men were hiding, but there were things still in sight which could raise a warning flag if the Germans were alert. The telephone wires were laying on the ground, not covered up yet. Signs of digging on the west ridge and a reel of wire near the knoll. Two backpacks by the edge of the bank. *God, please dull their senses,* he begged. He glanced at his watch. They'd been here forty-five minutes and this was the first traffic coming through. He'd been given more time than he'd hoped for.

He never knew a huge eastbound convoy passed across the bridge ten minutes before they'd arrived. It swept up all the other nearby eastbound vehicles so they could be under the protection of the convoy's AA guns.

# Chapter Twenty-One

Dane joined the men hiding behind the hut. The trucks topped the hummock and sped towards the bridge. Braun entered the hut and grabbed the first bottle he saw. Maria looked out the window and saw the same things which alarmed Dane. She grabbed Braun's arm and said, "I'm coming with you."

"No, you're not," he denied.

She motioned out the window, "If I'm with you, they might not see the turned earth and the telephone wire lying in plain sight on top of the ground."

Out of time to argue, Braun let her go outside with him. Holding the bottle and with Maria draped around him, he staggered to the middle of the road and held up an imperious hand. The trucks ground to a halt, but the last one stopped on the bridge.

The driver in the lead truck leaned out. "Get out of the way, you *dummkopf*."

While Maria lolled on the hood with a fatuous smile on her face, Braun staggered up to the door. "Gotta see your pass," he slurred, covering up his American accent.

"Pass, what pass?" the driver asked, disgust on his face. "Get your slut out of my way. We've got

169

to get this ammunition up to the front. It's urgently needed."

"This pass," Braun pulled out his luger and shoved it in the surprised driver's face. Dane ran to cover the other trucks, the other men following. The last driver tried to put the truck in reverse and Dane shot out its tires. It slewed to a stop. Faced with menacing guns, the three drivers surrendered.

While the drivers were being searched and led away, Raymond looked at Dane. "If you don't mind me asking, why do you want these ammunition trucks?"

Dane glanced at him. "Two reasons. First, it would hurt the Germans fighting west of here and we might get relieved sooner. And second, we're going to need more ammunition for the German guns we captured and Zimmerman is bringing."

"Oh, okay Sarge, just curious." With a puzzled expression at his sergeant's answer, Raymond went to work covering up the telephone wire.

Maria saw the puzzled expressions on Raymond and Braun's faces, who overheard the conversation. While Dane rounded up men to unload the ammunition, Maria asked Braun, "What is it you don't understand about *Zio* Sergeant wanting the ammunition?"

Braun shifted his attention to her. "I can understand depriving the Germans of ammunition, but I don't know why he wants them. German ammo doesn't fit our weapons and I don't know why he wants the German guns." He shook his head, then went to interrogate the prisoners.

Dane ordered the ammunition unloaded and the boxes stacked in the hut. Then the three trucks joined their companion as booby traps at the knoll. Several men cleared up evidence of the American's occupation.

\*\*\*

From his position on the ridge, Gates watched Dane position the trucks around the knoll before being booby-trapped. Gates turned his attention back to the road. Something moved due west of his position. Lying down with just his eyes over the top of the ridge, he focused his attention where he saw the flicker. Four German soldiers came into view, and a woman walked with them. He saw her stumble and start to fall. One of the men yanked on a rope binding her, which jerked her back to her feet.

Gates felt anger mount at the sight. These were the skulkers, the kind of men who were quick to run when the going got tough and eager to attack and plunder helpless people.

"Tennessee, you take the man holding the rope. Chilvers, the one on the far right, Conners, the one next to him and I'll take the left one." Gates

171

assigned targets to his men. "Wait until I shoot."

He waited while the enemy made their way to the foot of the ridge and started climbing. The woman lagged behind and her captor half turned to yank her up. Her slowness put her out of the line of fire. Gates saw the faces of the men: they were hard, vicious, and cruel, and he showed them no mercy. "Fire!" he yelled, and his men opened up. The Germans were blasted out of this life without knowing they were in danger.

He got to his feet and walked down the ridge to the bodies. The woman fell to her knees, terrified out of her wits. When he looked at her, gladness welled up in him for killing the men responsible for her condition. Her clothes were torn and there were fresh bruises on her face. He bent over to untie her, but she shrank away in terror. "It's okay, we won't hurt you," he said, trying to reassure her. She made animal like noises and cowered away, making it obvious she expected her new captors to attack her. Gates in a quiet voice spoke over his shoulder, "Tennessee, get on the phone and have Maria come on the double."

He continued to kneel and speak in a soft tone to the woman. Tennessee reported in and requested Maria to come at once. In a few minutes Maria made her appearance and broke into a spate of Italian. At first the woman shrank away, but as she listened she grew calmer. Maria untied the woman's hands and held them, still talking. At last they stood up and Maria led her back over the slope and to the stone building.

Inside the hut, Maria gave the woman some water which she gulped. Then uncontrollable shudders shook her body. Maria put her arm around her and said over and over, "*Sei sicuro, sei sicuro,* you are safe." The woman clung to her and started sobbing. At last she calmed down and released Maria.

Dane stalked in with his catlike walk and a glint in his eye. The woman, startled by his sudden, quiet appearance, shrieked in fear.

"No, no, he is a friend. He won't hurt you," Maria soothed in rapid Italian while Dane stood there, red staining his cheeks in embarrassment.

The woman stared at him while Dane explained, "I heard what happened and came to see how she's doing."

Maria replied, "She's shaken up and nervous." Maria knew she could only have a vague idea of the violence the other woman had lived through.

Dane turned to go. "That's what we were trying to warn you about yesterday, about not wondering around on your own. There are Americans who are as evil as those Germans were."

"*Si, Zio* Sergeant," Maria answered wide-eyed

as Dane left the hut.

The woman looked at Maria, "You called him uncle?"

Maria shrugged, "It is what I call him, he's been a friend to me."

The woman, Elena, shivered, "I think he's dangerous, like a predator."

***

Up on the ridge, Conners would have agreed with her. He thought again of the look in Shaw's eyes when he and Braun had fought. He remembered as a child when he visited a zoo. As he walked by a cage, he looked up into the eyes of a tiger. The big cat crouched and stared at him like he was the next meal. He remembered the look in the untamed beast's eyes. The same look which he glimpsed in the sergeant's eyes.

Conners glanced over at Gates. "Corporal, do you think Shaw is, um, sane?"

Gates looked at him in amazement. "What makes you think he's not?"

Conners squirmed. "I dunno, the look in eyes I think."

Gates snorted. "He's as sane as the rest of us, just intense." Gates added with a sardonic tone in his voice, "If you cross him, you pay, but if you do what you're supposed to and follow orders, he'll stick with you through thick and thin. He could be your best friend, or your worst enemy, it's your choice."

Tennessee, watching the road, interrupted. "Corporal, there're some vehicles coming." Gates looked through the binoculars at the approaching vehicles and spotted an ambulance with a red cross in the lead. He scanned the other vehicles and turned to the telephone.

"Gates here, tell Sergeant Shaw a convoy of what looks like wounded is coming." He paused, listened, and hung up. He ordered his men, "We're going to let them through. Keep your heads down and don't let yourself be spotted."

When the six ambulances and trucks rolled through the American's position, none of the Germans or Italians guessed they passed through the enemy.

More alarms kept coming through during the rest of the hot afternoon. An Italian family rode a donkey-driven wagon down the road. A messenger came from the east. A bullet ended his military career and the motorcycle ended up in the river. The Americans got his dispatches instead of the German commander.

"I hope it puts a crimp in the German defenses", Gates muttered.

Then about eighteen hundred hours, or six o'clock in the evening, a column approached from the west on the road. Gates watched them and swore. He rang up the phone. "Shaw, there's a group of prisoners headed our way. Two motorcycles in front with half a dozen guards." He listened and put down the phone. "We're going to take them at the bridge. Tennessee, Chilvers, and O'Halloran, get down to the hut. The rest of us stay put and hide. We're to keep any survivors from escaping this way."

Back at the hut, Braun stood in front the window. Maria and Elena disappeared up the stairs with Raymond and O'Halloran. Braun watched as Chilvers and Wilbers positioned themselves under the bridge. Two more men were behind the hut. Braun glanced at Shaw and Tennessee, plastered against the wall on both sides of him.

As the column made its slow way along the road and up to the bridge, Braun felt his muscles tighten. He felt so naked and exposed standing by the window in full view of everyone. If anything went wrong he would be the first target. He gulped as the two lead motorcyclists rode closer and closer.

# Chapter Twenty-Two

Dane, with his back to the wall, held himself ready for action. The sound of the motorcycles became louder. Braun leaned out the window, a bottle of wine in his hand. Dane heard one of the motorcycles stop running and the other slow down to an idle. Braun said something in German and yanked his pistol out.

Dane yelled, "Now!" He sprang through the door and ran towards the end of the column. Behind him guns bristled out the windows, covering the guards at the front of the column. The four men hiding outside leaped out and disarmed two of the guards. Before the startled Germans had time to react, they were menaced by guns held by Americans with determined faces. They held up their arms and surrendered, stunned by the sudden and unexpected attack.

Dane looked over the surprised American prisoners. "You're free now. Who's the senior man?"

A lean corporal pushed his way forward. "That'll be me. What's going on? Did we blunder into the front line?"

"No, we're miles from there. Come inside and I'll explain." Dane spoke over his shoulder,

"Chilvers and O'Halloran, see to the German prisoners."

When everyone gathered together, Dane sat down at the table in the building. "This is Corporal Buckman of the 82$^{nd}$ Airborne Division. He's the highest ranking man of the fifty prisoners we rescued, all of them paratroops. Sergeant Lassiter, Corporal Gates and Corporal Goldner," Dane introduced the four men to each other and they shook hands.

"Buckman, our orders are to seize and hold this bridge until relieved. We have one platoon and one squad of heavy weapons here. The rest of the company will arrive tomorrow. I'm glad to have you with us. Your outfit has some of the toughest fighting men in the army, almost as good as the First," Dane grinned as he referred to his division.

"We prefer to think The Big Red One is almost the equal of the All Americans," Buckman grinned back. The men chuckled.

"All Americans?" Maria asked with a puzzled expression.

"The nickname of our division, miss," Buckman explained.

"How did all of you get captured?" Lassiter asked.

The lean corporal stiffened in indignation. "Believe me, if we'd been all in one group we would still be fighting." He sagged a little. "The planes scattered our parachute drop over half of western Sicily. We were all picked up in ones and twos." He looked Dane in the eye. "We're thankful not to be on our way to a prisoner of war camp and ready to do some fighting, if we have weapons."

"We have enough captured German guns to arm half of your men," Dane said. "I'm putting you in charge at the knoll with your twenty-five armed men. You'll have a machine gun and three men from Goldner's squad with you."

Buckman nodded his understanding and asked, "Who's the officer in command of your company?"

"There isn't any. I'm in charge."

Buckman stared in surprise.

"We ran into some, uh, problems on the way here," Dane explained. He felt Buckman's speculative look as Dane turned to Lassiter. "You guard the hummock to the east along with a machine gun section."

"Gates," Dane switched his gaze to the last two men," you and Goldner get the ridge. Leave Tennessee, Braun and Raymond here. Goldner, you have the mortar, the last machine gun and the rest of your squad. Take five of the unarmed paratroopers.

"Buckman, have twelve of your weaponless men guard the twelve prisoners tied up under the bridge. I doubt they will give you much trouble,"

Dane said with a dry inflection in his voice.

Buckman gave a chuckle. "I don't think they will either, not with my guards."

Dane went on with his orders. "I'll have the last eight paratroopers with me. We're letting all traffic through tonight, don't stop anybody. Lay low and pretend you're not here. But we can't let anyone into the hut. If anyone tries, well, they won't make it.

"If there are no questions, then we'll eat supper and button down for the night."

After eating, Dane walked out of the hut, sat down with his back to the wall, and leaned his tired head back. With only the rations they'd brought and some food discovered in the hut, supper had been rather skimpy.

Dane thought over the sleeping arrangements. The women's beds were upstairs, while Lieutenant Crawford stayed downstairs. The rest of the men would take turns sleeping on the ground floor and standing guard outside.

Satisfied he'd done the best he could, he turned his attention to other matters. He reached for his Bible but remembered he'd given it to Maria. He closed his eyes and quoted some Bible verses, and then prayed.

"Thank you, God, for directing us here in time to prevent the bridge from being wired for destruction, for no casualties, and for the people we rescued. I ask you to watch over all the men under my command. I pray for their safety and for opportunities to witness. I pray for Maria's salvation. I ask you to work in her heart and bring her to a saving knowledge of You.

"Please take care of Sergeant Milne and the people at the Calvoratti farm. Keep the prisoners under control and not let them cause trouble.

"Watch over my sister Amy, and the baby they're expecting. It may have been born by now. I pray for a safe delivery with no complications."

And then he remembered Angelique. With a start, he realized he hadn't thought of her all day, although he'd been rather busy. He didn't feel the heart wrenching pain when her face came into his thoughts. For a moment, he held the picture of her in his mind, and then released it. He was over her. For the first time since their marriage he gave a sincere prayer for her and Drew. He drew a deep breath and released it.

His attention turned to Amy. With her due date last week, he might be Uncle Dane now. He wished he could be there with her. He pulled out her picture and studied it. Shorter than him and with lighter brown hair, she could be just as stubborn as Dane. He remembered some of the arguments they used to have.

He sighed and closed his eyes. His mind drifted back to the spring of 1938 and he recalled the last time he saw his parents alive. Eighteen and a new high school graduate, he and fourteen-year-old Amy waved goodbye to them. Another couple invited the elder Shaw's to go for a ride in their car. The four of them drove off for a carefree hour or two, only to meet up with some college boys with too much to drink. The boys took a corner too fast and plowed into the unsuspecting vehicle, killing all four of the adults. The accident shattered Amy's and his lives. Dane planned to go to West Point, and had all but been accepted. But then he withdrew his application because he needed to take care of his sister.

Both of their parents were only children, so there were no uncles or aunts, and their grandparents were all dead. The judge allowed Dane to be declared Amy's guardian so she didn't have to go to an orphanage.

Dane scrounged to find work to keep them fed and clothed. Things were tough until he got a permanent job. At first, Amy clung to him in shock and they were close. But as she grew older, she didn't like an older brother telling her what she could and could not do. But he brooked no insubordination and kept her under firm control. *Too much so,* Dane thought to himself, remembering some of his decisions. However, his suffering caused him to be overprotective of the only family he had left.

He remembered when she met Bill Franklyn and how she raved about his good looks and his kind nature. As they fell in love the relationship between Amy and Dane changed, and they became close again. He thought of their wedding day, of the radiant expression on Amy's face and the broad smile and the adoration in Bill's eyes. Dane liked his brother-in-law, a practicing Christian, and the way he kept his wife in hand. He enjoyed his all too rare visits with them. Maybe he would have a letter from them whenever the mail caught up to him.

Thinking of being an uncle caused him to think of Maria, and her calling him Uncle Sergeant. His lips curled in amusement as he thought of the imp. With her pretty face, vivacious personality, and a figure which would stop traffic anywhere, any man would be blessed to have her as his wife. Did he feel attracted to her? He examined his heart, but found no romantic inclinations, only an avuncular interest. In a sudden burst of insight, he felt a premonition it would be a long time before he fell in love again.

# Chapter Twenty-Three

During supper Maria's quick wit made for lively conversation with Tennessee and the others.

Afterwards she took Elena upstairs and had a quiet talk before Elena fell asleep, curled up in a German bedroll. Subdued at what she heard, Maria came back downstairs and wandered outside. Seeing *Zio* Sergeant sitting there, she dropped down beside him with her chin on her knees. In companionable silence, they watched the stars become brighter.

"How's Elena?" He broke the silence.

"She's sleeping." Maria shifted, uncomfortable at the story Elena related. "She told me she's married and her husband is in the army in Russia. She hasn't heard from him in weeks and doesn't know if he's dead or alive. She was on the way to the post office when those men took her." Her voice broke at the end. "How can people be so evil?" her voice rose, and she turned baffled eyes to him.

"Because of sin, Maria. All of us are sinners; all of us have broken God's commandments. God summarized them in the Ten Commandments: Thou shalt have no other gods before me, Thou shalt not make a graven image, Thou shalt not take the name of the Lord the God in vain, Remember the Sabbath to keep it holy, Thou shalt honor they father and mother, Thou shalt not kill, Thou shalt not commit adultery, Thou shalt not steal, Thou shalt not bear false witness, and Thou shalt not covet. If you break any of the laws, then you are guilty and must pay the penalty, which is eternal death in hell. So if a person has lied, stolen, disobeyed their parents, made something more important than God in their life or wanted something which belonged to someone else, then they're a sinner.

"Jesus further said if someone wants to sin, it is the same as if they did it. If a person says they hate someone, it is the same as murder. If someone lusts after somebody who isn't their spouse, it's committing adultery. God is righteous, which means God will punish sin. But God loves us, so He made a way for the penalty of sin to be paid so we can live forever with Him. Jesus Christ paid for our sins on the cross, and His blood washes away all of our sins. If we accept His sacrifice then we are saved. If we reject it then we are condemned to hell because we rejected it."

"But if God loves us, why did he let those men do what they did?"

He sighed. "It's hard for us to understand, but remember God has infinite knowledge and wisdom. We have to realize God loves everyone equally. He loved and died for those four brutes just as much as he loves and died for Elena. He gave them every chance not to do what they did, and now they have no excuse and are paying for their crimes, and they will suffer forever."

"They are in hell now?" Maria turned big eyes up to him.

"Yes, they are being tormented in hell now."

"I don't want to be where those bad men are. How do I not go there?"

"By admitting you're a sinner, that only the blood of Jesus Christ can cleanse you of your sins. You ask God to forgive you and ask Jesus to come and live in your heart. You have to believe in him."

"I believe, please help me, *Zio* Sergeant," Maria begged.

"Just pray to God and tell Him what is in your heart," came the answer.

Maria bowed her head and closed her eyes. "God, I am a sinner, I believe only the blood of Jesus can wash away my sins. Please forgive me." She raised her head, and her cheeks were wet with tears, but her eyes were wide with wonder as her sins were wiped away. Filled with joy, they shared an impulsive hug.

\*\*\*

Tennessee looked at the empty doorway. *She's been gone a long time. I'd better check on her.* He walked over and peered outside. When he saw their merged bodies a shock went through him. For a second, rage consumed him, and he wanted to tear the sergeant's head off, but then he sagged. *Who am I to compete for her affections? If they're in love and going to get married, Ah won't get in her way.* He turned and went back into the room, trying to hide his hurt. He poured himself a cup of coffee and sat down at the table, hanging his head in despair. He hoped the other men in the room didn't notice his changed demeanor.

A few minutes later, Maria floated into the room. When she spied Tennessee she exclaimed, "Van, you'll never guess what happened!" as she ran over to him.

He lifted his heavy head, and not wanting to hear the actual words of her claiming to be in love with Shaw, interrupted her, "Ah knows."

She gave him a puzzled look. "How do you know?"

"Ah saw when ah looked out the door," he replied, still in shock.

In her excitement, she didn't notice his eyes or the expression in his voice. "Isn't it wonderful? It's the most marvelous thing which has ever happened to me! I feel so…so… I can't describe what I feel!" Tennessee stared at her radiant face. He'd never seen anyone look so beautiful. Heartbroken, he looked away. Everyone in the room stared at them, and he didn't know where to look.

"Van, aren't you happy for me?" with a confused look on her face and a quiver in her voice she questioned him.

He forced himself to look at her and said with all the sincerity he could muster, "Yeah, ah'm glad for you." Her face brightened up and she hugged his arm, which sent daggers into his heart.

Shaw walked into the room, which made Tennessee embarrassed at being caught with another man's girl, but for some reason Shaw didn't notice. "I want all the lights out and this place to look like nobody's here." He turned to Crawford and saluted, "Sir, if you don't mind my suggesting it, make sure nobody goes up the stairs tonight to bother the ladies. Privates Raymond and Braun and these four men will be in here with you and under your orders," pointing to four of the men from the 82$^{nd}$. "I'll take Tennessee and the other four and stay outside. Remember, we don't want the enemy to take back this hut."

Shock hit the room like a bomb explosion. Eyes were cemented on Shaw because of his salute and words. Everyone forgot the scene with Maria.

Tennessee couldn't believe his ears. *A colored man put in command of white soldiers and in charge of protecting white women?* He saw the same surprise mirrored on Crawford's face as the officer returned the salute and said, "Yes, I will, Sergeant."

As Tennessee grappled with the novel idea, at least one man couldn't believe it either. One of the airborne men swore and sprang to his feet, "I won't serve under a…"

Shaw interrupted him, "You **will** obey orders!"

Tennessee saw Shaw's face change expression and wasn't surprised at all when the soldier stopped speaking and gulped. Tennessee witnessed the same savage look that Conners saw earlier which would stop anyone dead in their tracks, proclaiming no disobedience would be tolerated. The paratrooper collapsed in his chair as if his legs no longer supported him.

Shaw swept the room with a fierce glare and said with a soft voice, which made it all the more fearsome, "I trust I made myself clear?" Silence filled the room.

# Chapter Twenty-Four

Meanwhile, trouble brewed back at the Calvoratti farm. As soon as Zimmerman's men disappeared into the hills, Sergeant Milne looked over his small command. Besides himself, there were Corporal Brockhurst and Privates Pierce, Andreason, Smith, McFarlin, Heffernan, Davis, and Proskocil,-nine in all, to watch 110 wounded and 65 prisoners for at least two days until they were relieved.

"Corporal, you and Pierce man the machine gun, Andreason, patrol the fence around the prisoners, and Smith, watch the wounded," Milne ordered. "The rest of you get some shut-eye." He went and checked on the captured officers, which were kept separate from the rest of the prisoners. There were three, two of them wounded. Next he checked on the rest of the wounded and the German doctor, whom he viewed with suspicion. "How is it going, Doctor?" Milne asked.

Mueller looked up at him from the man he tended. "The men need vater, food, and shade," he stated in blunt terms. "This sun is dehydrating them."

It made sense to Milne, but, "I don't have anything to give them cover," he protested. "But I will get some water coming." He looked around and saw Lucia at the water pump with a container. He stopped Davis as he walked by. "Go pump water for Mrs. Calvoratti," he ordered.

When filled, Lucia walked over, carrying the filled pitcher with some glasses and started passing them out to the wounded.

"Do you have something to put water in, something big?" Milne asked her.

"Bigger than this?" she held up the pitcher.

"Yes," Milne nodded.

She and Antonio conversed. "Come with me," she said and they led him to an old wooden tub.

Milne examined the dried out tub. Other than cracks between the boards it appeared sound. "Davis, come help me," Milne ordered. They carried it over to the well, and Davis began pumping water into it. At first the water gushed out through the cracks, but as the wood swelled, they closed until it held water.

Milne and Davis carried the empty tub through the gate into the prisoner compound and set it down next to the fence. Next, they hunted up a couple of buckets. They filled them, carried them over to the tub and dumped the water in for the prisoners to use.

After the third trip Milne stopped and wiped his sweaty face.

"Sarge, we have a problem," Davis said.

"Yeah," Milne agreed. "In order to supply almost 200 people, over half of them wounded and almost all of them out in the sun, with the water they need, we're going to have to pump almost all the time." He sighed. Without the rest of his men, now resting, he didn't have the manpower to pump and distribute the water. Even with Antonio and Lucia's help they couldn't keep up, and how were meals going to be prepared for all of them? Sergeant Shaw had left the cook wagon, so they were supplied with everything they needed except for the bodies to do the work and watch over the prisoners.

"Davis, get the rest of the men up. I need them to distribute water to the wounded."

Antonio approached. "*Signore* Milne, I can pump water."

Milne smiled at him. "Thank you, Mr. Calvoratti, I can use your help."

Antonio worked the pump for almost hour before he tired out and stopped to rest. Milne stood there looking at the prisoners as Mueller walked up to him. "Sergeant," Mueller began, "the vounded are not getting enough vater."

Milne raised his eyes and looked at the men sitting and laying around the barn. Their moans and cries for water kept increasing. Lucia and the rest of his squad were trying to supply their needs, but things were getting worse. One solution jumped into his mind.

"I know, Doctor," he sighed. He looked Mueller in the eye and said, "The prisoners will have to supply their own water."

Mueller's eyebrows rose. "And how vill they do that?"

"You'll explain to them they're going to pump and distribute the water, four at a time. One will pump, one will carry water to the tub, one will fill canteens, and one will carry them to the wounded."

Mueller's eyebrows rose higher as he digested the words. "Vhat about meals? It is time for the food preparations to begin. The vounded would be much better off with a hot meal inside of them."

Milne looked around. "Mrs. Calvoratti, may I ask you a question?"

She walked over to them and asked, "Yes?"

"Can you supervise the meal preparation?"

She looked at him in amazement. "Food for two hundred men, *signore*? Me?" Then she looked at the pitiful sight around them, and her chin became determined. "I will need much help, but yes, it can be done."

"Okay then, Doctor, you explain what we need and get four volunteers to start the water. Then bring the cooks over to the wagon," Milne ordered.

"Davis, you watch the guys with the water. Heffernan will watch the cooks. Mrs. Calvoratti, please come with me to the wagon."

While Mueller explained the plan to the prisoners, Milne and Lucia hurried over to the wagon where Lucia did a quick inventory of the food while Milne searched for knives and weapons. She found several hundred-pound sacks of potatoes, sacks of dried vegetables and hanging sides of beef and pork.

"*Signore* Milne, we will have mashed potatoes, pork, and peas for supper," Lucia announced. When four Germans showed up, despite the lack of a common language and to Milne's amusement, Lucia managed to make the evening's menu known. The five of them soon had the food cooking. Milne left a suspicious Heffernan on guard.

Next Milne and Proskocil gathered wood for a bonfire and placed it on the opposite side of the prisoner compound from the machine gun.

"Hey Sarge," Proskocil asked," why are we piling the firewood down here for? It's a long ways from the cook fire."

"There's a waning three-quarter moon tonight but it won't rise until almost midnight. I'm worried about the darkness hiding an escape attempt. We'll light the fire when it's dark and keep it burning until the moon rises."

He also felt concern about the condition of his men. They were tired out after a long day's march and fighting two skirmishes in the heat. He wanted them to take turns resting this afternoon, but with so much to do there wasn't time. Needing a minimum of four men to stay on watch, this meant each man would only get about four hours sleep tonight. He sighed again. He devoutly hoped the relief forces showed up tomorrow.

After eating the evening meal, he saw Lucia speak to Antonio and then walk down the dirt track. Busy lining up the next group of prisoners to pump and distribute the water, Milne didn't think anything about it. No end of Germans volunteered for the extra duty. Either they were bored with sitting or standing around all day, or…Milne narrowed his eyes in suspicion. *Maybe somebody is hatching a plan.* He studied the prisoners with watchful eyes, but spotted nothing amiss. Still, it behooved him to cover all possible angles.

After a while he realized Lucia hadn't returned. He went and asked Antonio, "Mr. Calvoratti, where is your wife?"

"She is gone to see neighbors," Antonio explained.

Milne frowned. He thought it a poor time to go visiting, but he couldn't do anything about it now. "Please, it could be dangerous to travel around the countryside," he explained. "Neither of you should go wandering around."

Antonio only shrugged. Milne sighed again, but he had more pressing problems. Like keeping the guards awake all night, maintaining control of the prisoners, taking care of the wounded, and feeding and watering everyone. The squeaking of the hand pump made a monotonous rhythmic background noise to his troubling thoughts.

Lucia returned about an hour and a half later. Milne spotted her talking to her husband and strode over to them. "Ma'am, Mrs. Calvoratti, it could be dangerous to leave the farm. I must ask you not to do it again. One reason is we don't want to draw attention to ourselves here."

She looked up at him. "*Signore* Milne, don't worry so much. Everything will be better in the morning. Now if you will excuse us, we have had a long, hard day and are tired out." Turning their backs, Antonio and Lucia left Milne speechless and went into the house.

Grumbling at the perverseness of civilians, Milne set the night watches. "Heffernan and Proskocil, man the machine gun, Brockhurst, watch the prisoners, and McFarlin, guard the wounded. When it gets dark enough you can't see the prisoners, then light the bonfire and keep it going until the moon is bright enough to see by." He looked at his watch. "It's 2030 hours now, and it'll be dark in less than an hour. We'll stop the water pumping then and bed the wounded down. At 0200 hours, we'll change guards."

Milne spread out his blanket and dropped his aching, tired body onto it. The night passed without any interruptions, although the Americans on guard were tensed up all night, watching for signs of trouble.

\*\*\*

They weren't the only tired ones. *Hauptfeldwebel*, or First Sergeant, Feodant, the German company sergeant, tried to come up with an escape plan. Like the Americans, his troops were worn out too. They'd also marched and fought all day in the debilitating heat, and also endured a shattering defeat. Dispirited and at first sunk in shock, the hot meal raised their spirits. As he moved among them in the prisoner compound, his experienced eyes gauged their capabilities. Then he organized an unobtrusive conference with the remaining sergeants.

"The wire fence surrounding us isn't much of a barrier," one of them observed.

"Yes, but we can't go through it. We have to cut a hole in it, dig under it, jump over it, or go through the gate," Feodant retorted. "Check the men and see if any of them have something that can cut the wire."

While the sergeants questioned the men, Feodant pondered his options. The call for volunteers to pump and distribute water gave him hope for using the gate in some manner. His orders to the men to volunteer for the water and cooking details were to create an opportunity for a mass escape, but so far the American guards were too alert. The chance hadn't come.

The presence of their medic outside the compound must be used somehow. Word could be brought to him by the water detail.

The sergeants returned. "We don't have anything to cut wire," they reported.

Feodant thought. His men were too tired to run far tonight. He made his decision. "No escape tonight, everybody get their rest and wait for tomorrow. Besides," he gave a crafty smile, "we can rest, the enemy won't and they will be even more worn out tomorrow."

# Chapter Twenty-Five

As Dane and his men broke morning camp on the way to the bridge, a meeting between General Roosevelt and his commanders began, planning the second day of attacks by the 1$^{st}$ Division. As he marked out the battalion dispositions on his map, he looked at Major Hammond with a frown. "Major, why is your front so small? It should be half again as long."

"It's because I'm missing a company."

Roosevelt looked astounded. "Missing a company? How? Which company?"

"King Company. I was ordered to send troops through the hole in the enemy line to seize the Salso River Bridge."

"You sent a single company to advance twenty-five miles behind enemy lines?" Roosevelt stared at the hapless Hammond.

"I didn't intend to, sir. But right after King Company left, the Germans closed the gap before the rest of my battalion could advance."

Roosevelt scowled. "Where's the company now?"

Hammond gave a helpless shrug. "I don't know. We haven't heard from them since they left."

Roosevelt growled, "The company must have

been wiped out. What an unnecessary loss." He went on, "Make probing attacks all along the front to find weak points. Then we'll concentrate against them."

By midmorning, Roosevelt made his decisions and launched assaults. Artillery shells screamed overhead in limitless numbers. Khaki clad soldiers flung themselves at the stubborn defenders. Desperate to hold back the attackers until the rear echelon troops retreated, the Germans and Italians held on with all of their strength. But step by step, they were forced back.

The uncaring sun poured its rays upon all the combatants. The enervating heat drained men's energy. As the sun dropped below the horizon, so did the survivors, all of them exhausted.

They'd advanced another half a mile. Nobody knew it, but they were close to the place where the King Company ambushes occurred, two and a half miles from the Calvoratti farm. North of Hammond's battalion, the enemy line bent back several miles, creating a bulge.

***

The same morning, Milne watched the eastern sky turn grey with tired and gritty eyes. As the sun appeared in a clear sky, he sighed. *Another scorching day. I wonder what Shaw and the rest of the company are doing now.* He had no way of knowing both groups were eating breakfast before continuing the march to the bridge. When the sun shone bright enough to dispel shadows, he went to rouse up the doctor. He found him setting up and rubbing his bristling cheeks.

"Good morning Doctor Mueller." Mueller stared back and grunted. *Must not be a morning person,* Milne thought. "How are the wounded doing?"

"There are two vho if they haven't died in the last two hours von't live to see another sunset. The others vould be better off if they vere under some shade."

Milne sighed in frustration. *I seem to be sighing a lot lately.* "I wish it too, Doctor, but there's nothing I can do about it. If there's nothing else I'll get the water started.

"Breakfast vould be good, sergeant."

"I expect Mrs. Calvoratti will start soon, Doctor." He moved off, waking the rest of his command and calling to McFarlin, "Come with me to the prisoners." The two of them joined Smith and opened the gate, guns at the ready. Milne held up four fingers, "Four, now, *schnell,*" he hollered to the prisoners. Four of them walked over to him and passed through the gate. Milne got a good look at the leader and thought to himself, *tough and capable.* A warning bell went off in his head at the

201

glance he received back. Milne made a mental note; *He doesn't have the look of a defeated man. I need to keep an eye on this one.*

***

At the well Feodant assigned jobs to the others while he carried filled canteens to the wounded. He wanted to talk to Mueller. It took a few minutes, but at last Feodant brought some canteens into the barn where Mueller attended to the wounded.

"*Doktor* Mueller, do you still have your surgical knives?" he whispered while Mueller bent over one of the dying men.

Mueller stared up at him. "*Ja, Hauptfeldwebel*," he answered at last.

"Good, slip me as many as you can. The Americans must be stupider then I realized not to deprive you of them," Feodant added in a scornful voice.

Mueller gave his attention back to the wounded German soldier. "I can't," he said after a long pause.

"You can't?" Feodant asked in amazement, his voice starting to rise before he caught himself. "Why not?"

Mueller gave him a measured look before turning back to his patient. "In the first place I need those knives for the wounded." He nodded to the men outside. "I have some bullets I need to dig out

202

from some of them. Second, I gave my word that I wouldn't aid in any escape attempts."

"You...you gave your word?" Feodant stuttered. "Who to?"

"The American sergeant," Mueller replied in a calm voice.

Feodant gave a disparaging sniff. "You're a German, one of the master race. A promise to an American mongrel doesn't count. I order you to supply me with the knives."

Mueller sat back on his heels and looked at him with a wry look on his face. "Now here is a strange thing. The mongrel American, as you call him, was willing to accept my word of honor but you, a noble German, are telling me to break my oath. Besides, I'm an officer and you can't order me to do anything."

Feodant sputtered in outrage. Mueller turned back to his patient. "And *Hauptfeldwebel*, pass out canteens to the Americans as well as the Germans. That's an order."

Feodant sputtered again. He'd been giving water only to the German wounded. *After all, no member of a slave race should drink before their masters did.*

The American with three stripes on his sleeve and the Italian woman walked into the barn. . Feodant noticed the American giving him and

Mueller a long look. *He must have seen us talking and is suspicious,* Feodant thought. They said something in English to Mueller, who repeated it to Feodant. "The cooks are needed to start breakfast. I'll get them."

Mueller and the woman left and the two men stared at each other. Feodant spun on his heel and walked back to the pump to fill more canteens, followed by his opponent. When they arrived, the American switched jobs for the two Germans by pulling one, pushing the other, and pointing to Feodant and then to the pump.

Angry, Feodant shrugged off the hand. *How dare he, a Jewish infiltrated, Jewish led, racially mixed mongrel American touch a member of the pure Aryan Master Race?* As Feodant pumped, his anger turned to Mueller. Once they were liberated, he would bring charges up against the doctor for not aiding escape attempts. Feodant knew *Der Fuhrer* would overcome the recent reverses Germany suffered and sweep to victory, destroying all the enemies of the Fatherland.

# Chapter Twenty-Six

Mueller and Lucia walked to the prisoners where Mueller gathered the four cooks together and led them to the kitchen wagon. With Mueller translating, they planned the breakfast menu and began the preparations. Then Milne saw Mueller hurry back to the dying men, both Germans. Milne watched him disappear into the barn and then turned his attention to the German pumping water.

A few minutes later Milne sauntered into the barn and gave a speculative look at Mueller. "Doctor, may I see your knives?" Milne asked. Without a word Mueller got up, walked over to his bag, extracted the knife case and handed it to Milne. Milne opened the case, saw all the positions were filled and counted the knives He closed the case and the two men stood and looked at each other. At last Milne handed it back and said, "Better keep this on your person. I wouldn't want anyone to steal them." Mueller put it into a pocket with a glimmer of a smile.

Milne looked down at the patient. Once a handsome young man, but shrapnel from an exploding mortar shell had torn his body and now he lay gasping for air. Milne felt a strange emotion for the dying man. They were enemies and they'd

205

tried their best to kill each other, but now he thought of what a waste it all seemed. "Is there anything you can do for him, Doctor?"

"*Nein*," Mueller shook his head. "All anyone can do now is pray."

Milne remembered some of the stories he'd heard and said, "Sergeant Shaw would pray for him." He wasn't sure why he knew, but he thought he was right.

Mueller shot him a look of surprise, but a thoughtful look came over his face as he considered the remarkable sergeant. "I think you are correct," he agreed.

"Doctor, what's the name of the guy pumping water?" Milne switched subjects.

"Feodant. *Hauptfeldwebel* Feodant."

"Feodant," Milne muttered, committing it to memory.

Lucia appeared and announced, "Breakfast is ready for the first group."

Milne issued orders, "Brockhurst, take food to the wounded who can feed themselves. They will eat first along with half the squad. The second group will be the wounded who will need to be fed. The less severe wounded can help feed them. The rest of the squad will eat at the same time. Then the prisoners will be fed with all of us guarding them."

After the men ate and the dishes washed, the

cooks began a bread-making operation. Soon the smell of fresh baked bread filled the farmyard. While Antonio and Davis handled the choring the farm animals needed, Milne ordered Proskocil and Andreason to turn in for some shut eye. Being seasoned soldiers, they at once fell asleep.

Milne walked back into the barn to check on the young German. A blanket-covered form greeted him. Milne stared down at it, and then into the compassionate eyes of Mueller. Without a word, Milne turned and walked out.

He stood by the barn and forced himself to consider the myriad of problems he faced this day. A wagon pulled by a donkey coming down the road caught his attention. It stopped next to the house and a horde of Italian children spilled out from it, followed by three adults. Milne hurried over. Lucia spoke in voluble words to them and gestured to the wounded men lying around.

"What's going on? Who are these people?" Milne panted from the growing heat.

"*Signore* Milne, these are our neighbors. They have come to help," Lucia said with pride as another wagon bumped its way down the rutted road.

"But…but," Milne sputtered, "they shouldn't be here."

Everyone ignored him.

The Italian men unloaded poles and bedclothes from one of the wagons, and under Milne's bemused eyes began to erect sunshades over the wounded men. There were three men, all either too young or too old to be drafted, four women and half a dozen children. While the men were busy, Lucia put the women to work with the wounded. The children at first stood in a group, staring at the wounded men, prisoners and American soldiers alike with wide eyes. But the Americans, as usual, were quick to make friends with them and the children were soon running around enjoying themselves.

Too much so.

"Kids," Milne bellowed, "get away from there." Three of the children were playing between the machine gun and the prisoner compound, blocking the gun. They scampered away, only to return and be shooed away by Lucia.

\*\*\*

Feodant, his shift over and behind the fence again, noticed the Americans were distracted by the children and by a pretty girl. He checked his watch. *Almost time for the water detail to change,* he thought to himself. He gathered a group of Germans around him. If the Americans could be caught off guard, then perhaps a sudden rush would get them through the gate. Once among the Americans and

Italians the machine gun wouldn't do them any good. He curled his lip in derision. The weak Americans would never open fire on the civilians and their own men. They weren't strong like he and the German race were. If their places were reversed, he would have no compunction about opening fire.

A rumble of sound from the west interrupted him. His eyes widened as he exclaimed, "That's artillery! The Americans must be pushing us back." He whirled around to see the excited faces and animated voices of the Americans and the bewilderment of the Italians. "We must escape soon. Everyone, be ready for our chance."

# Chapter Twenty-Seven

Milne felt overwhelmed trying to keep tabs on everybody and everything going on. The artillery signaled help was getting closer, but also proving to be a distraction to everyone. The Italians were no doubt trying to be helpful, but Prosckocil and Andreason were awakened by all the commotion going on. Nobody could get any rest with all the racket going on.

"Men," Milne barked, "back to your duties. The artillery is miles away." He spared a glance at the prisoner compound. He noticed a group of Germans centered on the sergeant with undefeated eyes as he spoke to them.

His suspicions aroused, he watched the group spread out near the gate. He looked at his wristwatch. He'd been switching groups of prisoners each hour and it was almost time for the next group change. He changed his plans. "Brockhurst, have the Germans switch jobs, don't take them back yet," Milne ordered. Brockhurst looked surprised, nodded and hurried off to comply. As the prisoners switched jobs, Milne sneaked a glance at the group in the compound. Feodant looked chagrined at the change in routine.

Milne hid a grin and then watched in despair as

two more wagons filled with Italians arrived, followed by a third a couple of minutes later. He hurried over, wondering what to do with them. The sunshades were erected and the civilians were standing still, listening to the distant rumbling.

Antonio hobbled over. "*Signore* Milne, what other jobs do you want them to do?"

Milne got an inspiration. "We'll need more wood for the fire tonight. Can the men go get a big supply?"

"*Si*," Antonio answered. "There is plenty of wood two or three kilometers over there," pointing south. Soon all the men piled into the wagons and took off. The doctor and Lucia organized the women into helping the wounded.

Milne turned his attention to the kids. "Lucia, can you ask if the children can pump and distribute the water?"

Lucia looked up and nodded. "Good to keep them occupied," she said.

Milne gathered Proskocil, Smith and McFarlin and they escorted the four Germans back to the compound. With so many American rifles, as well as the manned machine gun, Milne knew the Germans wouldn't try an escape attempt. As he walked away, Milne felt Feodant's glare.

Lucia organized the children who were only too happy to pump water and carry canteens to the wounded. The Americans busied themselves with filling the tub with water for the prisoners. Afterwards Milne and five of his men laid down for a well-deserved rest, leaving Brockhurst and Pierce manning the machine gun and Heffernan watching the perimeter.

\*\*\*

Furious, Feodant growled at out his frustration at the lack of opportunity. The constant rumble meant time to escape was running out. As he wracked his brain for another plan, he watched how the Americans were distracted by the children running around. One of the teen-aged girls appeared to flirt with the guards. An idea popped into his head. He chose two men and said to them, "When they take us out to feed us, start yelling at each other and then fight each other." He picked out six pairs of men and gave them their orders. "When the Americans are attracted to the fight, each pair of you will attack an American. They won't fire the machine gun when everybody is in a tangled group together." The men agreed and they all went back to waiting.

\*\*\*

The sun hung high in the sky when the Italian men came back from their wood gathering expedition. The noise of their arrival woke Milne. He sat up, stretched, and swore at the heat. Wet patches of sweat marked his shirt and he made a face at his smell.

Lucia walked up to him and asked, "What about the noon meal, *Signore* Milne?"

Inspiration came to him. "Feed the prisoners with the bread you baked this morning," he directed. "That way we can keep them all inside the fence."

Lucia looked surprised but nodded and hurried off to gather the loaves of bread. Milne roused his men up as the women started preparing lunch. He ordered the tub filled with water and the loaves of bread hung in the squares of the woven wire. Then they allowed the Germans to approach the fence and gather their food.

*I wonder why I thought of feeding the prisoners like that*, Milne asked himself. Later, when he and Dane compared notes, Milne learned of Dane's prayer for wisdom in keeping the prisoners under subjection. It forever changed Milne's opinion of the power of prayer.

***

Feodant ground his teeth in anger at the thwarting of his latest escape attempt. He grabbed a loaf of bread and sat down. After lunch the Italians all took a nap, along with most of the Americans and many of the Germans. The heat sapped everybody's energy. Feodant lay on his back trying to come up with another escape plan.

Private Herschenkel moved over next to him. "*Hauptfeldwebel,*" he whispered, "there's a loose section of fence."

Feodant almost jerked upright but caught himself. "Where," he demanded.

"In the southwest corner, you have to lean on one section the right way and a gap opens up, just big enough for a man to wriggle through." Or a sheep, but neither of them ever found that out.

"How did you discover it?" Feodant asked.

"I sat down and leaned my back against the fence. When I squirmed for a more comfortable position the section of fence moved," Herschenkel explained.

"*Gute,*" Feodant breathed, "we will wait for tonight." He closed his eyes and made plans.

# Chapter Twenty-Eight

Tennessee crouched behind the building, hidden by the night. During his watch, sporadic traffic moved across the bridge, almost all of it from west to east. After a while, he checked on the men under the bridge.

"Y'all keepin' the prisoners quiet?" he asked the guards.

"Yep, we've got them hog-tied and muzzled," the man in charge responded. "All they can do is stare helpless at the sounds of their compatriots' crossing over the bridge."

"You spoke mighty poetical."

"Back home I'm a writer, well, trying to become one," the guard added in a bashful tone.

"Really? Ah never could figger out how some people can string words together that sound so fine."

"If I were writing for a newspaper, I came up with a good headline for our story." The man cleared his throat. "Steadfast Soldiers Defend The Salso."

"Yeah, ah like it," Tennessee applauded.

A burst of gunfire from the direction of the knoll halted their literary conversation. Tennessee climbed from the bench to the bridge. He breathed a sigh of relief at the sight of the empty road. For almost five minutes he listened to the firing before it died away. He waited for a sign to show who won the fight.

About ten long nerve-wracking minutes later he heard somebody approaching. Acutely aware he possessed the only gun among all the men here, he took a firm grip on his rifle. When he saw the tell-tale shape of American helmets he breathed a sigh of relief.

"Hello the bridge," a voice called out.

"Hello yoreself," Tennessee answered back. "What caused all the ruckus?"

"A group of Italians blundered into us," the paratrooper replied. His teeth shone white in the darkness. "We got six more weapons and we didn't take any prisoners. Corporal Buckman thought the extra guns might be useful here."

Tennessee thought about it. "There's more danger at the hut and ridge. Leave two guns here and take two up to Corporal Gates. I'll take the last two with me." He looked at his watch. "It's 2300 hours, mah shift is over."

He woke up the next pair of men to stand watch, handed over the weapons, laid down outside the hut next to Shaw, and closed his eyes.

But he couldn't sleep.

He struggled for hours but at last faced the fact

he'd fallen head over heels in love with Maria, only to discover she was in love with another man. At last he turned to the Lord and prayed for the first time in years. "Oh Lord, ah need help. Ah'm in love with Maria, and she's in love with Sergeant Shaw. God, ah ask you," he gulped and went on, "ah ask you to bless them." After a lengthy prayer he felt comforted and dozed off. He knew the next day was going to be a long and hard one, for more than one reason.

He felt like he'd just dropped off when the noise of a stopping vehicle woke him up. He slipped to his feet and saw Shaw rise up next to him. One of the two paratroopers on guard appeared. "A *kubelwagon* stopped out front," he whispered.

"We'll take them," Shaw whispered back.

The three Germans made a lot of noise getting out of the vehicle and walking up to the door. Shaw and Tennessee, knives in hand, slipped up behind them as 'quiet as moonshiners hunting revenoors', as Tennessee put it. Without making a sound they eliminated the two trailing Germans. One of the paratroopers' boots crunched the ground. The leading German turned. He got a rifle butt in the face. As Dane and Tennessee wiped off their knives, the last paratrooper lamented, "Why didn't you save one for me?"

Tennessee choked back a laugh.

217

Shaw ordered, "Search the vehicle and push it into the river. Give the three weapons to men who don't have any."

Tennessee fell asleep only to be awakened by a solid column of vehicles driving across the bridge. He peered out to see big guns traveling eastward. It appeared to him like the artillery train for a corps. He heard Shaw whisper, "Dear God, don't let them stop."

They didn't.

*\*\**

While Tennessee struggled with his thoughts, the German prisoners at the Calvoratti's farm plotted their escape. Feodant planned to wait until an hour after moonrise. The guard circling the fence would have to be disposed of first. Then one of his men would slap on the American helmet and continuing making the round. That should be able to allay any anxieties from the machine gun emplacement long enough to for his men to overwhelm it. Feodant nodded his head. *Yes, things are looking good.*

Milne went to bed after checking all the posts. The Italian women and children were safe in the house, especially the fifteen year old girl trying to act eighteen. The men were sleeping outside. The guards were set and the rotation established. He at once fell asleep, worn out by the long day.

Startled, Milne jerked awake. *Is it a dream? Did someone shout "Danger!"* He listened but all he heard now were snores. It must have been a dream or else others would have heard it too. Still, he couldn't shake the feeling of something being wrong. He pulled on his boots, grabbed his tommy gun and got to his feet.

He moved closer to the prisoner compound. The moon lay low in the east, giving fitful light and the bonfire had burned out. He made out a dark mass of prisoners at one end of the enclosure. The figure of the American guard with the distinctive helmet walked next to the fence. Everything seemed at peace. Chiding himself for being alarmed at nothing, he started to turn away when something about the guard caught his attention. It should have been McFarlin with his rolling gait, like a sailor walking on land. This guard walked ramrod straight. Milne looked again at the prisoners. Why were so many congregated at one end? The realization of what he's seeing hit him.

"Breakout!" he screamed and fired a burst from his tommy gun over the heads of the prisoners. They threw themselves to the ground. The shooting jerked Brockhurst and Davis, manning the machine gun, wide awake. In front of them, four figures leaped upright. Davis squeezed the trigger. The hail of bullets cut the escapees down just feet away. The

219

rest of the Americans came charging up, but the little fight was over. The few remaining Germans outside the wire enclosure raised their hands. As Brockhurst rounded them up, he discovered McFarlin, unconscious but unharmed. Milne lit a match to check the bodies and recognized one of them. Feodant lay facing the sky with sightless eyes.

# Chapter Twenty-Nine

As grey and pink stripes lightened the eastern sky on the third day, July 26$^{th}$, the sun peeked down at activity at several places.

Zimmerman oversaw the feeding of his men and the watering of the horses at the spring beside the white-scarred hill.

Keeler, the radioman, hollered from the top of the hill, "Sergeant Zimmerman, I made contact with an American unit!"

"What?" He stared at Keeler in surprise. "Stay there, I'm coming." He hurried up the hill and grabbed the hand-held radio. "This is Sergeant Zimmerman of King Company, 26th Regiment. Who's this?"

"Baker Company, 26th Regiment."

"Inform Regiment HQ we're on the way to the Salso River Bridge. A forward platoon may have already captured it."

"Affirmative. What's your location?"

"I don't know where we are. I don't have a map but I'm sure we're not far away from the bridge."

"Did you get cut off? The Krauts have been launching counterattacks. We've lost some men captured."

221

Zimmerman snorted. "You could say that. Over and out."

As he handed back the walkie-talkie, he said, "I can't believe we picked them up with this short ranged radio. They should be miles away." He took out his binoculars and scanned the horizon. "Maybe they're closer than I thought." He froze, looking at moving figures in the distance. "Get down," he yelled, pulling Keeler with him. "Those are Germans." He watched them for a minute. "They're moving north."

He scrambled down the hill and informed Jones and Grissom of the sighting and radio call. "I hope Milne and the Calvoratti's are safe. Okay, as soon as the meal is over, hitch up the horses. Let's get going," he ordered."

\*\*\*

Roosevelt wolfed down his breakfast with one hand and scanned reports with the other. "Aerial recon photos from yesterday afternoon show all the Salso River bridges still intact," he told his superior, Major General Terry de la Mesa Allen,

"At least that's some good news," the division commander grumbled. "General Patton ordered me to capture them today."

Roosevelt read some more. "Looks like the Krauts are getting ready to pull back. There's been a sighting of artillery on the east side of the Salso."

Allen frowned in thought. "They'll probably retreat and defend the river line." Both men bent over the map on Allen's desk, now adorned with food splatters. "I've ordered 26th Regiment to continue to push east and 18th to attack southeast towards the Route 120 Bridge. The attack is to kick off in," he glanced at his watch, "in half an hour."

A staff officer interrupted them. "Sir, we received a radio message from King Company of the 26th Regiment. They're nearing the Salso River Bridge. Another unit may have already captured it."

"What?" both generals exclaimed in unison.

"We've got to find out for sure. Ask for a recon flight to check the bridge," Allen ordered.

"Yes, sir," the staff officer replied and hurried away.

***

In Messina, another staff officer interrupted another meeting. "*Herr* Colonel, the engineer detachment to the Route 120 Bridge over the Salso River has not reported in."

The colonel frowned. "When was their last communication?"

"Yesterday morning. They reported they'd arrived, but we've heard nothing since."

The colonel continued frowning. "So we don't know if the bridge has been wired for demolition?"

"No, *Herr* Colonel."

"Send a recon unit and another engineer squad from Leonforte to investigate."

"*Jawohl. Herr* Colonel."

***

Dane sat up, wiped off the bottom of his socks and shook out his boots before he put them on. One of the paratroopers who'd helped Dane and Tennessee earlier that morning said, "That's how you moved so quiet." Dane nodded, checked the road for traffic, saw none, tapped on the door of the hut, announced himself and only then opened the door. He and Raymond grinned at each other over Raymond's ready rifle.

Dane called the ridge. "George, any activity?"

Gates replied, "No, all's quiet on this end."

"Okay. We'll eat a hot breakfast in shifts. I'll let you know when to send men over." Then Dane called Lassiter at the hummock with the same message. Dane cleaned out the ashes from the stove and began adding firewood when Tennessee walked in and began preparing coffee.

The noise from downstairs woke Maria. Not wanting to disturb Elena, Maria got up and dressed as quiet as she could. She floated down the stairs. "Good morning, everyone," she said, happiness evident in her voice and face.

Tennessee missed the fact Maria gazed at him first, but he caught the looks she and Dane

224

exchanged. He felt a dagger plunge into his heart and looked down at the pot he held. He felt surprised when Maria walked over and started helping him. He shot a glance at Dane, concentrating on lighting the fire.

"Why don't you help the sergeant?" he suggested.

Maria shot him a puzzled look. "He doesn't need it."

Others started helping with the meal preparation and soon the appetizing smell of hot coffee and warm food filled the room. With food ready to be served, Dane called both outposts and ordered, "Send half your men here to eat."

While the men stationed at the hut and the ones from the outposts were eating, Hemphill and Maria heated more food. Dane glanced at Tennessee's morose expression. *I wonder what's wrong with him?*

When the industrious cooks piled up more food ready to be eaten, Dane addressed one of the paratroopers. "Go tell Corporal Buckman to send half of his men over for breakfast."

The man left but a few minutes later appeared with the corporal and four other men. "We'll take the food with us and eat at the knoll," Buckman announced. He fixed Dane with a glare and said in a belligerent tone, "Half my men don't have guns."

Dane sipped his coffee. "There are guns coming with the rest of the company."

Surprised, Buckman asked, "But, where did you get the guns?"

"From a German company we wiped out on the way here."

Flabbergasted, Buckman said, "But…but, we'll need ammo for them."

"We have three truckloads of ammunition upstairs," Dane answered as calm as before.

Flummoxed, Buckman stuttered, "But…but…but, how did you know? Under normal circumstances we don't keep enemy weapons. Their distinctive sound leads to friendly fire incidents." He paused, thought, then added, "Except for the light machine guns. They're handy to have."

"Thought we might need them," Dane sipped his coffee again, giving Buckman a steady look. The room fell silent and everyone stared at the two of them.

Dane read their expressions: how could he possibly have known he would need weapons and ammo?

He didn't answer and the short sergeant became bigger than life to the onlookers for the rest of their lives.

Braun choked on his coffee. "That's what you meant when Raymond asked you yesterday about capturing the ammunition trucks. They're for Buckman."

"Yep," Dane smiled.

Braun stared at Shaw with an awed look. He muttered, "Gates said you always have a plan and I didn't believe him."

Dane looked at Buckman. "You can haul some ammunition from upstairs to your position."

"I'll get Elena up," Maria said and scampered up the stairs.

Buckman licked his lip and cleared his throat. "What are we going to do about the Krauts today? We can't hide 80 men now it's daylight."

"I know. We'll have to stop all traffic until Zimmerman arrives with the rest of the company, which will be soon," Dane replied as he took another drink of his coffee.

"But we've only got about sixty armed men, we can't hold this bridge against a determined attack," Buckman argued.

Dane snapped his head up. "We **will** hold this position until relieved," he flared with fire in his eyes and iron determination on his face.

Buckman gulped at the look he received and subsided.

"What makes you think we'll be relieved soon?" Crawford asked.

Dane turned his head to look at him. "All the

227

artillery we heard passing last night didn't stop, they kept moving. I think the front is only a few miles away." As if to punctuate his words, they heard the distant sound of artillery explosions to the northwest and the sound of shells passing overhead from east to west. Crawford, not used to hearing artillery like the others were, turned a nervous face upward. For several minutes they heard screaming shells and then they stopped. Everyone stared in awe at Dane again.

"Hurry up and finish breakfast. We're going to have company soon," Dane announced.

"After we eat, I'll send some men for the ammo," Buckman said. Then he and his men took food and left.

The men who'd eaten rotated with those the others, who gobbled down their breakfast.

"The prisoners and their guards need food. You four grab their chow and come with me," Dane ordered some men standing nearby. At the bridge he checked the men over. "Give the prisoners plenty of water, then tie them back up. I don't want any to escape and alert the Germans to how weak we are" he told the guards and returned to the hut.

As he entered the building, Crawford stood at the stove, pouring himself a cup of coffee. Hemphill told the pilot, "Boy, give me some coffee too."

Dane rocketed across the room and stuck his

face into Hemphill's. "He's an officer and you will call him sir!" he snapped. "And you get his coffee, he doesn't get yours."

Hemphill paled with mixed anger and fear but ground out, "Yes sergeant."

Elena, now downstairs, shrank back in fear from him. Although she didn't speak English, she heard the anger in his voice and felt the menace he exuded. He frightened her, this fierce American.

Maria stifled a shiver at the scary side of *Zio* Sergeant.

Dane took a deep breath to calm himself and added, "The main threat is from the west. Tennessee, Braun and Hemphill, come with me. Lieutenant, if you would man the telephone, please?"

Crawford nodded his curly head. "Of course, Sergeant."

Dane paused as more shells from the east passed overhead. Elena let out a scream and Maria cuddled her with a white, upturned face.

"Not to worry," Dane soothed. "They're aiming a few miles away."

With a head nod, Dane motioned the three soldiers to follow him to the ridge, joining Gates and Goldner.

# Chapter Thirty

The first attack, if it could be called that, came from a stream of stragglers coming from the northwest. These men, already defeated, were running away from the battlefield. Dane saw many were Italians and quite a few didn't have weapons. They came down the road. A burst of fire stopped them near the ridge. Some ran south but the majority turned north, crossed the ridge and tried to come down between the ridge and the river. They blundered into the knoll position and two of them were blown up by a land mine. After a brief firefight they turned north again and headed for the coast road. Dane estimated their number at five hundred.

When Dane heard the overhead artillery fire slacking off, he told Tennessee, "That should make the ladies happier."

"Yeah, especially your Maria," Tennessee replied in a strange tone.

Puzzled, Dane looked at him but the ringing telephone interrupted the conversation.

"Ridge," Dane answered.

Crawford's voice came over the wire. "Sergeant Lassiter reports a half-track and a truck coming from the east."

"Tell him I'm on my way," Dane said. He ran down the ridge and over the bridge to Lassiter.

Lassiter peered through his binoculars. "The half-track is mounting a machine gun and I see soldiers riding in it."

Dane's eyes searched the area around him, "Okay, we'll bushwhack them as they drive past. I'll hide behind the rock over there and try to lob a grenade into it."

Lassiter grinned at the western vernacular as he ordered his men into hiding places.

The lead vehicle ground to a stop just within tossing range. Peering from around the rock, Dane observed the driver and machine gunner scanning ahead of them. The men in the rear of the half-track were standing up, preparatory to their exiting the vehicle. The truck stopped behind them. With a quick prayer, Dane pulled the pin of his grenade and heaved it as far as he could. The grenade arched up into the sky and landed in the bed of the half-track. The explosion ripped into the men. With bursts from his tommy gun, Dane shot the driver and machine gunner before they could open fire.

He turned his attention to the truck as Lassiter's squad opened fire. The driver of the truck slumped over his wheel as the survivors from the half-track were wiped out. Men began jumping out of the truck but were mowed down. About half of them

231

made it. After several minutes of sustained firing two more Germans were killed and two were wounded. The last man surrendered. The Americans rose up and secured the prisoners.

"Lassiter, what casualties did we suffer?" Dane asked, concern lacing through him.

"Jest one slight wound," Lassiter answered. "The truck's carrying explosives, no wonder the soldiers in it baled out."

"Engineers, huh? The squad we wiped out got missed at last." Dane studied the surviving truck. "I'm going to drive it to the middle of the cut in the ridge to block the road. Riflemen on the crest of the ridge will cover all sides of it." He grabbed a German rifle and ammo, hopped in the cab and drove off.

When he arrived at the cut, he slid out and ordered, "Gates, wire some of these explosives to the truck. Use the rest to mine approaches to the ridge."

The next attack entailed harder fighting. This convoy came from the west. It consisted of a mixed group of a few vehicles and several horse-drawn wagons hauling wounded. A group of American prisoners guarded by some walking wounded followed behind. A staff car led the procession. When the lead vehicle saw the truck blocking the road, the column came to a stop.

Dane, his head hidden behind a bush, watched several men get out of vehicles. After a brief conference and nervous looks at the ridge on either side of the cut, two Germans walked up to the truck. Dane waited until they almost reached the truck before hollering, "Now!" He opened fire. Half a dozen Germans dropped. Gates led a charge down the slope, shooting as they ran.

When the prisoners saw the charging Americans, they jumped their guards. With a leap of his heart, Dane realized they were giving Gates and his men enough time to get in among the Germans. Fierce hand to hand fighting erupted.

Dane switched from his tommy gun to the rifle and fixed a bayonet. Followed by Tennessee, Braun and three armed paratroopers, they raced into the fight. Dane slashed his way to where the prisoners fought against hopeless odds. In rapid succession one, two, three Germans fell before his bayonet. A German officer pointed his Luger at him, but with incredible agility Dane spun away from the threatening gun and shot him between the eyes.

The fight became a kaleidoscope of sound and fury. Horses reared and bucked amid the deafening noise of the shooting and shouting. A wagon, its horses madden with fear and pain from wounds, careened off cross country, followed by a second wagon. Wounded inside screamed from the pain of

233

being tossed around.

Tennessee and a paratrooper flung themselves into another melee where prisoners with bare hands struggled with armed guards. A hard core of Germans formed themselves around a couple of vehicles. Dane pulled a pin on a grenade, leapt onto a wagon tongue, hurled the grenade into the group of Germans and jumped back off, all in one movement. Their cohesion destroyed by the blast, Gates led the attack which swarmed over them while Dane piled into the fighting around the prisoners. Again, his stupendous agility as he ducked, parried and slashed away kept him from harm while German bodies piled up around him.

At last the Germans had enough. Those that were able ran back down the road while the rest, most of them wounded, surrendered. One paratrooper lay dead while half a dozen men were wounded, none life threatening. Twenty-eight unwounded prisoners and six more with serious wounds were rescued, all from the 1$^{st}$ Infantry Division. Six of the ex-prisoners died in the fighting.

After sorting through the prisoners, Dane found himself saddled with some sixty German and Italian wounded, with no doctors or medical supplies. He looked the situation over and called Braun over. "Tell them we are letting them go. Take the wagons and head north to the coast road."

One of the Germans gave a violent protest, pointing to the wounded men. Dane interrupted, "Tell him we have no medicine or doctors. If they stay here they may die."

Braun repeated the warning to the German officer, who held his bloody arm, gave Dane a cold stare and then turned and issued orders to the others. After being stripped of arms and ammunition, they started on their way.

One of the released prisoners walked up and spoke to Dane, "I'm glad to not be going to a POW camp, but…" he shook his head as he looked at the six bodies.

"Yeah, I know, but they died fighting and saved some other lives," Dane said in a somber tone. He glanced at the other man, "Do you know how far away the fighting is?"

He stared at Dane in surprise. "Isn't this the front line? I thought we'd blundered into it."

Dane shook his head. "No, we're behind the enemy, holding onto the bridge."

"I guess we jumped from the frying pan into the fire," the man said, and then added, "The line must be about four or five miles up the road, but there's hard fighting going on. I don't know when they'll get here."

"Okay," Dane said. "Take your wounded back

to camp, grab some coffee and come back here. Arm yourselves and get ready for more fighting."

The ex-prisoner looked at Dane's sergeant stripes. "Who's in charge here?"

"I am. I'm Sergeant Shaw," and Dane moved off, issuing more orders.

# Chapter Thirty-One

Twice messengers from the east were intercepted, and as the morning wore on the artillery fire passing overhead became constant. A trickle of fleeing soldiers kept coming from the west, but a few well-placed bullets kept them moving northward.

At about ten o'clock came the sight Dane waited for: Sergeant Zimmerman leading the rest of the company from the south.

The men whooped and hollered as the column moved in and joined the defenders. Dane briefed Zimmerman on the happenings. "We captured the bridge and prevented it from being wired for demolition. We also released some American prisoners. We only possessed enough weapons to arm some of them."

"You did what?" Zimmerman looked astounded.

Dane grinned, then commanded, "Unload the weapons from your wagons and pass them out."

"Okay, but I don't have a lot of ammunition," Zimmerman said.

"We captured three truckloads. There's plenty on hand."

Zimmerman's jaw dropped. "You did what?"

he asked again.

Dane chuckled at Zimmerman's expression.

After the weapons were unloaded and issued to the unarmed men. Zimmerman turned worried eyes to Dane. "I've got good news and bad news for you."

"What's the bad news?" Dane asked.

"We had brushes with enemy patrols. They're between us and the Calvoratti farm."

Dane stared at him. *Now there's no possible way to get Maria out of here*. "What's the good news then?"

"We established radio contact with battalion and explained our situation."

"You did? Great." Dane felt elated. "I'll talk to them as soon as I organize the defenses."

"No go, Sergeant." Keeler shook his head. "I only made contact one time. The atmospheric conditions must have been perfect then for the walkie talkie to reach that far."

"Well, praise God for that much." Dane pursed his lips in thought. "We'll have a meeting in the hut with the platoon leaders and Corporal Buckman. I'll assign the defenses."

As Doc Pavel joined the others in the hut, introductions were made to Buckman, Crawford and Elena.

Dane huddled with his commanders.

"Zimmerman, how many men do you have in your platoon?" Dane asked.

"Counting myself, twenty-one."

"I'm assigning you to command the east side at the hummock. Take eight of the men we freed. Also five men from the heavy weapons platoon, a mortar and a machine gun."

Dane turned to Corporal Buckman. "Your forty-seven men cover the ground between the ridge and the river. Base your defense on the knoll. You get the three machine guns and two mortars we captured." Dane's eyes laughed. "All your weapons were made in Germany," Be sure to show the Krauts how excellent their guns are."

Everybody chuckled at the joke. "Four of our wounded will guard the fifteen prisoners under the bridge. Since we aren't hiding any more, the gags can be removed. Gate's squad and I will stay at the hut as reserve. Maria, Elena, Lieutenant Crawford and Keeler will stay here too. Keeler, keep trying the radio. Lassiter, your platoon and ten of the freed prisoners man the ridge south of the cut.

"Jones," Dane turned to him, "you get the last ten ex-prisoners with your platoon and guard the ridge north of the cut. Grissom, you divide the rest of your platoon between Lassiter's and Jones' positions."

Lassiter calculated in his head. "Thet means

ninety-nine men to defend the ridge." He shook his head. "I hope it's enough."

Dane's jaw firmed. "It must be."

"Hey," someone outside the hut interrupted. "There's an American plane buzzing us."

Everyone ran out and stared up at the sky as the plane circled around. "Jump and wave, all of you," Dane ordered. "Let him know there's Americans down here."

As the plane flew in low, Crawford exclaimed, "I recognize the insignia. It's my squadron. Gimme the radio," he ordered. Seizing it, he held down the send button. "Hey, you black man. Come in, talk to me. Over."

He repeated it twice before a voice came over the radio. "Who you callin' a black man? Who is you?"

"It's Cook Book. Who're you?"

"Steady Eddy. Is you by the bridge? We thought you were a goner, for sure."

"Nah, I bailed out and got a busted flipper. I'm with friends."

Dane noticed Hemphill give a start and stare at Crawford.

Crawford continued, "Are you looking for me?"

"No, I was sent to see if some GI company captured the bridge. From the jumpin' jacks I'm seein', it shore looks like it.

"D'ya want to try a pick-up? I'll look around for a landing spot but I'm not seein' anythin' close," Eddie added.

"Nah, I'm good. Don't risk a crack-up."

"We're having ribs tonight for supper. Is you sure you don't want picked up?"

"Ribs?" Crawford straightened up. "Now listen here, you hold off until I get back. You know the cook don't know how to make good sauce."

"If you was to give me yore secret recipe, we would save you some," Eddy said in a sly tone.

"Not on your life! You wait until I get back to fix those ribs."

"Okay then. Is there anythin' you be needin'?"

"A radio," Dane interjected.

"With a long antenna," Keeler added.

"Medical supplies," Doc Pavel put in.

"Roger. I'll tell the colonel. Mebbee we can do a drop later on."

The connection broken, Dane looked around. "The horses need to be taken care of."

Rosario volunteered, "I'll picket them behind the hut and water them."

"Thanks. Everybody to your posts", Dane ordered.

Doc followed the others into the hut and said to Crawford, "Let me take a look at your arm." With

Maria looking on with an anxious face, Doc examined it and pronounced, "Couldn't have done better myself." Maria beamed at him.

Doc turned to Dane. "I've got badly wounded men to take care of and there isn't enough space down here. What's the upstairs like?"

"There are still boxes of ammunition up there," Maria said.

Doc climbed the stairs, looked and came back down. "Not enough room to swing a cat." He glared at Dane. "I got to have a place to treat the wounded."

Dane looked at him and after a moment said, "The only other place is on the bench under the bridge."

"And share it with prisoners?" Doc asked.

"Make your choice," Dane said and turned away.

With a loud "Humph," Doc stalked outside. "Don't just stand there, take them down to my surgery," he barked to the stretcher bearers.

As Dane made a round of inspection of the perimeter, he overheard the two groups sharing their experiences since leaving the Calvoratti farm. When they heard how the force at the bridge at times lay hidden and let Germans pass through them, Grissom turned to Jones. "Didn't you call Sergeant Shaw a fox yesterday? The Krauts may have their Desert

Fox, but I think we've got one too." (If it were possible, the shades of several Germans and Arabs killed in Tunisia would have agreed.)

Jones thought about it. "I don't think Rommel would let enemy forces travel right through his position."

Dane saw the look of mutual agreement they exchanged.

When Dane returned to the hut, he walked into a discussion between Crawford and Hemphill.

Hemphill asked, "You have your own barbecue sauce?"

"Yeah," Crawford twisted around to face him. "That's the reason they call me Cook Book. I can rustle up some of the best ribs and chicken you ever did taste."

"I've got my own recipe too. I chop up two or three jalapeño peppers, gives it a zing."

"So do I!" Crawford exclaimed, and before the bemused gaze of the onlookers the two of them started talking about recipes and dishes.

In midsentence, Hemphill stopped speaking and stared at Crawford. Hemphill couldn't believe it. He was actually enjoying a conversation about cooking with a colored man. He got to his feet and rushed outside, ashamed and angry. But at who, and why?

Maria squeezed in beside Tennessee, much to

his discomfort and puzzlement. She pulled out a Bible and said, "*Zio* Sergeant gave me this, can you help me? Where should I start reading? I want to learn about it."

Tennessee couldn't stand it. "Why don't you ask '*Zio* Sergeant' fer help?" he snapped at her, stood up and stalked out. The sudden outburst stunned into silence everyone who knew the even-tempered Tennessean. Maria looked after him with hurt in her eyes.

# Chapter Thirty-Two

Under the bridge, Private Ralf Reissenhoffenberger, the captured engineer, rolled over on his side and squirmed at the same time. Shocked by the sudden and unexpected attack, he realized he talked too much when questioned. But for the life of him he couldn't see how his words would help the enemy.

After he got over his surprise, he wasn't worried about being rescued soon. There were only 25 or 30 enemy soldiers. As soon as a convoy came, they would be overwhelmed. But when all the prisoners were gagged, tied and hidden under the bridge, he became alarmed. Then when he heard a number of American prisoners were released, his heart plummeted. When he and his fellow prisoners realized the Americans were allowing German convoys to roll through their position, he became aghast. What kind of American officer was this? Did he have ice in his veins? As each unsuspecting German group passed overhead all the rest of the day and all through the night, he hoped each time someone would notice something wrong. But it never happened. His respect for the unknown American officer increased a hundredfold.

A serious, meticulous and observant young

245

man, his superiors pronounced him perfect engineer material. Now he used his abilities to look for a chance to escape. When they were first placed under the bridge, he swept the ground with his gaze and noticed a broken bottle among the weeds. Unfortunate for his planning, he wasn't the only observant one. When a dark haired sergeant arrived, he glanced around and said something to the guards. They searched the ground and picked up the broken bottle, as well as some other glass and sharp objects.

Reissenhoffenberger took a year of English in school because he liked to study, and after entering the army he learned all the ranks and rank insignias of all the countries Germany fought with just for fun. As he laid there listening to the Americans with their strange accents, he picked up a word or two here and there. Curious about the American commander, he listened for his name but heard no officer title. The only names he heard were a Corporal Buckman and a Sergeant Shaw.

Early this morning the dark haired sergeant appeared and the prisoners untied and fed. Reissenhoffenberger wandered over to the edge of the bank and glanced around while trying to be unobtrusive. In the two or three glances he allowed himself, he thought he saw where he could drop over the edge and make his way south along the bank, clinging like a spider to the steep side. If he slipped and fell into the boiling river, the chances were high he'd be killed. After being fed they were tied up. About mid-morning the gags were removed. *No more hiding, they're going to fight* he thought to himself. Sure enough, he heard firing several times.

He listened to a lot of movement going on, men crossing the bridge both ways. From the few words he made out he knew more Americans arrived. Several wounded men followed by an obvious doctor were carried down and laid under the bridge while the unwounded Germans were moved south of the bridge, but still on the bench. Still no officer showed up. With an operation this big there must be an officer, more than one, but where were they?

With a dry throat he called out, "*Wasser.*" The doctor looked up and said something to one of the guards who brought a canteen of water. Since his hands were tied behind his back he couldn't take it and the guard held it to his mouth. He spluttered and choked as some of the water went down the wrong way and the doctor hurried over. He frowned at the tied hands and said something to the guard. Reissenhoffenberger caught 'Sergeant Shaw' again. The guard left but returned soon, shaking his head at the medic and again Reissenhoffenberger heard 'Sergeant Shaw.'

As he sat there he observed a broken stone not too far away. It had a ragged edge but didn't look real sharp. So he lay back down and every so often rolled first one way and then back again. But as he squirmed each time he rolled, he got a little bit closer to it. Now it lay a few inches away. But a couple of the German prisoners looked at him as he moved, which caught the attention of one of the guards. Reissenhoffenberger lay still and the guard looked away. When he reached it he could start sawing away at his bonds, but then a thought stopped him. They were bound to free them for meals. If they saw the damaged rope it would give him away. He would wait for darkness.

# Chapter Thirty-Three

Colonel Manfred Schoerner, one of the regimental commanders of the 15<sup>th</sup> *Panzergenadier* Division, felt his nose twitch. There were those who'd fought with both the colonel and Field Marshal Rommel, the Desert Fox, and claimed both noses were equally adept in sniffing out danger. *But where was the problem?* He bent over his map. He couldn't see what caused the alarms in his head to go off. It must be coming from his subconscious, something he couldn't put his finger on.

He sat in his regimental headquarters about a mile and a half west of the bridge over the Salso River. His orders were to bend in his flanks, cross over the bridge and take up defensive positions on the east bank. But the Americans launched an attack before dawn. With grim determination he held on, giving ground yard by yard. He knew by experience it's almost impossible to attempt a retrograde movement while under attack.

Lieutenant Wurtzmeier walked in with the latest report from the fight.

Schoerner grabbed the paper and read it. "The enemy fight like demons," he growled.

Wurtzmeier said, "I've heard the propaganda claims that since the Americans are a mongrel race

249

they can't fight."

Schoerner snorted. "Then let those idiots come and face this Red One division. See for themselves how these Americans fight."

Again his nose twitched and he bent over his map. *Where's the danger? What's wrong? My front is stabilized; I see no immediate problem there. The divisional headquarters moved east across the river last night.* "That's it!" he exclaimed. He expected a courier with orders this morning. The general didn't want to broadcast them over the radio, and the courier hadn't shown up yet. He's hours overdue. Schoerner frowned. As a matter of fact, he hadn't heard of any communication from the east all day except by radio or of his ammunition delivery.

He looked up. "Lieutenant, check and see if the couriers have arrived yet."

"*Jawohl, Herr* Colonel," Wurtzmeier answered and left. A few minutes later he came back. "*Herr* Colonel, there's been no sign of the courier." He paused and Schoerner fixed his eyes on him. The lieutenant gulped and added, "There are reports of gunfire to the east."

Schoerner stared down at the map. To the east? How did the enemy get behind him? There were no reports of airplanes or a parachute drop. His lines were still intact. How…?

Two men entered the room and interrupted his

thoughts. "*Herr* Colonel, this man has a report I thought you should hear in person," the captain said.

Schoerner looked at the corporal, "Yes, what is it?"

"*Herr* Colonel, the Americans have captured the bridge across the Salso River."

Schoerner gaped while the words shocked the room into silence. "How do you know this for a fact?" Schoerner at last asked.

"*Herr* Colonel, I was a guard for a group of prisoners and wounded who were attacked at the bridge."

"Tell me exactly what happened," Schoerner ordered.

The corporal rehearsed the events earlier that morning and ended with, "And the wounded were released and headed north to the coastal road."

The colonel stared at the man while his mind grappled with the last fact. Released? But that must mean… He stared at the map then back to the men. "It's an isolated unit who somehow penetrated our lines. They're not connected with the front lines. Colonel Vessler is south of us. Get him on the radio," he ordered. A moment later he spoke to him. "Vessler, Schoerner here. Has there been a breakthrough in your lines?"

"*Nein*, Schoerner," Vesslers breathy voice

251

came over the line.

"Are you sure? Not even a temporary one?" Schoerner demanded.

"Well, a small one occurred two days ago, but we it plugged right away. Some Italians gave up, you know how it is," Vessler excused himself.

"An American unit has captured the bridge in our rear. They must have come through the gap. Can you send a company or two to recapture it? I am under heavy attack here and can't spare anyone."

"My dear Schoerner, I am under attack also and my orders are to retreat across the Salso River further to the east. I have already retreated over a kilometer and am in the process of swinging my regiment around to the east. I have no reserves right now to send to help you out."

Schoerner ground his teeth and said, "Very well, *Heil* Hitler," and dropped the phone down. "Get me Lieutenant General Rodt," he ordered the radioman, referring to the commander of the 15th *Panzergrenadier* Division, as he continued to study the map.

\*\*\*

Vessler hung up his phone as an aide approached him. "Colonel, the battalion commander says the company he sent after the American unit has not reported in."

"What?" Vessler stared at the aide in stunned surprise. "No word at all?"

"*Nein*, *Herr* Colonel, it's like they dropped off the edge of the world. There's no sign of them." Helpless, the aide shrugged his shoulders.

Vessler gripped his hands in frustration. Without that company he possessed no reserves. He bent over his map. After studying his options, he decided to bend his right flank to the river and then start retreating eastward.

# Chapter Thirty-Four

Schoerner told General Rodt, "*Herr* General, the Americans have seized the bridge across the Salso River. I'm under heavy attack. Can you recapture the bridge from your side?"

"Colonel Schoerner, I have no troops with me except for a couple of security platoons. All the troops are west or south of the river. You must recapture it from your side."

On the map Schoerner ran his finger up the Salso River and at last found what he was looking for. On the west side of the river a dirt track led up to the river and then turned north. On the east side of the river another minor road followed the river for a ways. "General Rodt, please have bridging equipment sent to," and he gave the map coordinates, "and stand by to throw a bridge across if needed."

"But Schoerner," Rodt protested, "all the bridging equipment is on the way to Messina."

"General Rodt, my command will be stuck on this side of the river if I can't recapture the bridge in time or if it gets blown up. I must have a backup plan. I need the bridge. Please get it for me!"

"I'll see what I can do," Rodt sighed, "and I'll see about putting together a force to attack from this

254

side."

"Thank you, *Herr* General. And send me more ammunition. The last convoy hasn't arrived. *Heil* Hitler," and Schoerner hung up the phone. He bent over the map again. If he moved this company back to this position, and slid this company over here, then that would free up this company. He could give it some artillery support, but all of his tanks were already engaged. He gave the necessary orders and within the hour a company began marching towards the bridge.

Just before noon, the gray skirmish line came out of the hills. With the speed and accuracy of veterans, they probed the American defenses along the ridge, determining the length of the defensive line. The German captain thought he perceived a weakness on the south side and tried an attack there. Half a dozen men penetrated over the ridge and reached the river side. But a few well-placed rounds from the hut stopped them. Then a German's feet slipped and with a scream he fell into the river below, where the rushing water washed his broken body downstream. The Germans ceased any more attacks from that direction.

Next he tried an attack from the north, coming down between the ridge and the river, right at the men from the 82$^{nd}$. Leaving one platoon to feint at the ridge, the German captain attacked with the rest of his company. Half a dozen or more men took shelter behind one of the parked trucks and laid down a covering fire while more men rushed the knoll. Immediately they ran into the minefield and six or eight men were blown up. Buckman then blew up the booby-trapped truck and sent those bodies flying. The attack wilted because of the intense fire laid down by the Americans and the Germans pulled back. In a matter of minutes they'd lost twenty-five men.

The captain got on the radio. "I need artillery support." While waiting, he organized his men for another assault on the knoll. Then shells began arching overhead and for twenty minutes they pounded the American position.

But the paratroopers were veterans and their foxholes deep. When the artillery ceased firing, they waited until the Germans were climbing the knoll before they opened fire. The hail of lead dissolved the attacking line and the Germans stumbled back, leaving their dead and wounded behind.

The captain got on the radio again, calling Schoerner. "Colonel, I'm taking heavy fire. My infantry alone can't take the position. I must have tanks."

Schoerner ground his teeth in frustration. "I can't spare them. I'm under heavy attack myself."

"Colonel, I can't take the bridge without armor

support. The enemy is too well entrenched and they have an antipersonnel mine field."

"Mines? How did they get those?" Schoerner rubbed his aching head. "Very well. The bridge has to be taken soon. I'll send one Mark II light and two Mark IV medium tanks, all I have left."

Half an hour later they rumbled onto the scene. They advanced towards the knoll and ran into the antitank mines. Within seconds of each other the two medium tanks exploded. A parachute trooper blew up the light tank with a *panzerfaust*, a single shot German equivalent of an American bazooka. Again the Americans forced the attacking Germans back. The German company lost over fifty men while the Americans suffered two killed and four seriously wounded.

As the Germans retreated, Corporal Buckman sagged in relief. "I don't believe it," he said to the men around him. "We withstood two attacks with artillery and tanks, but only suffered light casualties."

"Yeah," one of them answered with awestruck eyes. "The preparations Sergeant Shaw made with just the things he scrounged, are amazing."

"Not only that, he placed everything in perfect positions where they are the most effective," another man interjected.

"If we get out of this alive, I'm going to

recommend he get a field commission and join the paratroopers. He's as good an officer as I've seen in battle," Buckman stated. "Get the wounded back to the medic," he added.

The German captain radioed for the third time. "Colonel, the tanks were destroyed and I was driven back. I'm going to attack in a different place, but I need artillery support again."

Schoerner cursed under his breath. "Very well, but the artillery can't shell the bridge. I have to have it intact. Do you understand?"

"*Jawohl, Herr* Colonel. I'll leave a margin of error for the artillery."

Leaving the equivalent of one squad to give harassing fire at the knoll, the captain brought the rest of the company back over to the west side of the ridge. Again for twenty minutes German artillery rained destruction down while the Americans hugged the ground on the backside of the ridge. Most of the shells landed on the German side of the ridge. The few shells which lit on the far side of the ridge caused little damage. A shell needed to land on just the right spot at the top of the ridge to hit anyone. None did, nor did they hit the bridge or stone hut, although some came close.

This time the German captain ordered his men to the attack before the barrage ended. One shell fell far short, and a group of Germans flew through the air. The barrage ended and the Germans started climbing the ridge. Suddenly American helmets lined the ridge top. A withering firestorm of rifle and machine gun bullets along with mortar shells swept the company back.

The captain couldn't make any more radio calls. His body lay halfway up the ridge. The surviving senior lieutenant made the report. "Colonel, the attack failed and over half the company are casualties."

Schoerner cursed as he slammed the phone down. *Where can I scrape together another force? The American attack on my front is running out of steam, but so are my men.*

Then Wurtzmeier said, "You're wanted on the radio. It's General Rodt."

# Chapter Thirty-Five

All during the last attacks Tennessee watched Shaw sit at the table in the hut, listening to the reports and sipping coffee. All the preparations were made, reinforcements were not needed, and no crisis presented itself which he, as commander, needed to intervene on. Tennessee gave an approving nod. Many young officers think they need to be involved in every action of their unit instead of setting back and letting their subordinates handle their duties. The good ones quickly learn this important fact. His sergeant instinctively knew it. *He'd make a terrific officer,* Tennessee thought to himself. He took a closer look and saw Shaw mouthing words. Tennessee realized Shaw was praying, the only thing he could do.

When the artillery started shelling the ridge, everyone sat on the floor with their backs to the walls. Tennessee heard a commotion outside.

"The horses," Rosario exclaimed and flew out the door.

Tennessee peered out the window and saw Rosario approach the wild-eyed tethered animals. As he soothed the beasts, they pressed their trembling bodies as close to him as they could.

Tennessee sat back down and glanced around

260

the room. Elena huddled in a corner, starting and whimpering with each close explosion, while Maria cradled her, comforting her. The whites of Crawford's eyes showed and he winced once in a while. Tennessee saw the frightened look in Maria's eyes when a close explosion rocked the building. He stared at Shaw. Didn't the sergeant see his girl is frightened? Couldn't he see he needed to go to her, that she needed him? At last, Tennessee couldn't stand it anymore. He slid over beside her. She gave him a relieved smile, wrapped one arm around his and relaxed against him. He saw Sergeant Shaw glance at them and look away, unconcerned, and Tennessee's puzzlement grew. Why wasn't Shaw bothered about another man cuddling his girl?

\*\*\*

At the bridge Reissenhoffenberger and his fellow prisoners were heartened by the attacks. "We'll show these Americans how to fight," someone said.

"Yeah, they can't hold on for long, surrounded like they are," another person added.

"With no artillery or heavy weapons, two or three tanks will roll right through them." Many of the Germans laughed.

"Look, more American wounded are coming," the first speaker said as several were brought down under the bridge. Many of the Germans grinned at the sight.

Reisenhoffenberger watched the American medic bend over the bloody bodies. He felt an unexpected stab of sympathy for the groaning men. They were the enemy, but they were human beings too. Disturbed by his thoughts, he listened as another prisoner said, "Just wait until we get those wonder weapons we've been hearing about. We'll drive these Americans back into the sea."

"Yeah, then we'll invade their country and they'll see how they like it." Several of the men laughed, but Reissenhoffenberger noticed some men look away. *I'll bet they don't believe in them.* He didn't know what to think. He hoped they were close to being unleashed, but what if they weren't?

As noon passed and the early afternoon sun poured down its heat on their unprotected bodies, their laughter and talking stopped. After an eternity of being baked alive in this airless oven, Reisenhoffenberger had enough. He called out to the medic, "*Doktor, Doktor.*" When the doctor came over, Reisenhoffenberger said "*Wir brachen essen und wasser.*" talking in German because he didn't want the medic to know he understood some English.

The doctor said something to one of the guards who hurried away. In a couple of minutes he returned with the American who spoke German.

"What do you want?" the second American asked.

"We need food and water," Reisenhoffenberger repeated with pleading eyes.

"Listen, we haven't eaten yet. You'll eat when we do."

"But you must give us water. We are dying of thirst out here," Reisenhoffenberger exaggerated.

"Sure, we can give you water," and Braun pulled out a canteen.

Reissenhoffenberger indicated his wrists tied behind his back, "Free my hands so I can drink."

He saw an uncertain look cross the other man's face. "I don't know, the sergeant doesn't want you guys freed, not right now anyway."

"I demand to see the officer in charge, this is barbaric!"

"Sergeant Shaw is in charge, and he says your hands stay tied." Braun glared at the German. "I've heard some of the barbaric things you Nazis have done. Depriving innocent people of water is the least of your atrocities."

Reisenhoffenberger gulped and gave an inward squirm. So had he, some of them first hand. Abashed, his mind seized on the first sentence. "Sergeant Shaw? A sergeant is in command here?"

"Yeah, Dane Shaw, and he's as good as any officer I've seen," Braun bragged.

The medic came. "Braun, the prisoners need

water. Help the guards. I'll talk to Sergeant Shaw later about their bonds." After all the prisoners were given a drink, Reissenhoffenberger lay back down. *Dane Shaw. If all the sergeants in the American army are anywhere near as good as him, Germany is in trouble*, he thought to himself with a shiver.

***

"Colonel Schoerner," General Rodt's authoritative voice came over the radio, "have you succeeded in capturing the bridge yet?"

"*Nein, Herr* General. We attacked it three times but the assaults were beaten off. There must be more troops there than I thought at first."

"Have they armor and artillery support?" Rodt questioned.

"It does not appear so," Schoerner gave a cautious answer.

"I have two companies of Italian infantry which I'm sending in to attack. The artillery bombardment will commence at 1545 hours and the assault will begin at 1600 hours. You will attack from your side at the same time."

"*Jawohl, Herr* General." Schoerner hesitated and then asked, "May I have the panzer battalion?"

A pause and then Rodt answered, "*Nein*, I need the tanks on this side of the river. I'm ordering it to go with Vessler."

"If I'm to take the bridge, I need tank support."

"What happened to your tanks?"

Schoerner's jaw clenched. "They were destroyed."

He winced at the telling silence. At last Rodt spoke. "You may have one platoon. That leaves the battalion with only 22 tanks, and it started with 60 when the Allies landed."

"Am I getting the bridging equipment?" Schoerner pursued.

"I spoke to General Hube, commanding XIV *Panzer* Corps, and he's sending it to the coordinates you designated. They should be there early tomorrow."

"*Jawohl,* General, we will attack at 1600 hours," and Schoerner laid down the phone. He stood there for several minutes, deep in thought. *I need to check my front line, see the faces of my men. Are they up to more fighting? Then I'll focus on the bridge.* He called for his car and driver. They drove up to the front lines and Schoerner looked over the situation. He spoke to his battalion commanders.

"We're pulling back another half a mile. Major, bend your left flank back to the Salso River. Captain," Schoerner turned to his right flank commander, "make sure you stay connected to the Livorno Division."

"*Jawohl,* Colonel. It's a good Italian division, not trash like most of them," the captain said.

"By shortening the line like this, we'll free up another company which can attack the bridge," Schoerner explained. "General Rodt will attack from the other side. The two forces will crack the Americans like a nut." The officers grinned in anticipation of the victory.

Next Schoerner visited the field hospital. "We've quite a few heat related cases," the head doctor explained. Schoerner nodded as he looked over the suffering men.

"When will you move the wounded back?" the doctor asked.

"As soon as we can, doctor, as soon as we can."

While the troops were adjusted, Schoerner watched and judged them. They held their heads up, they weren't defeated, but they were tired. He saw the lines of fatigue etched on their faces. They'd been fighting now for two weeks here in Sicily, and they'd been engaged in battle since before dawn this morning. But he had to ask them to fight another battle this afternoon. The heat drained men of their energy, but they must keep going.

The captain of the freed company appeared. "We're ready, *Herr* Colonel."

"Go down the road to the bridge. You'll find part of a company already there. You'll attack at 1500 hours along with two companies of Italians from the east side. I believe you're facing two companies of Americans. You'll have artillery and tank support. You must take the bridge."

"*Jawohl, Herr* Colonel." The captain saluted.

Schhoerner drove back to his headquarters where Wurtzmeier informed him, "The tank platoon is here."

"Good, we have them now. The Americans haven't a chance."

# Chapter Thirty-Six

At the bridge the fighting died down, although sporadic firing came from the west and north sides where the Germans kept up pressure. During a pause in the attacks, a voice came through the walkie talkie in the hut. "Hey Cook Book, I got a drop for you."

Crawford grabbed the radio and stuck his head out the door. "I see you," he said as he stared up into the sky.

Everyone ran outside and watched a white parachute billow open and drift down. Without any breeze, it came straight down and landed between the ridge and the hut.

"Good shot," Crawford exclaimed as Dane and Keeler raced to the capsule lying on the ground.

Dane cut away the parachute cords, then helped to open the container. Keeler grabbed the radio and tore off the protective packaging. The antenna and medical supplies were removed. Rosario began assembling the antenna while Braun carried the supplies to Doc. The squad fastened the antenna to the hut and Keeler attached the radio and tried it out.

"Do you read me?" he asked over the radio to the plane above.

"Loud and clear," came the answer.

As the plane flew away, Dane ordered Keeler, "Ring up battalion." When connected, Dane took the headset and reported, "This is Sergeant Shaw commanding King Company. We have captured the bridge and have fought off several assaults. We are awaiting relief."

"Sergeant? Where are the officers?"

"All dead or wounded."

After a moment of silence, Dane heard Major Hammond say, "I can't help you right now. I'll forward your message to Regiment. Your orders are to hold on until relieved." *Just as I expected,* Dane thought. But when he asked for artillery support, he hit a snag. "We're at the bridge crossing the Salso River," he reported to divisional artillery. "Map coordinates? I don't have any...I don't have a map...Listen, we need artillery support...Yes sir, I realize I'm talking to an officer...But...Sir, please...If you could throw a shell we could call corrections...No sir...Yes sir," and he flung the phone down in disgust.

"We can't do it that way, it isn't in the regulations, we have to have map coordinates," Dane repeated in a disgusted voice.

Crawford, an interested listener, said, "Let me see if I can some help from the squadron. Give me the radio."

It was Dane's turn to be flummoxed. "You mean you can give us air cover? Close air support in Sicily is unheard of, and you're offering it?"

"If the colonel can spare the planes," Crawford answered. "We have a lot of missions on the board, but if he can free up some planes, he will. Besides," he grinned, "I am rather important in the mess hall."

He put on the headset. "Alpha Tango Oscar Ought Ought, come in, come in." He repeated it four or five times before he got an answer.

"Alpha Tango Oscar Ought Ought here, come in."

"This is Cook Book. Can air cover be provided at my location?"

"Let me check."

Several minutes of silence passed. Nervous, Dane bit his lip and rocked on his feet.

At last, "The colonel can send over two flights, but not until later this afternoon."

"Thanks, man. Talk to you again, over and out." Crawford turned and gave Dane a thumb up.

Dane sagged in relief.

Dane's radio message was forwarded to Regiment, who sent it to Division, where it was handed to Major General Terry Allen. He read it and handed it to a visitor, a big man with a rather squeaky voice and three stars on his helmet.

"You gotta keep attacking and secure the

bridge," the visitor ordered.

"General, we've been attacking since before daylight and my men are exhausted. I need some time to form up a new attack," Allen protested.

General Patton swore. "The Krauts are tireder than your men. Keep attacking, don't give the enemy time to rest."

Allen hesitated. "Yes sir, we'll keep the pressure up and launch a new attack as soon as we can."

"Sooner," Patton demanded and stomped back to his car. As he sank into his seat, he scowled and said to an aide sitting in the back seat, "Ed, I think Allen's lacking fighting spirit."

"I'm sure he is doing the best he can," Ed said, trying to diffuse Patton's ire.

"Humph," Patton snorted.

After Patton left, a subordinate came into the headquarters with another message for the division commander. "The Germans are pulling back."

Allen looked up. "Keep the pressure up, we'll attack again in the morning." He wiped his streaming face. "This heat is awful."

\*\*\*

"Gates, we'll take advantage of the lull to feed the prisoners," Dane ordered. "Start the preparations while I go check with Doc."

Reissenhoffenberger lay with his eyes closed,

trying to rest. If his plan succeeded he wouldn't be getting much sleep tonight. He heard voices and opened his eyes to see the dark-haired sergeant talking with the medic. They visited with the wounded and then wandered over by the prisoners. He heard the medic call the other man 'Shaw'. Reissenhoffenberger gave the sergeant all of his attention. So this was the wily man, this...this...fox who fooled everyone all night long. If his escape attempt were to succeed tonight, he must outwit this man.

The medic said something which caused the Fox to snap something back. All at once, as if feeling eyes upon him, the sergeant spun his head and stared right at Reissenhoffenberger. Shocked at the savage look in the other man's eyes, Reissenhoffenberger looked away. Could the Fox read his mind?

\*\*\*

Doc said to Dane, "Shaw, I'm not sure we can hold out against a determined German attack."

Dane's face set in determination, "Doc, we WILL hold on, we will NOT give in!" Feeling someone's eyes on him Dane turned to look and saw a trussed up German prisoner staring at him. The German looked away and a warning bell went off in Dane's head. The German's eyes were not showing a defeated nature, but rather a considering look. *He's up to something, but what?*

"Have you had any trouble with the prisoners?" Dane asked.

"No, and I need to talk to you about them," Doc blustered, shaken at the look in Dane's face. "It's inhumane to keep these men tied up in the sun like this. They need some freedom of movement."

"I don't want them getting free, Doc. I don't want to have to shoot them. They stay tied up. It won't be for much longer, I think we'll be relieved tomorrow," Dane explained.

Surprise washed over Doc's face at Dane's words as Dane left him and went back to the hut. "Braun, Raymond, Rosario and Chilvers, when you finish eating go help with the prisoners. As soon as they are fed and watered, tie them back up and get back here. Gates, get the others to digging foxholes and maybe a slit trench or two. We're going to need more protection outside the hut before we're through. I'll take some food over to Zimmerman. I want to talk to him."

Dane crossed the bridge and met Zimmerman. With a worried look on his face, Zimmerman said. "Shaw, there's dust clouds over there. They're moving troops up. If they hit us hard enough, I don't know if we can hold on."

Again the look of iron determination came over Dane's face, "We WILL hang on. You will NOT retreat. THEY WILL NOT PASS!" Dane spaced his words out.

Zimmerman retreated a step from the savage aura emanating from the smaller man. He caught the intensity and his head went up. "We will stay," Zimmerman promised. He found his own courage and determination fueled by the sergeant and he in turn issued orders to his men. "We stay and fight here and if necessary, we die here. We won't retreat."

# Chapter Thirty-Seven

When Dane returned to the hut, he discovered Maria sitting outside with her back to the east wall, facing the bridge and thumbing through the Bible. She looked up with a smile and asked, "*Zio* Sergeant, can you show me where to start reading?" With a troubled look she added, "I asked Van but he wouldn't, he was upset about something."

Dane sat down beside her. "Yeah, I noticed he's not his usual cheerful self. You don't know why?" Maria shook her head. "You should read Genesis first. It lays the foundation for the entire Bible." Dane hesitated then went on, "Maria, I owe you an apology." She gave him an enquiring look. "I never wanted you to be mixed up with this fighting, I wanted to send you back to your home when we got here, but there just hasn't been the opportunity. If anything happens to you, I could never forgive myself."

"Oh no, *Zio* Sergeant, it's not your fault I am here. I needed to come because…" her voice trailed off as the look on his face changed from surprise to suspicion.

"Why did you have to come? You have something up your sleeve, don't you?" At the guilty look on her face a memory of something she said

275

once dropped into place. "It's something to do with farming, isn't it? You said yesterday a farmer was the most important thing to you."

Maria looked into his eyes and again decided it would be best to tell the truth. "I love this land, I love the farm, but Papa cannot keep it up. He needs help, but we can't afford to hire someone. Therefore I have to find a husband who knows how to farm and in exchange for marrying me and living here with us will inherit the farm. That's why I needed to come, to find someone, and I have!" she said with pride in her voice.

Aghast, Dane stared at her. "Maria, you can't marry someone just to provide a farm help, to bargain away yourself for a farm. You have to marry for love. Only God and love are the reasons to marry. And since you are a Christian now, God wants you to marry only a Christian. The only way to true happiness is living in God's will."

"He is a Christian," Maria interrupted.

"Well that's something at least." Dane marshaled his thoughts. "Maria, when a man and a woman marry, they have to give themselves one hundred percent to each other. They have to help and support each other, or the marriage will break down. It is the man's job to love his wife and to provide for her. It's her job to support him."

"The farm will do that," Maria interrupted,

eager to explain. "Once it is up on its feet it can provide for all of us."

"But Maria," Dane said in a gentle tone, "these men are Americans. The United States is their home. If you marry him and he wants to go home and live in the United States, it's your duty to support him and go with him and leave the farm."

Maria looked at him with a stunned look on her face. "It is?"

"Yes, imp. If you love him like you need to, you will love him more than the farm, and if necessary give it up for him." Maria sat there with a blank look on her face as Dane got up, walked around the hut and into another conversation.

Gates and the men were digging in front of the hut. Crawford helped as much as he could. O'Halloran stopped to take a breather, looked at Crawford, and said in a sudden burst of candor, "You know, I've never met a colored person before."

Crawford looked at him. "Yes, you have. You're a colored person yourself."

"What? No I'm not!" O'Halloran protested.

"Isn't white a color?" Crawford asked.

"Well, yes it is," O'Halloran admitted.

"We're all colored, it's just you're colored white and I'm colored black."

Maria wandered around the corner and heard

what Crawford said. "It's terrible the way your people were treated, but at least you're free from the terrible curse of slavery now."

Crawford looked at her with a grim look on his face. "Freed from slavery? Maybe in some legal fashion, but we're still treated as slaves, as second class people. There are restaurants which we can't eat in, hotels we can't stay in, bathrooms we can't use. When we meet a white person on the sidewalk we have to step aside. Yes massa, no massa, whatever you say massa." His voice became bitter. "I remember my mama on a bus. Even with a baby and a toddler and two bags of groceries, she had to give up her seat and stand so a big fat white man could sit."

Everyone was quiet as what Crawford said sunk in to their consciences. Dane's soft voice broke the silence. "I pray if ever I find myself in that situation, I would have the moral courage to not take the seat."

Hemphill jerked and stared at Shaw. Hemphill remembered the times he took some colored person's seat without thinking. It's just the way things are done. He detected no accusation or blame in Shaw's voice, only a thoughtful reflection. And then the thought came to him. *Would I have the courage to refuse the seat and face the scorn of the white people on the bus, even my friends?* He saw

Crawford give the sergeant a long careful look with surprise in the pilot's eyes, as if he too was thinking of what it would cost a white person to do such a deed. Without another word the men went back to their digging.

Dane looked at Crawford, "If you don't mind, Lieutenant, would you call and see if we can expect any planes soon? It appears we're about to be attacked."

Crawford looked surprised at the information and said, "Sure thing, sergeant," and went inside to make the call.

\*\*\*

Colonel Schoerner decided to ready the assault from the west in person. He arrived with the company of infantry and five tanks. After issuing orders, he checked his watch for the time. 1530 hours, the artillery bombardment would start in fifteen minutes, the attack in thirty. He paced as he waited.

\*\*\*

Lieutenant Crawford came out of the hut. "Shaw, they're on the way, four planes, two loaded with bombs."

"How soon 'til they get here?"

Crawford shrugged, "Fifteen, twenty minutes."

With Teutonic timing the German barrage cut loose at precisely 1545 hours. For five minutes the ground shook and quivered from the blasts and the Americans hunkered deep in their foxholes. The radio blared, "Tango Alpha Oscar One Seven, come in Tango Alpha Oscar One Seven."

Crawford grabbed the phone and over the noise of the explosions screamed, "This is Tango Alpha Oscar One Seven, come in!"

"We are here," came the welcome voice. "Man, is you being blasted!"

"I noticed," Crawford yelled back. "Can you spot where it is coming from?"

"Sure can, we'll see if we can put a damper on it." In about five minutes the shelling slacked off, and then came another call. "Hey Cook Book, there's a mess of soldiers coming at you from the east. We'll see if we can kinda discourage them."

Dane grabbed Crawford. "Ask them if they see any other attackers."

Crawford passed on the message. The reply came back, "Yeah, there are some tanks and men to your west, but a lot more men and artillery to your east."

Everyone dashed out of the hut and stared at the eastern horizon. Four planes dropped out of the sky and made strafing runs. Dane grabbed Hemphill. "Run to Buckman. Tell him to send twenty men to help Zimmerman. Gates, follow me." They took off running towards the ridge.

# Chapter Thirty-Eight

While artillery hammered the area, Reissenhoffenberger, bound and helpless, came as close to praying as he'd ever done in his life. "Please don't kill me, please don't kill me," he begged. When the shelling stopped, he breathed a sigh of relief.

However, Schoerner, watching through his binoculars, cursed the premature stopping of the shelling. "*Achtung*, attack," he ordered. He knew the attack would succeed. Even if the American force consisted of two companies as he suspected, they were surrounded and without artillery or armor support. His forces numbered between 600 and 700 men and were attacking from two sides with artillery and tanks. There could only be one outcome.

But unknown to him the eastern attack unraveled. On the first swoop by the American planes on the artillery positions, while other planes strafed the startled gunners, one plane dropped a 250 pound bomb on a battery. On the second run the pilot dropped the other bomb onto the ammunition dump. The resulting cataclysmic explosion not only destroyed most of the ammunition, but it put out of action many of the guns and gunners, at least for a while.

Then they began strafing the advancing Italians which broke the back of the attack. They made one half-hearted assault which Zimmerman's reinforced platoon beat back with little difficulty. The Italians broke and ran for the rear.

*** 

Dane lay on the ridge, sweat trickling into his eyes as he watched five squat monsters clanking down the road towards him, followed by lines of grey-clad infantry. "Hold your fire until I give the word," he ordered, and turned to Grissom. "Where is the *panzerfaust?*" he asked, referring to the one they captured two days ago. The paratroopers possessed the ones from the ammunition trucks.

"It's on the other side of the cut," Grissom said.

The leading tank, with a second tank following close behind, entered the cut and with contemptuous ease started pushing the truck blocking the road out of the way. Grissom pushed the plunger and the explosive laden truck blew up, taking the lead tank with it. The trailing tank started to back up when Dane leaped to his feet, took a running jump and landed on the moving tank. While German bullets ricocheted around him, with frantic haste he shoved three hand grenades into a port and jumped off again. The exploding tank gave impetus to his leap. He lit and rolled over on the north side of the cut.

The remaining three tanks stopped and Dane imagined the conversations flying around. Then they turned and began climbing up the ridge abreast of each other, the cut now blocked by the burning tanks. "Give me the *panzerfaust*," he ordered and Wilbers passed it to him. Lining up where the lead tank would come over the crest, Dane lay on the back side of the ridge, blind to the approach of the tank, feeling the ground quiver as it came closer and closer. The nose of the tank appeared over the top of the crest. For a brief instant the weak underbelly showed. At point blank range Dane fired the *panzerfaust*. Desperate, he rolled out of the path as the machine teetered at the top of the ridge. The explosion ripped the turret loose from the rest of the tank.

The second tank passed over one of the hidden charges. Jones ignited it and the tank blew up. But still one more tank kept coming.

"Bazooka, bazooka," Dane yelled but rescue came from another direction. An airplane dropped out of the sky and laid a 250 pound bomb next to it. The tank exploded. The pilot dropped the other bomb into the German infantry and with a last strafing run all the planes flew away, out of ammunition.

*\*\*\**

The German line broke and retreated while

283

Schoerner cursed. This position had cost him eight tanks. Eight! And he hadn't reached the top of the ridge except for one tank. But the Germans were veterans and Schoerner an excellent officer. In only moments a new assault began.

The grey lines of men laid down covering fire, leapfrogging their way across the valley, to the base of the ridge, and then up the slope. Closer and closer they advanced, not heeding the falling bodies around them. But their own fire now took a toll and Americans were screaming in pain or dying. Everybody was yelling and shooting. Mortar bursts went off everywhere and still the Germans kept coming. The cacophony of noise was deafening and now the Germans were reaching the crest of the ridge here and there. A group of Germans reached the top of the ridge. The American line sagged back and started to crack.

*** 

Dane saw the line breaking. His men were being driven back, they were being killed. HIS MEN! He felt fury rising up from deep inside him, like the berserker fury of his ancient forbears. His iron will strove to contain it, but then for the first time in his life he released his control. A red mist of rage dropped over his eyes. With a savage primordial yell, he threw down his Thompson submachine gun, seized a rifle and leaped into the midst of the Germans.

He became a whirling shifting dervish, ducking and blocking all the blows aimed at him by the Germans surrounding him. They couldn't fire without hitting one of their own. They used rifle butts and bayonets to try to bring him down.

Dane blocked a swung rifle butt and then jammed his rifle barrel into a stomach. The soldier howled in anguish and dropped. In the same motion Dane smashed his rifle butt into the face of a second man. A German swung a rifle at Dane's head while another thrust a bayonet at his stomach. Somehow Dane ducked, twisted and turned and both missed.

The fighting took place on the crest of the ridge and in full view of both forces. Unaware of being the cynosure of all eyes they fought on. Two Germans side by side thrust bayonets at him, but he swung his rifle and blocked them. The sweep of his gun smashed the head in of another German. The German who had the rifle barrel buried in his stomach scrambled to his feet. With four Germans surrounding him, Dane danced and weaved and ducked and blocked.

As the seconds ticked away it seemed impossible for the unequal contest to continue. Each onlooker, Colonel Schoerner included, felt the American couldn't continue the unequal battle. He must go down with multiple wounds. But still he kept on his feet and fought on.

Again two Germans thrust with their bayonets, this time one in front and one behind him. Dane tossed his rifle up in the air, twisted sideways and grabbed both barrels stabbing at him. He pulled the rifles toward each other and around his body, adding to the impetus behind the thrusts. One bayonet plunged into the other German's body while the second one cut the other man's side open. Dane snatched his rifle out of the air and swung at an opponent's neck, trying to slash the carotid artery with the gun sight. He missed and gashed the jaw to the bone. With a shriek the stricken man fell back and Dane whirled to face the last German standing. His gun was already swinging and Dane only had time to raise his rifle. The smashing blow tore the gun out of Dane's hands. But as the German swung, he exposed his abdomen. Dane buried his hand into it and twisted, the force of the blow lifting his victim off of the ground. The German's mouth dropped open and his eyes bulged out as he felt his internal organs rupture. He fell to the ground, dying.

Dane dove down the backside of the ridge to retrieve his submachine gun. German bullets split the air behind him. The German with the lacerated jaw jumped to his feet into the line of fire. He fell, mortally wounded.

Through the roaring in his ears Dane heard Rosario shout, "Let's go!" In the red mist clouding his eyes, Dane saw him and 'Pache lead the American charge back up the ridge. They cheered, heartened by what they saw while the Germans, stunned by what happened, tried to recover. Dane slid down the slope, grabbed his submachine gun and scrambled back to the crest. More Germans were climbing the ridge. Dane sprayed bullets at the advancing enemy. A swathe of them fell. Jones ignited another hidden charge. A group of Germans flew into the air. Their dying screams added to the ear-splitting noise of battle. More Germans reached the crest. Where Dane fought, the American line held firm. But to his right and left, the struggle swayed back and forth.

Dimly, Dane became aware Zimmerman fought at his side. Later Dane learned Zimmerman, after driving off his attackers, saw the battle on the ridge. He took the twenty paratroopers and ten of his own men and took off on the run. They pounded across the bridge, up the slope, and smashed into the Germans.

The reinforcements knocked the Germans off the crest. But the Germans were veterans and didn't run. They slid down the slope and prepared to make their stand.

But the berserk fury still filled Dane. With a

scream he jumped to his feet and led the charge down the slope, his men following him. His machine gun ran out of bullets and he threw the empty gun down. Spotting an abandoned Garman light machine gun he picked it up and continued running down the slope, firing it at the wavering and retreating German line.

The Germans broke and streamed back across the valley. With red rage still in front of his eyes, Dane began to chase them. He felt someone grab him by the shoulder. He whirled around to kill whoever pulled him. The horrified look on Gates' face shocked the berserk fury out of Dane.

The wildness died and sanity returned. As the adrenalin poured out of him, Dane's body trembled and he staggered. He felt bewildered at where he stood on the valley floor. What happened? He didn't remember running this far. He only remembered bits and pieces of the fight. A kaleidoscope of stricken faces danced in his mind. But he did know he stopped the German attack. A new sense of pride at his achievement wisped into his mind, like a seed sprouting. Pushing the thought away, he took a deep breath to steady himself and gave a weak grin to Gates.

Then he issued orders. "Pick up our wounded and take them to the medic. Retrieve all the weapons and ammo. Then go back to the ridge."

The Americans plodded back up the slope, picking up their wounded as they went. Half a dozen lightly wounded or stunned Germans were herded up also. An American started to pick up the German with the slashed side but Dane stopped him. "Leave him for the Germans."

"But Sarge," he protested, "he needs medical attention."

"I know, Wilbers," Dane explained, "but we don't have the medical staff to help him. The Germans do, let them take care of him." With a reluctant expression, Wilbers left the German.

At the ridge, Dane gathered the platoon leaders. "How many casualties did we take?"

Lassiter answered, "Dead and those with serious wounds, twenty."

Gates added, "O'Halloran's dead. He's got a hole in his chest you could put your fist into."

Dane pursed his lips together in grief. "How about the lesser wounded?"

Grissom responded, "They just poured sulpha powder into their wounds, bandaged themselves and climbed back into their foxholes. They're ready to fight again."

"We have the best soldiers on the planet," Dane exclaimed. "And you're all doing an outstanding job." Dane beamed at the platoon leaders, then added, "But return to your posts. I expect another attack soon."

As Dane prowled the perimeter, he overheard 'Pache tell Wilbers, "Shaw, he's a killing machine."

Wilbers replied with awestruck eyes, "Counting the crewmen in the tanks, the Germans lost almost a hundred men, killed, wounded and captured, and he caused about a third of them himself."

"From what I heard, add to them the score from yesterday and last night, and he inflicted fifty casualties by himself."

Dane felt again the frisson of pride at the praise. But he was busy and shoved the sensation aside.

# Chapter Thirty-Nine

Colonel Schoerner kept his glasses on the fight at the top of the slope and then on the same American who led the furious charge down the slope. Although too far away to see any facial features, he had a good idea about the size and build of the man and saw his easy and graceful walk. He saw them pick up their own dead and wounded and some prisoners, but not the bulk of the German wounded.

"Those callous Americans, leaving our wounded like that," an officer standing next to Schoerner sputtered with outrage.

"No," Schoerner lowered his glasses. "The Americans must have straitened medical services. They can't take care of them."

He scanned the grey uniforms littering the ground and his jaw tightened. He faced a horrible decision.

The German soldiers were veterans, Colonel Schoerner an excellent combat officer and in a short time they were reorganized and ready for another assault. He hesitated but then called up his artillery chief. He felt the eyes of the surrounding men boring into his back, but he didn't see any other choice. He could not send in his men without

291

artillery support to attack such a position. He would simply be signing their death warrants. "Commence firing," he ordered. Guns and mortars slammed into the ridge. He lowered his field glasses, glad he couldn't hear the shrieks of the doomed wounded men lying in the open.

Again the lines of Germans swept across the valley under the protection of the artillery until they reached the slope. "Cease fire!" he hollered into the phone and the Germans scrambled up the slope, only to be met by sheets of fire. The Americans, all of them born scroungers, supplied themselves with so many captured German machine guns they had the firepower of a force two or three times their size. Nevertheless, the Germans swept up to the crest, wavered, and fell back. Again they only retreated a little ways down the slope and shot at any heads which appeared over the crest. Then they heaved grenades up and over the top of the ridge.

As Hemphill hugged the ground, one of them burst close to him. He yelped as pain lanced his leg. Raymond and Gates scrambled to his side. They tried to stop the bleeding while Hemphill clenched his teeth and clutched his bloody limb with both hands. Somebody yelled a warning. They looked up to see a grenade float in the air towards them. Time stood still as it got bigger and bigger. A body flashed as Dane raced across the slope and threw himself forward. He snatched the grenade out of the air, twisted in midflight and tossed it back over the crest. He lit on his shoulder and rolled. The three men let out pent up breaths and stared in astonishment at the acrobatic feat.

Dane scrambled to Lassiter's side. "We can't stay here and take this. I'll tell Jones and Grissom. We'll throw grenades and then charge."

Once organized, Dane pulled out a grenade and yelled, "Throw on my command, now!" He launched his grenade over the top and a dozen more followed. As they exploded he yelled, "Charge!"

The Americans flung themselves at the surprised Germans. A fierce fight broke out for a few moments. Then their line broke and they ran back across the valley, leaving more bodies lying still on the slope of the ridge.

The Germans were veterans, Colonel Schoerner a very good officer, and they all realized they could not launch another assault. He gave a long look through his glasses and turned to a lieutenant who spoke English. "Prepare a white flag and come with me. I want to talk to their commander."

A few minutes later the Americans were surprised to see two Germans approaching with a white flag. They walked to the base of the ridge and stopped. Dane looked at Braun and said, "Come with me." Both of them walked down to meet the two officers.

At the foot of the ridge, Colonel Schoerner glanced at the American heads looking at him. The experienced officer estimated their numbers at between one and two platoons. He mused out loud. "If they're equally divided between west, north and east, then not less than one nor more than two companies." He refused to look at the bloody rags around him. He couldn't tell which bodies were the result of American fire or his artillery, and he didn't want to know. He looked up and watched two Americans coming down towards them.

When they arrived, the lieutenant said, "This is Colonel Schoerner. We wish to speak to your commanding officer."

Dane replied, "You're looking at him." The lieutenant looked puzzled at the expression and Dane explained, "I'm the one in command."

The lieutenant translated and Schoerner glanced at Dane's sergeant stripes. He knew as well as Reissenhoffenberger the American rank insignia. If a sergeant was in charge of a unit this big then it must mean they'd suffered gigantic casualties among the leadership. He whispered into the lieutenant's ear a change of plan.

The lieutenant drew himself up as stiff as a ramrod. "We have come to discuss surrender terms," he stated.

Dane looked at him with a gleam of humor in his eyes. "We would be glad to accept your surrender. Advance halfway across the valley, lay down your guns and put your hands on top of your heads."

The lieutenant looked at him in astonishment and then said with a haughty lift of his head, "Not our surrender, yours. You are surrounded and cut off from all help and with no chance of relief. It would be the humanitarian thing to stop the continued suffering of your men."

Dane threw back his head and laughed. "Colonel, if you want to stop the suffering of men, then I suggest you surrender. You are not crossing the bridge." He said the last line with a steely look and a determined jaw. "Furthermore, if you don't want to kill your own people, don't try to shell the bridge."

While Schoerner considered the younger man's determined face, the lieutenant made the translation, and then repeated back the colonel's response. "You on purpose placed prisoners as shields to safeguard the bridge? That is against the Geneva Convention!"

"No, Colonel," Dane shook his head. "There isn't much room and I put them in the safest place I could. It just happens to be next to the bridge."

As Schoerner hesitated, he heard moans

coming from wounded men. He looked around and met the beseeching gaze of a sufferer, his face twisted in agony. Schoerner turned to Dane and asked, "I would like an hour's truce to gather my wounded," and indicated the men on the slope.

The two men stared into each other's eyes. Schoerner tried to gauge his opponent, but the brown eyes facing him gave nothing away.

"You ordered your own artillery to fire on your wounded," Dane snapped.

Schoerner winced but then stared back, stone-faced.

"You're a hard man, but I see you have a heart also. I'll agree to the truce but you'll stay on the other side of the valley. My men will bring the wounded off of the slope and down to here. Then you can come and collect them. None of your men will climb this ridge."

Schoerner looked into Dane's implacable eyes as the lieutenant translated. This American learned something about him, Schoerner, but he'd discovered something too. This man would fight long and hard to keep the bridge.

The silence lengthened and then Schoerner nodded. As Dane turned and glided up the slope Schoerner noticed something: that walk, that build! Is this the man who fought six of his men up on the ridge and, although surrounded, killed them all? He wasn't even wounded! More shaken than he wanted to show, he turned and began the walk back to his own lines.

They completed the transfer of wounded by 1900 hours. Schoerner lowered his glasses and turned to the senior lieutenant. "I'm going back to my headquarters now. You're in charge here. Keep the pressure up."

"*Jawohl, Herr* Colonel," the lieutenant saluted. Schoerner spun on his heel and left.

***

Half an hour later, Dane stood on top of the ridge and sniffed the air like a fox searching for danger. "There's no artillery bombardment and the gunfire is desultory. They aren't going to attack any more today."

Sergeant Jones looked at him. "What about tonight?"

"Maybe. I think they're more apt to early in the morning. The prisoners we picked up are worn out." He looked at the sun. "We'll start the evening meal now. Let the men eat in shifts, and then let them sleep. Rotate the guard so everyone gets some shut-eye."

Braun turned a worried face to Dane and asked, "Do you think the colonel might be right? Are we not going to be relieved?"

Dane said, "Listen." Everybody stopped what

297

they were doing. Off to the west they heard a steady rumble like thunder from the clear sky. "That's our artillery. They'll be here tomorrow," Dane stated. Heartened, they all returned to their duties.

Tied up prisoners and wounded crowded the bench. The Germans looked with hopeful eyes at the growing number of wounded Americans coming in. Then they sagged in disappointment when new prisoners were brought in and they related the events of the day.

Hemphill, carried by Raymond and Rosario, refused to join the overflowing bench. "Don't take me down there," he begged when he saw the conditions. "Take me to the hut."

The two stretcher-bearers reversed directions.

Meanwhile, all during the long afternoon Maria huddled with Elena in the hut, listening to her whimpers and feeling her body shake as they heard the explosions. Maria tried to comfort the poor girl, scared out of her wits at the possibility of being captured by Germans again. She clutched Maria and said over and over again, "Don't let them take me."

Maria tried to comfort her by saying, "*Zio* Sergeant will protect you. He won't let them come," but to little avail.

But Maria wrestled with her own problems. What seemed like such a simple plan to a girl had turned into a complicated one for a woman.

What if Van didn't want to live in Sicily? What if she had to make a choice between him and the farm? She loved the farm. She couldn't see herself living anywhere else, so she would have to tell Van goodbye. But then the thought of not seeing his long face and never hearing his soft drawl again became too much to endure and she would have to say farewell to the farm. But she couldn't do that either. Her emotions see-sawed back and forth as the day wore on.

The door opened with a bang and two men carried someone in, feet first. "Oh God, no!" she prayed as she got to her feet, her face white as a sheet. "Not Van, please God, not Van, not dead, please God." All thoughts of the farm went out of her head. Then they turned and she saw Hemphill's face. Her knees almost buckled in relief. Then her practical side came to the fore and she bustled about making him comfortable.

"How is...everybody?" she asked Hemphill after the other two men left.

He looked at her, hesitated, and at last said, "O'Halloran bought it. He's dead."

"Oh," a long pause as she looked down, thinking of the Irishman. "Anybody else hurt bad?"

"Nah, minor scratches is all." He squirmed from the pain in his leg and bit back a groan.

She felt an almost overpowering desire to fly to

Van and tell him of her decision, that she loved only him, but she held herself still. The battlefield wasn't anyplace for her to be in.

# Chapter Forty

To take his mind off of his pain, Hemphill told the people in the hut some snippets of the victorious battle. "The Germans asked for a truce to collect their wounded," Hemphill added.

"Then they will get the medical care they need," Maria exclaimed. Then she felt tears in her eyes as she said, "The poor families of all those who died. Now they'll suffer for the rest of their lives."

A somber silence fell over the room.

Maria shook herself and translated Hemphill's news for Elena. Then she smiled and added. "See, I told you *Zio* Sergeant would protect us."

Wide-eyed, Elena asked, "Are the Germans gone?"

"No, but *Zio* won't let them come."

Then Maria's mind switched to another thought. *Maybe Van will come and I can tell him.* But as she waited with her heart in her throat during the truce period, he never came.

The radio blared, startling her. "Tango Alpha Oscar One Seven, come in. Tango Alpha Oscar One Seven, come in."

Crawford answered, "This is Tango Alpha Oscar One Seven. Start talking, Steady Eddy."

"The colonel wants to know if you need any more missions. He don't want to launch any more flights unless absolutely necessary. The pilots have been busy all day and they needs their beauty sleep."

"I'll ask the commander," Crawford began when Dane walked in the door. "Wait a minute, he's here now.

"Shaw, the colonel wants to know if you need more air cover. The pilots are worn out and he doesn't want to send them if they aren't necessary."

"Not right away, sir. It looks like the German attacks are over for now. I expect we'll need help in the morning, though."

"You can tell the colonel they can stay home," Crawford told Eddy. "And mind you save some ribs for me, and without any inferior sauce on them."

"Sure thing, Cook Book. Roger, over and out."

Crawford leaned back in his chair and cuddled his aching arm.

"Shall I get the doctor for you?" Maria asked, concern written on her face.

"No, I'll be all right. Just need to rest a little," Crawford reassured her as he closed his eyes.

Dane looked at Keeler. "Radio battalion and let them know we're still here."

"Maria," Dane turned to her, "we're going to eat now. Will you start the meal? About thirty men to a shift."

"*Si, Zio* Sergeant."

While she told Elena about supper plans, Dane stoked the fire in the stove. He checked the stock of firewood and told Keeler, "We need more wood. When you've finished with the call, grab an axe and follow me."

They walked outside and Dane spotted a dead tree on the south side of the hut. He glanced at Keeler. "Have you ever cut down a tree before?"

"No, Sarge."

Dane grinned. "Neither have I. Let's see how we do."

They did manage not to drop the tree down on either themselves or into the river.

They carried enough chunks into the hut to sustain the stove. The aromas of fried spam and hot coffee filled the room. Maria, with perspiration on her brow from the heat of the stove, said, "We can start serving."

"I'll let them know. Keeler, go tell Corporal Buckman to send a squad at a time and to replenish his ammo from upstairs. I'll call Lassiter and Zimmerman and tell them the same."

After making the calls, Dane walked back outside. With hands on his hips, he scanned the area around the hut. *The horses have eaten all the grass on this side. I'll have Rosario move them to the other side.* He studied the dried brush south of the hut, extending along the river bank.

As the first group of men arrived to eat their meal, Dane left to walk around the perimeter to check everyone's condition. He told Lassiter, "Send Gate's squad last. I'm keeping them at the hut tonight." He accompanied Zimmerman's remaining squad to the hut, picked up food for the prisoners and wounded from the hardworking women, and ordered a squad who'd finished eating to follow him to the bench.

Dane visited with Doc about the wounded and helped the prisoners, six at a time, start to eat. He paused when he started to leave. Something niggled at the back of his mind, something he should remember. But he was tired. His head buzzed with the questions and orders he'd given during his tour of inspection. Ideas, plans and worry chased themselves around in his mind like a dog chasing its tail. He put the feeling out of his head. If it was something important he would remember it later.

*** 

Reissenhoffenberger watched him leave with a sigh of relief. If the Fox followed the same pattern as yesterday, he wouldn't be back until morning. Reissenhoffenberger finished eating, and obedient to the guard's gesture, held his hands behind his back to be retied. Then he sat down to have his feet bound. When he laid back he felt the sharp rock in the small of his back. He tried to relax as much as possible and waited for darkness to fall.

# Chapter Forty-One

All the time she worked, Maria's eyes and heart yearned for sight of Van, but he never appeared. When Gates and his men arrived for their turn, she stared at the door. But Van didn't show up. At last she asked Raymond, "Isn't Va…Tennessee coming to eat?"

Raymond looked around. "Funny, I could have sworn he was right behind me when we left the ridge. He's around here somewhere." He shrugged and went on eating.

Tennessee stood outside the hut, feeling disconsolate. The sound of Maria's voice coming from within felt like hammer blows upon his heart. *Ah must forget about her. She belongs to someone else.* Immersed in his thoughts, he failed to notice Shaw's approach.

"Have you eaten yet?" Shaw asked, making him jump. Tennessee shook his head. "Neither have I. Let's go and see if Maria saved anything for us."

Tennessee hung back, surprised. *Didn't Shaw want to eat alone with his beloved?*

He turned an inquiring eye as Tennessee didn't move.

"Ah don't want to intrude," Tennessee mumbled.

306

"Intrude?" Shaw looked puzzled.

"Uh, ah know what happened last night," Tennessee explained.

Shaw's face lit up. "You do? Isn't it wonderful! I rejoice so much whenever it happens."

Tennessee gaped at him. *Whenever it happens? How many women has Shaw been engaged to?*

"The last time was back in Tunisia, there were two of them. They're married now," he added with a faraway look in his eyes.

Tennessee's mouth dropped further. *What kind of womanizer is he? Two women at a time? But...married?* "What are you talking about?" Tennessee sputtered.

"Why, people getting saved, of course." Shaw looked at him in surprise. "You said you knew Maria accepted Jesus as her savior last night."

"Ah did...ah didn't...Aren't you going to marry her?" Tennessee stuttered.

"What?" Shaw's jaw dropped open. "The imp? Of course not! Why do you...?" and his voice trailed off.

"But ah thought...," Tennessee began.

"You're not thinking," Shaw chided. "She's got someone else on her mind."

"It's that Chilvers, he's such a smooth talker," Tennessee said with a glum expression.

Shaw gave him a friendly but exasperated look,

"It's not Chilvers either. She wants a farmer." Tennessee gave him a puzzled look and Shaw gave a sigh. He stepped to the doorway and said, "Maria, will you come out here, please?" When Maria appeared he said, "Talk some sense into this lunkhead, will you?" He went inside to find something to eat.

Maria came to the door without her usual bounce but face lightened up with a brilliant smile when she saw Tennessee. "Why did he call you a lunkhead?" Maria asked.

Tennessee stammered, "Uh…ah…uh…" Then he said in a rush, "Maria, do you want to marry Sergeant Shaw?"

The shock on her face convinced him as no protestations could have. "Me? Marry *Zio* Sergeant? Of course not! Whatever made you think I wanted to?"

He didn't answer her question. "Do you want to marry Chilvers?"

She shook her head, "No." And then greatly daring she smiled up at him and said, "I want to marry you."

She saw the answer in his face and her heart melted with happiness. Tennessee looked around. There were too many curious eyes around so he took her by the arm and led her around to the south side of the hut where they found a little privacy.

"You love me?"

"Yes, Van," and then the whole story poured out. Of how she loved the farm and planned to find a husband to work it so she could live there. "But...but when they brought Hemphill in and I thought it was you and...and...I thought you were dead, I would have given up the farm for you." She looked up at him with tears in her eyes.

Tennessee looked at her with tender eyes, but then his expression changed. "Maria, ah cain't ask you to marry me."

Maria froze, only her eyes alive as several thoughts chased themselves through her mind. *He can't marry me? Is he married already? But Zio Sergeant pushed us together and he wouldn't do that if Van has a wife.* She waited with bated breath for his next words.

"Ah'm in this war fer the duration and it's going to last fer a long time. Ah cain't ask you to wait fer me."

"I will wait."

"It'll be years 'fore it's over."

"I will wait."

Despite his words his hands of their own volition reached out and took her by the shoulders. His fingers tingled when he touched her. "Ah might be killed or crippled or...or...."

"I will wait. Van, I will wait for you until you

309

come back for me. If you will live her in Sicily I will stay with you. If you go back to America I will go with you. If you are killed I will wait until we are in heaven together."

"Oh Maria," Tennessee breathed. He leaned down and their lips met in a tender, passionless kiss, a kiss of promises made to each other.

"Shaw just told me you accepted Jesus." Maria nodded. "Ah haven't been living the way ah promised to when ah accepted Jesus as mah savior. Last night ah asked God to forgive mah broken promises and I would live fer Him from now on, and now He has brought us together." Both of their faces were beaming. "Ah will need you to help me keep mah promise to God. Will you pray fer me to live like ah should?"

"Yes Van, and you pray for me to be the wife God wants me to be."

"Ah will." Tennessee answered it like a marriage vow. Hand in hand they walked back into the hut. He saw Shaw's eyes laughing at them.

# Chapter Forty-Two

After Schoerner's call earlier in the day, Colonel Vessler studied his maps. He ordered his headquarters and rear units to move east of the Salso River. Then he drove up to the front line. He examined the terrain with his glasses and turned to his left flank commander. "Major, you will counterattack the Americans in front of you. While they scramble to hold you off, my other two battalions will move east behind you. You will then break off the attack and act as rear guard as they cross the Salso River. Then you will cross, destroy the bridge and deploy on the north bank. By then Colonel Schoerner will have also crossed the river and we can hook up with his left flank."

"*Jawohl, Herr* Colonel. *Heil* Hitler." The major saluted and went to work.

With the sun low in the west, Vessler sent a message to General Rodt. "Movement across Salso River executed. The Americans were taken by surprise by our attack and we slipped away. However, I have not been able to make contact with Colonel Schoerner. Has he crossed the river yet?"

Vessler received Rodt's terse reply, "No, he's hung up at his bridge."

When Vessler's regiment disappeared, Major

311

Hammond sent out patrols to probe the hills, looking for the missing German army. The sergeant leading one such patrol topped a ridge and saw farm buildings across the way. He lunged to the ground. "Hit the dirt," his order rang out.

"What is it?" A soldier behind him asked.

"A lot of Germans," the sergeant replied.

For a minute they studied the situation. "Sarge, they're just standing or sitting in a group," the private said. "What are they doing?"

"I don't know, but let's get closer."

They wormed their way halfway down the ridge and hid behind a tangle of bushes. "Sarge, they're inside a fence," the keen eyed private said. "And I don't see them holding any guns."

"Who's that?" asked the sergeant, as an American holding a rifle came into sight and circled the enclosure.

"Why, the Germans are prisoners," the private exclaimed.

A few minutes later a relieved and happy Sergeant Milne shook their hands.

"How did you capture all these Germans?" the sergeant asked. Milne related the events of the last three days.

"I knew we seized the bridge, but this is the first I've heard of the two ambushes and King Company being led by a staff sergeant," the sergeant said in amazement. "I'll inform battalion." In the mysterious way which news travels, by dusk all of 1$^{st}$ Division heard the story and of their comrades still holding on to the bridge after three days without support.

As night fell, conferences were held at three headquarters.

Dane told his platoon leaders, "From 2100 to 2400, four guards each on the ridge, at the knoll and at the hummock. One guard here by the building looking south. From 2400 to 0300 the same number. At 0300 get everyone awake. The Germans will hit us sometime before dawn." After the others left, Dane and Gates stood outside the building. Dane looked south. "Have Rosario move the horses to the east side of the building and tether them there. Finish digging foxholes and slit trenches here. We're going to need more protection. Gather up a big pile of dried brush from the river bed and stack them about fifty feet south of the hut. Siphon gas from the trucks by the knoll and soak it down. Lay a fuse to the pile. The Germans haven't attacked from that side for a while. I think they'll try again."

General Allen finished his preparations for the next day. He looked at his officers. "Gentlemen, we'll launch our assault at 0400 hours beginning with an artillery bombardment. We'll attack and we won't stop until we reach the bridge. Tell your men our own First Infantry boys are holding out there and they are counting on us. Dismissed."

Colonel Schoerner received his written orders. They came from General Rodt via the coastal road. "I'm to cross the Salso River and join the new defensive line being built at Troina. I'm to make every attempt to destroy the bridge to deny its use by the Americans," he read out loud to Wurtzmeier."Call my officers and have them assemble here," Schoerner commanded.

While he waited, he looked over his map. When they arrived, he issued his orders. "The men are worn out after fighting since before dawn and all day. I'll give them a chance to rest before the next attack. The enemy sergeant will be worried and feeling in over his head, so he'll keep his men up all night, waiting for our attack."

"Maybe," muttered the English-speaking lieutenant. Remembering the sergeant's face, doubts plagued his mind.

"One platoon will infiltrate from the south, one platoon will feint at the ridge and the rest will advance from the north. The darkness will cover our approach, so there'll be no need of a preliminary bombardment. It'll be a surprise attack. The platoon from the south will not move in until the other two attacks take place. Get the men up at 0300 hours, we attack at 0330."

314

At the same time Schoerner issued his orders, Reissenhoffenberger braced himself and started sawing at his bonds with the sharp rock. He used small movements to avoid alerting the guards or his fellow prisoners around him, lest by their actions the guards become suspicious.

Meanwhile in the hut, the two women climbed the stairs after the newly engaged couple wished each other goodnight. Exhausted by the long day, Elena fell right to sleep. Although just as tired, Maria lay awake for a while, a tender smile on her lips as she reviewed the highlights of the day.

All during the night the Germans fired off bursts of small arms fire directed at the ridge to try to rattle the young commander and keep the Americans from resting. The Americans grumbled or cursed and fell back asleep after each episode. Dane kept on sleeping.

\*\*\*

The English-speaking lieutenant woke up at three in the morning and joined his men. They gulped their hot coffee, downed some food, and traveled to their positions. He felt the tension in the air, like a tangible thing which could be touched. He cursed under his breath. He knew experienced soldiers could feel the upcoming attack and be warned. He hoped this attack without a preliminary artillery barrage, unlike all of the other attacks, and the new direction of attack would surprise the Americans.

The lieutenant's confidence in his colonel remained steadfast. Schoerner was in his late forty's and the sergeant less than half his age. Colonel Schoerner had fought in Poland, France, Russia and North Africa. The young sergeant could only have battle experience from Tunisia. Colonel Schoerner commanded a regiment, the sergeant at the most two battered companies. Colonel Schoerner had an excellent battle plan. There should be no way the sergeant could hold on. But as the lieutenant waited with his under-strength platoon, ready to attack, he felt apprehension. He'd looked into the man's eyes and felt this was no ordinary sergeant. *I wonder what surprises might lay in store?*

***

Dane rolled to his feet on the fourth morning, 27 July. His watch read 0300. Alone or in small groups, men grabbed coffee and a bite to eat. They made their way to their positions.

"Ladies, time to rise," Dane hollered up the stairs. He heard the women rouse up. "Rosario and Braun, take the BAR, go upstairs and cover from the windows. Keeler and Conners, stay down here with Crawford and Hemphill. I'll be here too. Gates, take Tennessee, Raymond and Chilvers outside and guard the south approach."

316

Dane's watch read 0335 when multiple explosions rocked the night. Dane cocked his head. "Sounds like the Germans stumbled into the minefield," he murmured out loud. A crescendo of small arms fire erupted from the direction of the knoll, followed by more bursts from the ridge. Dane sat and sipped his coffee, listening.

Tennessee scratched at the door. "Somethin's moving out here."

Dane glided to the window. He made out dark figures creeping closer and closer.

"Now, Gates," he whispered out the window. Gates lit the fuse. The gasoline soaked brush pile ignited, backlighting the surprised Germans. A storm of lead from the hut and from the men outside cut down the advancing Germans like a deadly scythe. The few survivors tumbled back out of the light, and then laid down a harassing fire.

The door burst open. Dane lowered his gun. "Son, that's a great way to get yourself shot," he reprimanded.

The young paratrooper gasped and then recovered himself. "Corporal Buckman says he is being hit hard."

"It sounded like the minefield worked," Dane said.

"Yeah." The paratrooper gave a wolfish grin. "They liked the shelter of the trucks too, until we blew them up. Then we picked them off like flies while the trucks burned. They've retreated but Buckman thinks they'll be back and wants some reinforcements.

Dane listened to the shooting, and then called up the ridge. "What's it like there?"

"Just a lot of noise," Lassiter reported. Dane gave a nod. "The main attack is from the north, and a smaller one from the south. Send a squad over to help Buckman."

Dane then called Zimmerman. "All quiet over here," he reported.

"Send a squad to Buckman and half a squad to the building."

The men arrived and Dane waited until the brushfire burnt out, not wanting the flames to illuminate his men. "Keeler, stay here with Hemphill and Crawford and provide covering fire. Gates' squad shoots while the half squad advances, then they fire while your squad makes a rush. Let's go," Dane ordered.

The first rush over, Gates and his men dashed forward. Braun screamed and doubled over. Raymond saw what happened and rushed over to help. Bullets slammed into him and he fell, limp. Then Dane and Gates smashed into the Germans. The Germans wilted before their assault, and the Americans swamped the remainder. None escaped, and the lieutenant and a number of his men joined the wounded on the bench.

Dane dropped on his knees beside his two men. Braun groaned from a bad wound in his abdomen, but Raymond lay dead.

***

In all the confusion, Reissenhoffenberger strained his muscles and the torn rope binding his hands burst. He laid there for several minutes while his circulation returned to normal, and then rolling to his side he brought his knees up until he could reach the knot. Using minimal movements he freed his feet. Nobody, not even the prisoners on each side of him realized what was happening. Groggy from sleep, they were barely conscious. *If I leave the ropes behind, they'll realize I'm escaping.* Picking them up, Reissenhoffenberger, without making any noise, slithered to the edge of the bank and slipped over. His feet found the narrow ledge he'd seen earlier. He dropped the ropes into the darkness below and edged along the bank, southward. His felt his heart beating as he listened for the shout, which meant they'd spotted him. It never came.

***

Schoerner got the news of the failed attack and scowled. The bridge the engineers were building wouldn't be finished until dawn. He needed both bridges to get his forces across the river as fast as possible. One bridge might cause a bottleneck to form and the Americans would be quick to take advantage of the situation. He called up the artillery. "Pound the north side, and then we'll attack again."

His mind went back to yesterday. He'd chosen to see the American commander face to face in order to gauge his opponent, but the caliber of man he saw surprised and dismayed him. He should have no problem smashing the Americans, but so far he'd met defeat at every turn. This new attack should carry the day. But he saw again in his mind's eye the grim face and the declaration 'you are not crossing the bridge', and he wondered.

***

Explosions rocked the knoll as the German artillery opened fire. Dane looked up from where he staunched the flow of blood from Braun. "Take him to Doc," Dane ordered a nearby figure.

"Sergeant Shaw," a voice called out.

"Over here," Dane answered while he wiped his red-stained hands.

A grey-faced American with a bloody arm staggered into view and leaned his back against the hut. "Sergeant Shaw," he gasped, "Corporal Buckman is unconscious."

Dane ran into the building and grabbed the phone while the paratrooper slid down and sat on the ground. "Sergeant Lassiter, Corporal Buckman is wounded. You get over there and take command."

He ran back outside. "Follow me," he ordered the men with him. As they ran the artillery stopped firing and he heard the sound of the Germans attacking between the ridge and the river. Under intense pressure, by the river the paratroop line began to waver and pull back.

When he saw the paratroopers retreat, Dane felt the feeling welling up from deep inside him, the feeling that he would never give up, that he would never surrender, that he would fight on until his last gasping breath, scratching and clawing with every atom of his being. The green flecks in his eyes glowed and burned. Like an ancient Viking berserker he threw himself into the fray, followed by his cheering and yelling men.

Firing his tommy gun at his hip as he charged, the German line came to a wavering stop. Dane threw himself down at a machine gun. He shoved aside the dead body of the erstwhile gunner and opened up a lethal fire. Half a dozen or more Germans fell. Then the enemy surged forward again and the fighting became hand to hand. The Germans possessed the advantage of numbers but Dane rose to the occasion. With a rifle, with a knife, with his hands and feet, he fought with a fury which couldn't be stopped. All enemies who came within arm's reach were killed, maimed or injured. Shots fired missed the flashing, weaving figure. The assault wavered to a stop. It became the Germans turn to fall back.

Then both sides heard the distant thunder of massed artillery to the west. It was 0400.

# Chapter Forty-Three

Colonel Schoerner grabbed the phone and screamed into it over the noise of the shelling, "Have you captured the bridge yet?" He listened and without another word slammed it down. Another defeat! How could that sergeant be victorious at every turn? And now this artillery barrage signified a major attack on his front and he couldn't spare the manpower for another attack. He toyed with the idea of knocking out the bridge with his artillery, but he'd failed to make any kind of lodgment in the American defenses so there weren't any artillery spotters to direct the shellfire. It would be hit or miss, with his captured men taking the brunt of it. With relief he rejected the thought. He still suffered from the shelling of his men yesterday. He turned to the problem of extracting his force across one bridge while undergoing an attack.

\*\*\*

Dane came to a halt. As the adrenalin flowed out of his system he felt weak and shaky. He passed his hand over his eyes as the green faded back to brown and he looked around. A mental image of blurred German faces that'd he fought and killed ran through his mind. The noise of the artillery caught his attention. *Help is getting closer.*

323

He looked around again. "Gates, gather the wounded and take them to Doc. Then everyone back to your posts. I'm going back to the hut."

He reached it, collapsed in a chair and held his head in his hands with his elbows on the table. Maria came, sat beside him and put her arm around him. He muttered, "Oh dear God, all those men dying, and now so many of them are burning in hell. Oh God, when is it going to stop?"

Maria whispered to him, "You have no choice, *Zio* Sergeant. It is they who started it and they are the evil ones. They must be stopped before they destroy everything."

He sat still for a couple of moments. "I know, and God has made me very good at killing soldiers, but I still don't like it. I wish I would never have to fight again." He pulled himself upright and said in his normal voice, "But I know it's not over and I have to continue."

Tennessee poked his head in at that moment and saw the two of them sitting close together. For a second his face closed up, but then they smiled at him and he relaxed. Dane got to his feet. "You have a wonderful, sensitive fiancée, congratulations."

"Thank you, ah'm mighty happy about it." Tennessee and Maria exchanged a long, loving look.

As Dane went back outside to reorganize the

defenses, Schoerner's phone rang again. "What is it?" he barked.

"Colonel, a Tiger tank has shown up," said an excited voice on the other end. "It's separated from its unit. The commander heard about the bridge being built here and came to cross the river. But the bridge won't hold it, the tank is too heavy. What should I do?"

Schoerner's mind raced. "You say the tank is on the west side of the river and can't cross?"

"*Jawohl, Herr* Colonel. The way north to the coast road has been cut. The only way across the river is here."

"Send the tank down here. Tell the tank commander if he can capture it, there's a bridge here which will support the weight of the tank."

"*Jawohl, Herr* Colonel," and the phone went silent.

Schoerner bent over his maps again. *I'm being given another chance,* he thought. With the huge tank, surely the American sergeant couldn't stop another attack, as long as it launched before daybreak.

"Wurtzmeier, have the men ready to cross the bridge as soon as it is finished. I have to scrape up some infantry to assault with the tank."

Light began to spread across the eastern sky when the monstrous tank rumbled down the road, followed by one hundred fifty combat soldiers. While locked in a titanic struggle just a couple of miles to the west, nevertheless Schoerner worried about the battle for the bridge. The attack must succeed. The Germans were determined to hold their positions until the bridge could be seized and they escape over it. But the ferocity of the American's attack informed him they were even more determined to reach the bridge and relieve their comrades.

When he reached the German line, the tank commander stopped and poked his head out of the hatch. "Where's the best place to attack?"

An officer answered, "The cut through the ridge is completely blocked by two destroyed tanks and a burnt out truck. The defenders have bazookas so going over the top will expose the bottom of your tank. The best way to the bridge is by the knoll. It's held by a group of paratroopers."

"All right." The commander waved his arm to the infantry behind him. The machine clanked its way towards the knoll, leading the way.

The first that Dane knew about the attack was when a runner came gasping into the hut, "Sergeant, there's a tank coming towards the knoll, a huge one!"

Dane jumped to his feet. "Are there any infantry?"

The runner nodded. "A whole lot of them, maybe a company, Sergeant Lassiter said."

"Gates, you and your squad come with me." Dane and his men raced to the knoll. The biggest tank Dane ever saw clanked up and over a hump between the ridge and knoll. Its machine guns rattled and it drove right through the American opposition, with German soldiers close behind. Dane saw a paratrooper fire a *panzerfaust* at the side of the monster, but the projectile exploded harmlessly.

The heavy tank turned to go behind the knoll when Dane saw out of the corner of his eye a bullet hit Rosario and spin him to the ground. German troops gained the hump and fired in all directions. The tank stopped turning and rumbled forward, its machine guns spitting death, heading for Rosario's crumpled body. The horrified Americans saw him trying to drag himself out of the way, but he couldn't move fast enough. The firing from the tank and soldiers kept everyone pinned down.

Dane lay there, watching the approaching monster with narrowed eyes, calculating angles and trajectories. When the tank came within three feet of Rosario, Dane lunged to his feet and raced towards the prostrate form. Bullets whined around him until the tank blocked the German soldiers' fire. He grabbed Rosario's belt with one hand and

327

the neck of his shirt with the other. With a mighty heave from his powerful shoulder muscles, Dane snatched him from off the ground only a foot or so away from being ground into pulp. He threw himself forward and rolled the two of them to safety.

Dane looked around and saw a paratrooper with a *panzerfaust*. "Gimme that," he ordered. The paratrooper tossed it to Dane who caught it and aimed, not at the impervious hide, but at the nearest track. He fired and the track exploded, neatly sheared in two. One side immobilized, the tank swung around. "Another *panzerfaust*," Dane demanded.

Lassiter slid down next to him. "This is the last one," he shouted to Dane over the deafening sounds of firing and tank noise. He gave Dane covering fire, but then Lassiter jerked from the impact of bullets hitting him. Dane heard him say, "I'll never see my son," and he fell limp.

For a second Dane stared at the body. Anguish tore through his soul at Lassiter's words. *Lord, when will this end?* Then with grim determination, Dane drew careful aim and blew the other track off.

\*\*\*

Back at the hut, Crawford saw the battle raging at the knoll. He grabbed the phone. "Sergeant Zimmerman, this is Lieutenant Crawford. Are you being attacked?"

"No, no action here. What's happening at the knoll?"

"They are under heavy attack, take half your men and get over there!"

"Yes," a pause, "sir."

Crawford called the ridge. "This is Lieutenant Crawford. What's your situation?"

"We're fine here, Sergeant Grissom is leading men over towards the knoll. He's going to set up fire teams on the ridge to hammer the infantry, but we can't stop the tank." Jones' voice contained a hint of panic.

"Sergeant, do you have bazookas?"

Jones gave a little gulp, "Yeah, one."

"Try...try hitting the wheels or track or something. Do something to slow it down." Crawford grasped for something, anything which might help.

"Okay, we can try it," Jones' voice became steadier and Crawford heard him giving orders before the line disconnected. Crawford went back to the window to look out. Unknown to both of them, the tank was already rendered immovable.

***

Like a wounded animal, the tank searched for an enemy to strike out at. Its machine guns chattered nonstop, but it searched for a target for its

88 millimeter. The big gun could do little against the scattered enemy soldiers, but it looked for a target to blast, and found one. Seeing the stone hut and reasoning the Americans must be using it, the tank commander aimed the gun and yelled "Fire!"

Crawford heard the shell burst into the upstairs room, filling it with lethal steel and stone shrapnel. The explosion shook the building to its foundations and part of the upper floor began to drop, right above where Hemphill lay. The two women, cowering in the corner, scrambled to safety. Seeing the danger, Crawford jumped across the room, grabbed Hemphill by the arm and wrenched him to safety before the ceiling collapsed.

Hemphill gazed up at Crawford in amazement. "Why did you risk your life for me?" he asked.

Crawford looked puzzled for a moment and then a big grin split his face. "You haven't given me your recipe for barbecue sauce yet."

Hemphill looked at him for a moment, then looked down and with a gruff voice said, "Thanks...sir."

***

Dane searched his pockets. "Grenades, anyone got grenades?"

"Here," shouted a paratrooper, tossing him three. Dane looked at them. Two were smoke and one a fragmentation. Thoughts whirled in his brain.

"Cover me!" he screamed. He leapt to his feet. With bullets striking all around him he raced to the tank and jumped onto it. He armed the two smoke grenades and thrust them into a view port. With bullets pinging all around him he crouched, waiting until smoke poured out of the ports, waiting until the crew couldn't stand it anymore. The commander, choking and coughing, threw open the hatch and fired at Dane. He shot the commander with his pistol and jumped for the hatch, dropping the last grenade inside the tank. It exploded, filling the inside with deadly shrapnel, ricocheting around and cutting everyone to shreds. He rolled off the tank and back to the ground, unhurt.

He saw Zimmerman's reinforcements pounding towards him. "Over there," he shouted, motioning to the east of him. "Catch the Krauts in a crossfire." Then Grissom's men laid down a fierce barrage of machine gun and mortar fire. Without the help of the tank, the Germans faltered.

But they still outnumbered the Americans. Determined to take the bridge, they attacked again. The situation hung in the balance.

Salvation came from above.

Four planes dove out of the sky. Machine guns tore into the grey uniforms. Bombs blew holes in the ranks. Pummeled from above and with Americans on three sides of them, the Germans pulled back, the attack over.

# Chapter Forty-Four

Lieutenant Wurtzmeier oversaw the loading of the last of the headquarters' equipment. "All ready to leave, Colonel," he announced.

Colonel Schoerner nodded. He cocked an eye to the west. "They're fighting less than a kilometer away. I'll drive over to the bridge, be ready to follow me over the river." They exchanged salutes and Schoerner drove off.

The driver parked at the base of a slope. Schoerner climbed up and peered through his field glasses towards the ridge which he'd been trying to capture for two days. He looked, searching for a sign of victory. Instead he saw his infantry heading towards him, streaming across the valley.

He lowered his glasses, too shocked to swear. Beaten again! How did this sergeant do it? He saw a solitary figure standing on top of the ridge. He focused his glasses and the sergeant jumped into view. They stared at each other across the landscape. "I'll see you again, my friend, and you won't be so lucky next time," Schoerner said under his breath.

Schoerner watched as the sergeant turned and disappeared down the far side of the ridge at the same time as a rifle barked nearby. Schoerner jumped and saw the marksman about ten feet to his left. "Did you try to shoot him?" Schoerner asked him.

"*Ja*, Colonel, but I missed," the rifleman replied, chagrined.

"I'm not surprised," Schoerner said with a soft tone. "I'm not surprised at all." He turned and slid down the ridge.

"Captain," Schoerner ordered the senior commander there, "pull your men to the north and cover the withdrawal across the other bridge." Schoerner turned and glared at the unseen enemy. "The Americans have won this bridge."

\*\*\*

At General Allen's headquarters, a jeep drove up. General Patton hopped out and strode into the building. "Have you reached the bridge yet?" he demanded in his rather squeaky voice.

General Allen looked up. "Almost, general," he replied. "We're within half a mile and the reports say the Germans are retreating northward, away from the bridge."

"Good, I'll wander up to the front and see how it's going." They saluted each other and Patton left.

\*\*\*

An hour later, Dane stood in the cut, watching some newcomers pulling the burnt tanks out so the road could be used. A jeep carrying a pennant with three stars rolled up and stopped. He, and everyone else, snapped to attention when the familiar form of Lieutenant General George Patton got out. He returned their salutes and asked, "Who is in charge here?"

A portly captain said, "I am, sir."

Patton looked at him. "Did you capture the bridge?"

"Uh, no, sir. We're, uh, the relieving force, sir."

"Who did capture the bridge?" Patton swore.

"We did, sir." Dane answered.

Patton looked at him. "Where is your commanding officer?"

"Dead, sir."

"Killed while defending the bridge?"

Dane felt embarrassed. "No sir. He died before we got here."

Patton fixed him with an eagle eye. "What officer took over command?"

"Uh, none of them, sir. They were all killed or wounded, so I took command of the company and completed the mission, sir."

Patton swore a blue streak. "That's what I like to hear. You took command and finished the job. You commanded the whole company, you said?"

"Yes sir," Dane replied with a gulp.

Patton looked at the wreckage in the cut and the three destroyed tanks on the ridge. "What artillery support did you have?"

"None, sir."

"Tanks?"

"No,sir."

"It looks like you did a magnificent job here, Sergeant." He swore again. "I'll give you a field commission. Ed," he spoke to the captain in the back seat of the jeep, "stay here, get a report and bring it back to my headquarters."

The captain removed himself from the jeep. "Yes sir."

"Carry on." Patton got back in the jeep and the driver sped off, back up the road.

Dane felt dazed. "An officer?" he repeated.

"Let's go get those reports written up," suggested Ed. "I'll need reports from the other noncoms also."

"Yes sir." Dane shook himself, looked around and issued orders. "Sergeant Jones, get all of our men over to the hut, including the paratroopers."

Ed's eyebrows rose at the mention of the airborne men, but they rose higher when he arrived at the hut and saw Lieutenant Crawford, Maria and Elena. He watched as men gathered around.

Dane looked over the survivors. Counting the freed prisoners, there'd been almost two hundred men in the operation at the bridge. Less than half of them stood here, and quite a few sported bandages.

"Men," Dane addressed them, "I want to thank each and every one of you for your efforts and valor these last four days. Without your tireless efforts, your grit and your determination, this mission could not have been accomplished." He paused and gathered his composure, wetness in his eyes. "I want to lead all of us in prayer to the great God who gave us this victory." Some feet shuffled.

He bowed his head and spoke in a voice audible to all. "Lord, we humbly thank you for the victory you wrought here. We thank you for those of us whom you have safely brought through the vale of danger. We pray for those who have died. We pray you will comfort their mothers and fathers, the brothers and sisters, their wives, their children who will never see their daddy again." His voice broke on the last few words and he paused to recover himself.

He thought of his own sister and how close she came to getting a letter from the War Department. There were more than a few damp eyes when he continued. "We pray for the wounded and for their rapid and full recoveries. In Jesus name we pray. Amen." A chorus of amens echoed him.

Dane lifted his head up and looked at the crowd. "Since none of us ate much of a meal this morning, go ahead and eat and then catch up on some shut eye until we get some orders." His words were greeted by a cheer as the men separated. Dane and Ed returned to the hut and sat down at the table.

"Do you have something I can write on?" Dane asked.

In reply Ed opened his briefcase and extracted some blank paper. "Have you ever filled out a post action report?"

"No," Dane answered, "but I have read a few. If you have any suggestions please feel free to offer them, sir." He sat there for a couple of minutes to organize his thoughts and began writing. Ed left him and mingled outside, listening to the comments being made by the ex-bridge defenders.

"I thought the sergeant was nuts when he said to lay low and let the Krauts drive right on through the first night," said a private standing with a group of 1st Infantry and 82nd Airborne men. Ed's eyebrows shot up.

"Yeah," agreed another man. "But he sure fooled the Germans, just like a fox fools the hounds."

"Fox, hey, I like it," said a third. "Shaw out thought, out schemed, out tricked and out fought the Germans."

"Did you see him fighting on top of the ridge those six Germans?" asked someone.

"Who didn't?" the first man replied. "And he took out how many tanks by himself, including the

Tiger?"

"I don't know, I couldn't keep track," someone replied.

"He's a pretty good commander, for an infantryman," said a paratrooper. "You guys were lucky we were here to bail you out," he teased.

"But we rescue d you," the first man bantered back. "And don't tell me you have a better commander than our Fox."

"You got me there," the paratrooper shook his head. "I haven't seen a better sergeant who did what he done."

A thoughtful Ed walked back into the hut. He glanced over Dane's finished report and made a few suggestions.

While Dane made the corrections, he glanced out the window where the prisoners were being loaded up. He jumped to his feet, yelled "Stop!" out the window and ran outside, followed by the others in the building.

Dane braked to a halt and looked the prisoners over. He turned to the guards. "You're missing one."

"What?" the guard asked, staring at the men in grey.

"You're missing one," Dane repeated. "The engineer we captured first."

Everyone looked at Dane and the row of

prisoners. One of the guards said, "This is all there were this morning."

*That's what I forgot last night, to have a guard keep an eye on him. I knew he was up to something,* Dane thought. "He must have escaped during the night then," Dane answered and walked back into the hut, leaving an even more thoughtful Ed staring after him.

A couple of hours later, while Dane finished another report, he heard a jeep brake to a stop outside the building. The women, sitting at the table with him, and Ed, in a corner reviewing the other NCOs' reports, looked up.

A loud voice said, "I'm looking for Company K, 26th Regiment."

"You found it," came Tennessee's laconic answer.

"Who's in command and where is he?"

"That would be Sergeant Shaw and he's in the hut," Tennessee answered.

The man entered the hut and looked at Dane. "Are you Sergeant Shaw?" he barked.

Dane rose to his feet and saluted the lieutenant, "Yes sir, I am."

"I'm Lieutenant Honeywell and I'm the new commander of this company."

"Yes sir," Dane said in his quiet voice.

Dane recognized that the lieutenant, plainly

upset, felt the need to establish right off the bat who was in charge.

"Why are those men loafing around?" he demanded. "I run a tight command and there will be no lollygagging around."

"Sir," Dane explained with an expressionless face, "those men were just surrounded and fought off repeated attacks for three days."

Thwarted, the lieutenant switched targets. "What about those two women? What are they doing here? What's been going on in here?" He glared at Dane.

Dane looked back. "One guided us here and we rescued the other from being a prisoner."

"Well, I want them out of here, right away," he snapped. "What are you doing?"

"I'm finishing up a report about the action here."

"You can give it to me as soon as you're done. I'll need to read and approve it."

For the first time Dane felt ill at ease. Ed came to his rescue. "Lieutenant," he said as he moved forward.

Lieutenant Honeywell gave a start and said, "Oh! I didn't see you." He saw the captain's bars and belatedly saluted.

"Lieutenant, General Patton wants to see these reports this evening and he ordered me to deliver them to him in person."

"General…General Patton?" Honeywell's voice squeaked.

"Yes, Lieutenant. I'm sure once General Patton has perused them, he will pass them down the chain of command and you will get to read them," Ed offered in smooth tones.

"Uh, I…uh…well…uh…carry on then, Sergeant," Honeywell stammered and tottered out the door, flummoxed.

Dane glanced at Ed's impassive face but caught the gleam of humor in his eyes. Dane glided to the door. "Corporal Gates," he said, not raising his voice, but Gates replied at once, "Yes?"

"Lieutenant Honeywell is taking over command of the company and his first order is for the ladies to be returned safely to their homes." Dane paraphrased the order and Ed ducked his head to hide a smile. "Get the Calvoratti's wagon, hitch up the two best horses and escort them home with your squad. He wants the ladies returned at once."

"Yes sir." Gates stood at attention and saluted.

"Oh, stop it!" Dane felt embarrassed.

"I wanted to be the first to call you sir and salute you," Gates grinned, which made Dane grin back.

It didn't take long to get the wagon hitched up and the men ready to set off. Maria walked up to

Dane and looked at him, "Thank you so much, *Zio* Sergeant, for telling me about Jesus, and for, oh, everything." Impulsively she hugged him and he hugged her back.

"Thank you for showing me I was self-centered, concerned only with my hurt. I'll pray for you every day. Do you have your Bible?"

She patted her skirt pocket and nodded.

"Thank you for being our guide and all the help you have been, imp," he added, with a teasing gleam at the last word.

Dane watched them leave. Gates, his usual steady self despite a blood stained shirtsleeve, led the way. Conners, of course untouched, rode in the wagon with Chilvers. A bad gash on his face scarred his handsome face, making it unhandsome. Tennessee and Maria walked hand-in-hand, happy smiles on their faces. As Dane looked at Maria, he knew he would never see her again.

Doc appeared at Dane's side.

"How's the wounded in my, Gates' squad," Dane asked, correcting himself.

"Braun has a bad wound and will be sent home. Rosario and Hemphill have flesh wounds and will recover soon."

"And Patterson, O'Halloran and Raymond are dead," Dane murmured. "Lassiter's dead too."

Doc looked at him in surprise. "No, he's not.

He's got multiple wounds and a bullet broke his arm, but he'll live. He'll be invalided home." Doc cleared his throat. "You did the best you could. You did good, Sergeant."

Dane stared at Doc's retreating back. *He actually said something complimentary,* Dane thought in surprise. "So Lassiter will hold his son, after all," Dane said in relief.

# Chapter Forty-Five

Early in the evening Ed slipped into General Patton's office and watched as the general rubbed his tired eyes. He waited until Patton glanced at him, then the general resumed rubbing.

"I have the reports from the sergeant at the bridge you wanted."

"I realize the bitter fighting that must have taken place. The sergeant must have a lot of courage and knowhow to have succeeded in capturing and holding the bridge. Just read me the highlights," Patton said as he pressed his tired eyes.

Ed glanced at the papers in his hands. "King Company, 26th Regiment, orders were to penetrate behind enemy lines and seize the bridge over the Salso River. After traveling a short distance Germans ambushed the company and all the officers and senior sergeants were killed or wounded. Sergeant Shaw assumed command. They ambushed a German company and wiped it out."

Patton stopped rubbing his eyes and listened with intense concentration.

"They traveled the twenty miles to the bridge and captured it with an advance unit. The first night they hid and allowed superior German forces to cross while they remained undetected."

Patton dropped his hands and stared at the captain.

"They rescued fifty prisoners from the 82$^{nd}$ Airborne, a downed flier and a group of 1$^{st}$ Infantry prisoners, arming them with captured German weapons. For two days they held off six separate assaults, three of them with tank support. All the tanks were destroyed."

"Let me see that," Patton held out an imperious hand. He read the report, flipping the pages. At the end he looked up with an incredulous look. "Is this verified by the others?" he asked.

"Yes, general. I showed it to the surviving NCO's and they all corroborated it's 100% accurate. Here are their signatures and comments." Ed handed over more papers.

"Best company commander I ever served under," Patton read aloud, turning the pages over. "Outfoxed and outfought the Germans. If Sergeant Shaw transferred to the airborne, I would be proud to serve under him. Sergeant Shaw showed tremendous organizational and combat skills, he fabricated a communications center, planted effective mine fields, used reserves and pulled troops from one line to a threatened line in an efficient manner." Patton looked up, "Lieutenant Crawford? I thought all the officers were out of action."

"The flier, sir."

"Oh."

"Here is a list of suggested medals and promotions from Sergeant Shaw," Ed handed over another paper. Patton took it, read it over and then handed it back. "Send it to the battalion commander. Tell him I looked it over, but of course he has the final say on them."

Ed hid a smile as he took the report back. No mere major would dare to deny any award after General Patton tacitly agreed to it.

"Here is another report, sir, signed by every NCO and a number of privates," and Ed handed it over. "It's a request for the Medal of Honor for Sergeant Shaw, sir."

"Medal of Honor?" Patton sat up straight as he snatched the paper. "Single handedly stopped one attack in hand to hand combat while surrounded by enemy soldiers. Single handedly destroyed a tank by jumping on top of it while under enemy fire and tossing hand grenades into it. Single handedly destroyed a Tiger tank by blowing out its tracks, jumping on top of it and throwing smoke grenades into it. When the hatch opened shot the German and dropped a hand grenade into it, all the while under enemy fire. He destroyed another tank. When out of danger, he ran towards a thrown grenade, snatching it out of the air and throwing it back, saving the lives of three men at great danger to himself. While under fire, ran up and pulled a wounded soldier out of the way of an enemy tank which almost ran over them. He led numerous charges. He showed exceptional valor and courage." Patton stopped reading out loud, stared at it and then at Ed.

"I overheard the men talking, sir. They're very impressed with his fighting prowess, as well as his leadership. They have also given him a nickname. They call him The Fox because of the way he tricked the Germans."

Patton read the report over again, wrote a notation on it, signed it with a flourish and handed it back. "Send it to Ike with my recommendation." He took the post action report again, looked at it and said, "I promised him a commission, didn't I? What rank is he?"

"Staff sergeant."

"How long has he been a sergeant?"

"Since February."

"Best company commander I ever served under." Patton swore, "I can't promote a staff sergeant to captain, no matter how much he might deserve it, or how much I would like to. These new lieutenants they're sending us are trash." Patton paused. "Write up a commission for a first lieutenant. That'll give him a chance to learn something of how a company is run. If he's as good as they say, he'll get his company sooner."

\*\*\*

At almost the same time, Colonel Schoerner arrived at General Rodt's headquarters at Troina. Covered in dust, tired and not in a good mood, he stomped into the building. He walked into Rodt's office, barely noticing a tall private in the room. General Rodt looked up and returned Schoerner's salute. "Report," Rodt snapped.

"I crossed the Salso River over the bridge the engineers built with my entire command. Now we are making a fighting retreat to the new defensive line, the Etna Line."

"You didn't capture or destroy the bridge," Rodt stated rather than asked.

Schoerner's lips tightened. "*Nein, Herr* General. All of my assaults were beaten off."

Rodt indicated the other man. "Private Reissenhoffenberger was a prisoner there and managed to escape. He's going to tell us what he learned while there." The general and the colonel turned their attention to the young man, who flushed but began his tale. When he got to the part about the Americans hiding while German convoys passed through, Rodt interrupted, "Nonsense! I myself went over the bridge that night. There were no Americans there."

Reissenhoffenberger, with respect but firmness,

denied it. "General, I was tied up and lying under it when you drove over the bridge."

Shocked, General Rodt stared while Reissenhoffenberger went on. "The sergeant in command, he's a fox! I saw him, he...he," words failed him.

"A fox in deceit and a tiger in battle," mused Schoerner out loud, remembering the cat-like walk and the fierce fighter. "Do you know his name?"

"*Ja*, Sergeant Dane Shaw."

"Dane Shaw," Schoerner repeated, committing it to memory. "Dane Shaw."

# Chapter Forty-Six

Gates halted the small cavalcade once they were out of sight of Lieutenant Honeywell. "Maria, ask Elena where her home is," Gates said.

After a brief conversation with Elena, Maria turned to him. "She lives in a village west and south of here."

They traveled the rest of the day and part of the next before reaching their destination. When they arrived at her home, everyone in the village ran out to welcome her. Maria watched with tears in her own eyes as Elena's loved ones wailed and cried in their relief at seeing her once again. From overheard comments, Maria learned they believed Elena to be dead and the outpouring of emotion came from the relieving of their grief.

When Elena's father heard of the Americans rescue, he came to Maria, his cheeks wet with tears. "Can you stay the night? We wish you to join our celebration."

With hope in her eyes Maria passed on the request to Gates. She would grab at any reason to prolong Van's staying with her.

But to her disappointment Gates shook his head. "I'm sorry Maria, but we have many hours of daylight left. We need to move on."

351

Hiding her disappointment, Maria gave the answer to Elena's father and then took her leave of Elena.

Elena hugged her tight. "Tell the Americans I will pray every day to The Blessed Virgin for their safety. I cannot find words to thank them enough for..." Her voice trailed off and she shuddered.

"They understand. I will tell them of your prayers." Maria hugged her back.

Elena drew a ragged breath. "If only my husband were with me, then today would be perfect." (Elena's husband was imprisoned with the rest of his division by the Germans when Italy surrendered on September 8th. Freed after Germany's surrender in April, 1945, he made his way back to Sicily and rejoined his wife.)

Waving their goodbyes, they resumed their journey to Maria's home, and arrived the following afternoon. During the whole trip Maria stayed by Van's side, as much as possible. Hand in hand, Maria bounced along beside Tennessee's loping stride.

They talked almost nonstop about every subject under the sun, such as raising sheep and fertilizer. They compared notes about life in America. They talked about the scriptures they read together each night. Maria asked questions about what they read, but too many times Tennessee didn't know the answer.

Tennessee looked at Maria. "Ah don't know enough about the Bible to tell you, but ah promise to learn as much as ah can."

Maria gave him a beaming smile. "I know you will do the best you can."

When they arrived at the farm, Maria proudly led Tennessee up to her parents and introduced him. "Papa and Mama, this is Van Norton, the man I'm going to marry." The explosion she feared from her father didn't happen. He merely gave a loud rumble.

Maria glowed with happiness as she watched Van win over her parents by his obvious love for their daughter and his practical common sense.

The next morning they made a protracted goodbye, knowing this could be the last time they might see each other again, not daring to voice the possibility that Tennessee might be killed in this war.

"I'll write to you every week," Maria promised with tears in her eyes, holding on to him as if her life depended on it, which in a way it did.

"Ah'll write as much as ah can, but ah don't know about the mail. You might not get mah letters."

"I know, the mail service here in Sicily is not good and it'll probably get worse. But God is merciful and He can get them through, at least

353

enough of them."

After a last long, passionate kiss and hug, he wrenched himself free and joined the others, walking back to the front. Maria watched Tennessee turn and give one last wave, keeping the picture of him standing there in her mind for almost two years.

Instead of going cross country like before, the squad walked to Leonforte where a MP attempted to arrest them for desertion. Gates convinced him they were trying to rejoin their unit. They cadged a ride and caught up to their company.

The following Monday Maria walked to the nearest village and posted a letter to 'her Van', the first of 96 straight weeks.

In September she got two letters from him on the same day, dated two weeks apart. Just before Christmas she got a third letter, with a plaintive question wondering if she'd gotten any of his letters as he hadn't received any from her. It tore at her heart and she prayed long and hard for him to get her letters. The sale of one of the horses got them through the winter.

Spring came before she heard from him again, joyfully announcing he'd gotten six letters at Christmas, 'The best Christmas present ah ever got.' He also hinted he was a long ways away from her. She helped her father with the sheep shearing, which provided some needed revenue for the three of them, but not much. A handsome young man who frequented the post office tried to catch her eye, but she ignored him.

Maria read her Bible out loud every day. After several months, Lucia began listening. At first Antonio rejected any interest in God or the Bible. But after hearing discussions between his wife and daughter for weeks, he became curious. One of the happiest days of Maria's life was when both of her parents bowed their heads and accepted Jesus as their savior.

In June she, as well as the world, heard about the landings in Normandy, and she wondered if Van was there, not dreaming he'd been on Omaha beach, the bloodiest of them all. The young man asked her to join a group of youths to go watch a cinema, but she turned him down. "I'm engaged to be married."

She didn't get another letter until October, just a short note written in haste of his recovery from his wound which he'd told her about and he'd just received her first letter, wasn't that funny? The young man appeared in the post office with a girl on his arm and pretended he didn't know her.

The winter storms were severe. The barn suffered heavy damage from a bad wind storm. The young man, alone now, tried to engage her in conversation.

Spring rolled around again. They heard news of

the Allied invasion of Germany. After the sheep were sheared, Maria dropped off her letter and the postmaster gave her one back. It was only a month old. "Ah'm glad yore in warm Sicily and not battling the fierce cold in Europe," he wrote. She spied the young man with a different girl hanging onto his sleeve.

One beautiful day in June Maria took her six letters and climbed up a ridge and sat there reading them over again. The early ones were thin and trying to tear so she had to be extra careful with them. She'd read them so often she'd memorized them, but she still loved to read them over and over. After all, his hands had held them.

With slow steps, a tall, gaunt man with haunted eyes, carrying a back pack and dressed in an American uniform with sergeant's stripes on the sleeves, walked along the road. When farm buildings came into sight he stopped. He surveyed the scene and the broken down barn before resuming his way up to the farmstead. When he reached the house, the door flung open and Lucia Calvoratti stood there in shock, her hands on her cheeks. "Van, you have come back," she gasped.

"Yes ma'am." He dropped his pack with a weary sigh and looked around, eagerness brightening his face. "Is Maria here?"

Lucia indicated the ridge, "She is up there."

He turned and walked up the ridge, his pace stronger and faster. Maria sat, the opened letters on her lap, with a faraway look in her eyes when something caught her attention. She focused on the figure climbing up to her. At first she thought it was her daydream. But then reality burst upon her. It was really him! "Van!" she screamed, jumping up and scattering her precious letters. "Van, Van, Van," she screamed at every step as she ran down the slope and threw herself into his arms.

Long minutes later, they separated and stared at each other with hungry eyes. She touched his face with wondering fingers. "You've come back."

"Yes, Maria," and then with deliberation added, "Ah've come home." She squeezed him tight, realizing he meant they would live here, in Sicily. "Ah see the second job ah have to do is repair the barn."

"What's the first job?" she asked.

"Marryin' you, if you still want me." Her answer left him in no doubt of what she wanted. Hand in hand they turned and walked down the slope, where her parents stood and waited at the house.

# Epilog

On a hot day in July, a few weeks after Tennessee's homecoming, Jonas Hemphill got on a bus in his hometown in Mississippi. The crowded bus held no empty seats. He saw four middle-aged colored women with tired faces, each holding a grocery sack. He guessed they were returning home from their shifts at the factory, having done some shopping on the way. The four looked at each other, and then one of them prepared to get to her feet, giving him her seat.

He stared at them as a memory exploded into his mind. The scene in the stone hut by the river in Sicily, almost two years ago, when Lieutenant Crawford told about his mother on a bus. He remembered Shaw, he'd been a sergeant then, saying something about having the moral courage to not accept the seat. All this flashed through his mind in a second. Standing proud in his army uniform, Jonas told the woman, "No, you sit and I'll stand."

Surprised, the woman sat back down. "Thank ya, sah," she mumbled.

He stood there, ignoring the stares of his fellow white passengers, and it felt right. He felt good.

# The Tuskegee Airmen

During the 1920's and 30's there was considerable agitation to allow Colored soldiers into combat roles, especially as pilots. Instead they were relegated to menial labor battalions. In 1931 the War Department stated the Air Corps had always selected men with technical and mechanical training, that Colored men weren't attracted to flying like white men, and it had received so many applications from college trained white men that many of them had to be turned down. This was despite the fact there were over one hundred trained Negro (as they preferred to be called) flyers in the country.

On April 3, 1939, Congress passed a bill authorizing the Secretary of War, in conjunction with the Civil Aeronautics Authority, to train Negro Air Pilots at civilian aviation schools, such schools to be chosen later. The War Department and the Civil Aeronautics Authority interpreted the law to mean they could train pilots, not they had to. In June 1939, a congressional hearing asked Secretary of War Harry Woodring if Negro pilots were going to be trained. He answered they were planning to do so. However, whenever a Colored youth applied for training he was told 'It has been a policy of the War

Department not to mix Colored and white enlisted men in the same tactical organization, and since no provision has been made for any Colored Air Corps unit in the Army, Colored persons are not eligible for enlistment in the Air Corps.'

Finally, under Congressional pressure, in the fall of 1939 the C.A.A. designated some college campuses as training centers for Negro pilots. Included in the list was the Tuskegee Institute. However, pilots were still denied the right to enter the Army Air Corps.

The Selective Training and Service Act of 1940 did state that there should be no discrimination on account of race, creed or color. But there were loopholes the War Department used to effectively bar the use of Colored soldiers in combat units. It wasn't until the fall of 1940 President Roosevelt directed the War Department that 'Colored men will have equal opportunity with white men in all departments of the Army.'

Meanwhile, in June 1940 the first pilots started their training at Tuskegee, and in July advanced training classes were begun. In December 1940 the Air Corps began planning for a Negro pursuit squadron and attached ground support. It wasn't until March, 1941, that the Army started accepting applications from Colored youths. The first Army class began training on July 19, 1941 and graduated

March 6, 1942. The five young men were Benjamin Davis Jr, Charles Debow Jr, Lemuel Custis, George Roberts and Mac Ross. These men formed the nucleus of the 99th and 100th Pursuit Squadrons.

The 99th Squadron, under Colonel Benjamin Davis Jr., remained in training until April 1943. While white squadrons were shipped overseas earlier in their training, the 99th was held back. While this was discouraging to the men, the added training did allow them to be more proficient when they finally arrived on the battle front than the white squadrons which preceded them.

The squadron arrived in Tunisia on May 31, 1943, where they served alongside the 33rd Fighter Group. On July 2, 1943, Lieutenant Charles Hall became the first Afro-American to shoot down an enemy plane. He was personally congratulated by General Eisenhower, General Spaatz, General Doolittle, and Air Marshal Cunningham.

The 99th flew missions over the islands of Pantelleria, Lampedusa and Limosa. All three islands surrendered without being invaded, the first time in history air power won surrender of a ground target. Then they conducted missions over Sicily after it was invaded. Colonel Momyer, commander of the 33rd Group, did not want the 99th. He relegated the squadron to missions where they were unlikely to encounter enemy planes, and then criticized them for lack of victories. He wrote such scathing and prejudicial reports that some high level brass considered disbanding the squadron. In October 1943 the 99$^{th}$ was transferred to Italy and joined with the 79$^{th}$ Group. Colonel Bates of the 79$^{th}$ was a fair-minded man and gave Colonel Davis more missions. The 99$^{th}$ responded.

It wasn't until January 1944 that the 99$^{th}$ scored its second downed enemy aircraft. On the 27$^{th}$ the squadron shot down five planes in one day and the next day they shot down five more. Their morale went sky-high.

In March of 1944 General Eaker of the 15$^{th}$ Air Force sent for Colonel Davis. White fighter squadrons assigned to protect bombers were chasing enemy planes and allowing other enemy planes to shoot down his bombers. Fighter pilots were trained to be aggressive and attack enemy planes. Unfortunately the bomber crews paid the price. Colonel Davis assured General Eaker his pilots would stay in close support of the bombers.

In May 1944 the 332$^{nd}$ Group under Colonel Davis, consisting of the 99$^{th}$ and 100$^{th}$ pursuit squadrons, was equipped with P-47 fighters. The group painted the tails of their new planes with bright red paint, gaining the nickname Redtails.

Colonel Davis soon found out his pilots were no more fond of 'close support' than their white colleagues. Davis threatened his men with grounding and court martial if they chased after enemy aircraft and left the bombers. The men disliked nothing more than being grounded. They obeyed.

From then until the end of the war the bombing groups in the Mediterranean welcomed the sight of the Redtails flying overhead. With Redtail escorts, the losses from enemy planes dropped. Contrary to legend, bombers under their protection were shot down, but far fewer than average.

On March 24, 1945, the 332nd Group scored one of its greatest victories. While escorting bombers attacking Berlin, they were jumped byME-262 jets. The Redtails shot down three of them.

The 332nd earned several commendations including the Presidential Unit Citation and 96 Distinguished Flying Crosses, making it one of the most decorated air groups.

After the war its men returned to a segregated and prejudiced America. Crack pilots who applied for jobs as civilian pilots soon found out the airline companies would only hire whites to fill their cockpits. White commanders, including General Eaker, who during the war commended and praised the Colored squadrons, reversed themselves. They claimed the Afro-American squadrons were inferior to the white squadrons and their men, with a few exceptions like Colonel Davis, were harder to train and not up to white men's standards.

But the wheels of change had begun and in 1948 President Truman desegregated the Armed Forces by executive order. Black units were broken up and the men transferred to other units. In many cases the transition worked smoothly and men of whatever color accepted each other as fellow soldiers.

Americans can be proud of men like Lieutenant General Benjamin Davis Jr. who helped pave the way for desegregation and wrote a glorious chapter in the annals of warfare. The Tuskegee Airmen were truly one of the great units of World War 2.

www.ingramcontent.com/pod-product-compliance
Lightning Source LLC
Chambersburg PA
CBHW060157260626
47160CB00001B/310

\* 9 7 8 0 9 9 1 1 1 6 7 3 7 \*